'Hands down one of my favourite reads of the year'
**Freida McFadden, *Sunday Times* bestselling author
of *The Housemaid***

'Absolutely remarkable . . . Do yourself a favour – clear your
schedule and crack open this novel'
**Lisa Gardner, *Sunday Times* bestselling author
of *Before She Disappeared***

'A true classic in the genre'
**Lisa Jewell, *Sunday Times* bestselling author
of *None of This Is True***

'A propulsive story that haunts and mesmerizes'
**Karin Slaughter, *Sunday Times* bestselling author of the
Will Trent series**

'Noelle has mastered the art of keeping readers on
the edge of their seats'
**John Marrs, *Sunday Times* bestselling author
of *The One***

'An immersive, spine-tingling, deeply visceral experience.
I recommend reading it with the lights blazing'
**Heather Gudenkauf, *New York Times* bestselling author
of *The Overnight Guest***

FORGET YOU SAW HER

Noelle lives in Idaho with her husband, two sons and two cats. When she's not plotting her next thriller, she's scaring herself with true-crime documentaries or going for a trail ride in the foothills (with her trusty pepper spray).

Forget You Saw Her is Noelle's eighth thriller-suspense novel. You can find her on Instagram @noelleihliauthor

FORGET YOU SAW HER

NOELLE W. IHLI

PAN BOOKS

First published in the US 2025 by Dynamite Books

First published in the UK 2025 by Pan Books
an imprint of Pan Macmillan
The Smithson, 6 Briset Street, London EC1M 5NR
EU representative: Macmillan Publishers Ireland Ltd, 1st Floor,
The Liffey Trust Centre, 117–126 Sheriff Street Upper,
Dublin 1 D01 YC43
Associated companies throughout the world

ISBN 978-1-0350-8004-5

1 3 5 7 9 8 6 4 2

A CIP catalogue record for this book is available from the British Library.

Printed and bound in the UK using 100% Renewable Electricity by CPI Group (UK) Ltd

MIX
Paper | Supporting
responsible forestry
FSC® C116313

Visit **www.panmacmillan.com** to read more about all our books
and to buy them.

Please note that this book contains content that may be sensitive for some readers, including descriptions of domestic abuse, death of a child, and non-explicit references to sexual assault.

For Cathy, Alexis, and Kathleen.

JULY 31, 2015

Dear Ms. Turpin,

The Ogden Utah Police Department recently recovered the body of a seventeen-year-old girl. Despite our best efforts, the condition of the remains has made it difficult to identify the individual using standard methods.

That said, based on certain physical attributes and personal effects recovered with the body, we have reason to believe that the remains may belong to Andrea Beaumont, who was reported missing three months ago.

In order to confirm or rule out this possibility, we are requesting a DNA sample from you for comparison purposes. Your timely cooperation in this matter will greatly assist us in our investigation.

Enclosed, you will find a DNA collection kit along with instructions for its use. Please return the sample using the prepaid envelope included in this package as soon as possible.

Should you have any questions, you may contact me directly.

Sincerely,

Detective Monte Barker

1

SABINA TURPIN

NESKOWIN, OREGON

August 18, 2015

I'd been tracking my mail deliveries for two weeks now, clocking the postal vehicle's daily arrival with the intensity of a child waiting for Christmas morning.

Except the only thing I felt was slick, stomach-turning dread.

Don't let it be a match. Please, God, don't let it be a match.

My palms prickled with sweat every time I heard the hum of tires coming up our private lane. Whenever it was a package delivery driver, I breathed through the rush of nausea and forced my gaze back to my computer screen, where the landing pages I was supposed to be designing blurred and swam in front of my eyes.

When it was the postal service truck, I tensed and counted the seconds until I could get my hands on the mail.

Today was no different—at first.

When the mail truck appeared around ten a.m. like a boxy white ghost materializing through the ever-present coastal fog, my heart rate spiked as if I'd just downed a caffeine pill. Like always, I crept downstairs and waited beside the front door until the driver had deposited the day's mail in the box at the end of the driveway.

My husband, Joel, was shuffling papers around on his desk down the hall. I knew he was watching, too. The second I came back inside with a handful of letters, he would open his office door and wait while I sorted through the envelopes, ready to place a hand on the small of my back if one of the return addresses read, OGDEN POLICE DEPARTMENT.

I pressed my wedding band into the skin of my finger until it hurt, watching as the postal worker straightened the thin pile of envelopes in his hand before placing them carefully into our box. He frowned, rubbed his mop of stick-straight gray hair, then ducked back inside the vehicle.

Hurry up and go, goddammit, my mind screamed. But I stood silently on the cold entryway tile, staring through the blinds that covered the window beside the door, like I was the woman from *Rear Window.*

After what felt like days, he leaned back out of the mail truck's cutout and deposited one more letter in the box.

Somehow, I knew it was *the* letter. As if my desperation had finally mounted so high, I'd actually made that letter appear out of thin air.

The letter that would tell me whether my own DNA matched the girl whose body was so badly mutilated that the police in Ogden, Utah couldn't identify her without my help.

The letter regarding the girl whose name had been a whisper in my ear during quiet moments for the past seventeen years.

Andrea.

When the mailman finally closed the lid of our box and gunned his truck back up the lane, I didn't even take the time to put on shoes as I yanked open the door, rushed down the driveway and pulled down the sun-warmed metal flap.

And there it was. Right on top of the stack, the words OGDEN POLICE DEPARTMENT stamped in bold black letters in the upper left corner.

The detective I'd spoken to two weeks earlier said that someone would call me when his department received the DNA results. I wasn't banking on any calls, though. "I apologize in advance if the letter from the lab reaches you by mail before I get a chance to touch base ..." he'd said, like we were talking about the results of a yearly physical. Like the letter I'd received asking for my DNA with a cheek swab was really that clinical. Just cells and DNA.

Then again, cells and DNA were the only things that tied me to the six-month-old baby girl I'd voluntarily given up for adoption when I was sixteen.

The girl would be seventeen now. I had no claim to her anymore, legally or otherwise, but I'd never stopped thinking about her.

Something sharp bit into the ball of my bare foot as I hurried back up the walkway toward the door I'd left open. Warm liquid oozed between my toes, but I didn't stop walking or even look down.

Joel was waiting for me in the kitchen, standing with his arms crossed and a crease running between his hooded blue eyes. "It's here?" he asked, and reached out a hand as he stepped toward me. When he read the look on my face, the hand fell to his side and he didn't come any closer.

I swallowed, grateful and guilt-stricken that he'd understood without me saying the words. I needed to open it by myself. It wasn't fair to shut him out, but some part of me needed to be alone in this moment. As alone as I'd been when I held my baby for the last time in the lobby of the Oregon Department of Health and Welfare Child Services.

Joel wasn't Andrea's birth father. Her father had been a senior at a neighboring high school who'd signed the adoption papers as fast as he could grab the pen from my own father. I wouldn't meet Joel for another decade.

Hands shaking, I moved into the open laundry room, tore open the top of the envelope and blinked. The faint smell of fried eggs and hashbrowns lingering downstairs, comforting a few minutes earlier, now made me sick.

"Sabi?" Joel asked softly after a few seconds, knocking on the laundry room door.

I stared at the single sheet of paper unseeing, letting the words blur and swim in front of my eyes.

When Andrea went missing three months ago, I hadn't been notified by the police—or her adoptive parents. It had been a closed adoption, which meant that nobody had my contact information readily accessible. So the first time I'd learned that my daughter had disappeared was when I read Detective Barker's letter two weeks ago, requesting my DNA.

"We didn't have a way to contact you at first..." The detective had trailed off when I'd called the number in the letter and demanded to know why it had taken three months to notify me. The police had started tracking down the court adoption records, but it took them a while. It was clear enough that notifying me of her missing-person status wasn't a priority. Not until the police found that body and needed my DNA.

There was also the fact that Andrea wasn't necessarily missing, Detective Barker explained. She was presumed to be a runaway. And while she was technically still a minor, there was every reason to think she'd left of her own accord based on what her adoptive parents had said.

This theory—that Andrea had merely run away—should have been slightly comforting, if I'd heard it three months ago. But hearing it while Detective Barker was backpedaling to explain the letter requesting my DNA offered me little hope. There was a dead young woman lying in a morgue somewhere, who might or might not be the daughter I'd given up so she could have a better life.

The words *missing, remains, impossible to identify* had burned themselves into my brain like brands.

"Sabi?" Joel asked again as he pushed the laundry room door open. "What does it say?"

I gripped the edges of the letter, vaguely aware of how slowly I was reading the words. Words I'd been waiting for with every waking moment since I'd provided my DNA sample.

My eyes landed on the bold phrase in the center of the letter: **Not a match.**

A strange, wolflike whimper escaped my lips. I read the words again and again, desperate to be sure I wasn't misunderstanding.

Not a match, not a match, not a match.

2

SABINA

NESKOWIN, OREGON

It wasn't her.

The body the Ogden Police had recovered wasn't my Andrea.

I shook my head over and over as I held the letter out to Joel so he could read it himself, while I turned my eyes to the tiny blue flowers in the wallpaper. They were forget-me-nots. I hadn't even realized that until that very moment.

"Oh, thank God," Joel breathed, as relieved as I was numb. "This is … this is …" He let the sentence fade, giving up on finding the right words. "I'm so glad it wasn't her."

When he said that, I finally felt the tears start to burn behind my eyes. I tore my gaze away from those forget-me-nots blurring on the walls and looked at him. "She was supposed to … I thought I was giving her a better life than …"

I couldn't complete the thought. Couldn't even feel the relief of knowing that the body I'd pictured mangled and bloody was not, in fact, my daughter.

I was grateful it wasn't.

But nothing felt remotely okay.

The horror had just shifted gears. And all I could think about was the face of that little girl with enormous hazel eyes. The baby

I'd last held against my chest in the basement of my parent's house a little more than seventeen years ago.

Andrea had cried nearly every moment she was awake for three months, from the day she was born. So did I. Silently, in contrast with her loud, hiccupping, machine-gun wails pinging off my eardrums as I held her against my shoulder and patted her back, trying to help her find the burp that would ease her tummy. I paced back and forth, back and forth, while I held her in the tiny basement bedroom I'd slept in since I was a baby, desperately trying to lull her back to sleep.

My mom wanted to help me during those first dark weeks after Andrea arrived, but my dad stopped her every time. *"She has to do this on her own, Janine. This is the bed she made. She's gotta sleep in it now."*

It nearly made me laugh out loud when he said that, because I was getting so little sleep at the time. All I wanted was a bed to lay in—made or unmade—where I could close my eyes, knowing I'd get a few hours of uninterrupted rest.

When Andrea wasn't crying, she was nursing. It was the only thing that seemed to soothe her, so I fed her as often as she'd latch until my nipples cracked and bled.

By the end of those first three months, I was desperate. For sleep, for someone to tell me that things would get better, for someone to hold *me* while *I* cried.

The first time my baby girl smiled at me—docile for once, hazel eyes clear and searching instead of scrunched and angry—I burst into loud tears I couldn't turn off. She was just so beautiful. That smile broke my heart and lifted it up at the same time. It also told me how depressed and awful I felt, if one small smile could shatter me like glass.

I knew I couldn't survive on a smile, even one so perfect.

That day, the heavy footsteps on the stairs made me wipe my eyes as quickly as I could. From the clomping rhythm, I knew it was my dad, not my mom. I pulled my maternity shirt down to cover myself up and wiped Andrea's milky mouth with my sleeve. She puckered her lips in frustration and prepared to scream, not finished nursing yet. The footsteps came down the hall then stopped. The door to the basement nursery stayed closed.

After a few seconds, a red-and-white striped envelope I recognized from my mom's collection of stationery came through the crack beneath the door. Then the footsteps thumped back down the hall and upstairs.

Not daring to put Andrea down in her crib for fear she'd let loose the wail building in her throat, I tucked her against my shoulder and bent to pick up the letter lying on the floor.

The note was in my dad's handwriting. As I read the words, I imagined his low, gentle voice that called our backyard chickens into the coop at sundown every night.

To our dearest Sabina,

Your mother and I want what's best for you. You understand that now, because of the beautiful little girl you've brought into the world. I know you want what's best for her, too. You are a good girl, and you want to be a good mother.

But sometimes wanting the best for our children isn't enough. Not when you're sixteen.

Watching you struggle through a pregnancy and now motherhood hasn't been easy. There have been so many times we've wanted to step in and save you from your choices. However, being a parent means making tough decisions.

Andrea deserves the best life with a mother <u>and</u> a father. A stable home. There are so many parents who desperately want a baby. You can give her that life. You won't be giving her up. You'll

be giving her more. And someday, when you're truly ready, you will
have the opportunity to be a mother in the correct way.

We love you. And we love Andrea. We know you'll do the
right thing.

Love,
Your parents

As I read the letter a second time, Andrea made an unhappy squawking noise against my chest, and I realized I was gripping her chubby thigh too tightly. She hiccuped, then squealed, and I sank to the carpet, looking at the letter in my hand.

My parents had tried to tell me the same thing before the baby came. They warned me that as an unwed mother who hadn't even managed to finish high school, my life would be difficult.

It wasn't that I thought they were wrong, before. I was terrified to have a baby while I was still a kid myself. But I was already falling in love with that miraculous moving blurry blob I'd seen on the ultrasound screen at my first doctor's appointment.

Still, the love I felt for my baby when she arrived was more complicated and painful than I could have imagined. And the threads of doubt and terror that had grown while I paced and nursed and cried and longed to sleep, quickly turned into what felt like a rope around my neck.

For the first time, I looked down at my baby's chubby, tear-stained cheeks and let myself feel the horror of the decision I'd made.

I wasn't enough for her.

I was never meant to be a mother like this.

She deserved the world. And all I had to offer her was this cramped basement room with faded wallpaper and a low supply of milk.

I held her to my heart and stumbled upstairs before I could change my mind. Before the voice in the back of my head begging *no, no, no,* could convince me otherwise. That voice had started as a scream when my parents first brought up the idea of adoption. Now it had dwindled to a frantic, threadbare whisper.

"Okay," I told my dad, even though the word burned like acid in my mouth.

He nodded sadly then reached out his arms, beckoning for the baby. "I'm proud of you, Sabina. That's real love right there."

I just nodded again, because I couldn't speak.

Andrea nuzzled her cheek against his shoulder and sighed, calming down, like she'd been waiting for me to come to my senses this whole time.

My dad smiled. "Why don't you get some sleep for a few hours while I hold the baby? We'll sort it all out with your mother when she gets home from the grocery store."

* * *

After I read the letter from the lab declaring my DNA was not a match to the girl the Ogden police had recovered, I went outside and sat on the back deck facing the ocean. Then I watched as the sky darkened, wind churning the waves in the distance like frothed cream.

The irony was, even though Joel and I had wanted them, I hadn't been able to have more children. I'd just assumed I would be able to get pregnant easily when the time was right, since I'd done so at sixteen by accident. That was before a diagnosis of endometriosis in my late twenties. The doctor assured me it had nothing to do with my earlier pregnancy as a teen. And I knew, logically, that it had nothing to do with my decision to give my baby up for adoption. But that didn't stop it from feeling that way. Like the universe had meted out yet another punishment.

Joel sat next to me on the swing, leg touching mine, until I fought through the haze of my memories and turned to look at him.

There was a thought pushing its way to the front of my brain that I couldn't ignore any longer.

"I have to know what happened to her. I owe her that," I said, finding my voice for the first time since I read the letter an hour earlier.

He turned his hand palm up and beckoned to me, slowly, gently, like he might approach a frightened feral animal. "This isn't your fault."

"I know that," I said so sharply that it was clear I knew nothing of the sort. Whatever had happened to Andrea *was* my fault. It was one thousand percent my fault. She was my baby first.

"What can I do to help?" Joel asked, his voice low and kind, his eyes clear blue like sea glass in the sun.

I took his warm hand in my freezing one and closed my eyes as the first drops of rain tapped on the porch roof. "Tell me I'm allowed to get involved."

He huffed, taken aback. "*Allowed*? What do you mean?"

"I'm not her mother anymore," I said, feeling my body shake as the wind rustled the leaves of the potted plants creeping along the deck boards at our feet. "I gave her away when she was a baby."

Joel squeezed my hand. "You've carried that little girl with you every day of your life. She's part of you. You're still her mother, and you love her," he said with so much conviction I actually believed him.

I blinked rapidly, but it didn't stop the warm tears from spilling down my cheeks.

A clap of thunder rolled, and a second later lightning split the clouds hanging heavy over the surf.

"I need to go to Utah," I whispered, making my decision the second I said the words out loud.

Joel drew me closer, and I let him pull me against his chest. "I'll come with you, then."

I shook my head. "No." I shifted to face him as the wind swept sideways, sending cold drops of rain onto my cheeks where they mingled with the warm tears. "Your mom needs you here."

Joel was the primary caregiver for his mother, Irene. Part of the reason we'd moved to Neskowin was to be near her as she got older. Then, last month, she'd broken her hip in a bad fall. The idea that both of us might leave the state right now was out of the question.

"I won't be gone long," I added. It was the first lie I'd ever told him. I had no idea how long I might be gone.

I didn't even know where to start.

Didn't even know what I thought I'd find.

I wasn't the police. I wasn't an investigator. And I had zero legal claim to that child.

But within the hour, I was racing the storm to Ogden.

THREE MONTHS
EARLIER

3

ANDREA

OGDEN, UTAH

May, 2015

Sometimes, I had this thought that maybe Dennis wasn't my real dad. And that maybe Bunny wasn't my real mom.

But what sixteen-year-old girl hadn't entertained that fantasy? That maybe there was somebody out there who loved me more?

Or at all.

I never followed the thought very far. The girls at school complained about their parents all the time. As soon as one person started bitching about phone limits or not being allowed to wear makeup, it was off to the races. Nobody at Ogden High School spoke the words "Mom" or "Dad" without a roll of the eyes.

Still, I'd never seen welts on the hidden parts of their skin when we all changed for gym. And believe me, I'd looked.

Sometimes, I found myself daydreaming about scenarios where my parents died in a car crash and I had to go live with distant relatives. But I didn't really know any of my aunts or uncles. Bunny said we used to host Christmas when I was little, and I had vague memories of clattering dishes and the smell of turkey and stuffing. There had been some kind of falling out, though, and that was the last time anyone got together for the holidays, or anything else.

I felt so guilty for those kinds of thoughts when Dennis and Bunny got me the new jeans I wanted for Christmas, or let me choose a restaurant for dinner, or bragged about my grades to the employee at Ralph's when we took my report card there for free ice cream. Especially because every once in a while, Dennis gave me this squinty-eyed, questioning look, like he could read all the mean thoughts running through my mind.

Sometimes, I wondered if that was why he treated me the way he did. Because he knew what I was thinking.

I got my answer the day I turned seventeen.

Bunny had ordered a cake from Baskin Robbins, which was something special all by itself. It had purple frosting roses, rocky road ice cream layered between slabs of chocolate cake, and my name written in loopy cursive on top, HAPPY BIRTHDAY, AN-DREA!

When I opened the freezer that morning and saw it there like she'd promised, I just knew it was going to be a good day. My mouth watered every time I thought about it that Friday at school.

I was feeling so good, in fact, that I nearly asked Paloma if she wanted to walk home with me after school. I wanted her to see that beautiful cake, share it with me, pretend I was just a normal seventeen-year-old girl on her birthday.

The words almost tumbled out of my mouth when Paloma surprised me with a cupcake and some monarch butterfly earrings in first period, along with a note saying she'd made the earrings herself—and calling me her BFF.

The only reason I didn't ask her over was because I thought that if I opened my mouth, I might cry and wouldn't be able to talk properly. Nobody had ever given me a gift like that before.

The earrings were partially translucent, like a real butterfly, and the delicate red-and-black wings looked like they might take flight at any moment. I'd never had a best friend. Not really. Not since the time in elementary school that I'd worn the same shirt three days in a row—a gross, stained Mickey Mouse button-up that was way too big for me—and got sent to the office to change into a loaner. After that, nobody was lining up to be friends with "And-reek-a," the nickname Nova Tomlinson gave me.

So when Paloma gave me that note, I really wanted to invite her over to share the cake we were going to eat after dinner. But Bunny had been extra high-strung ever since she'd started a new job at the dairy plant a few months back. I told myself I didn't know how she'd react if I invited a friend over without asking.

That wasn't the real reason, though.

The real reason was knowing that the second I got home, I'd have pretty much no choice but to peel off my ratty red hoodie.

That was a problem. The school classrooms were air-conditioned, so I could wear the long-sleeved hoodie all day long in front of my classmates. But we had a swamp cooler at home, and with the temperatures already tipping past eighty degrees in April, I was going to sweat through my hoodie while I walked home along the canal, and I'd definitely have to take it off the second I stepped through the front door into our muggy house.

The raised pink cuts on my forearms hadn't quite finished healing yet, and the thick, blue-black welts on my stomach definitely hadn't.

The marks were my fault. I was the one who made the cuts on my arms so low, down past my elbow. Slicing the skin shallowly, one drag of the safety pin at a time, impossible to stop, like eating potato chips.

It didn't feel *good,* exactly.

It just felt *better*.

Because for one moment—which I could draw out for nearly a minute if I really took my time—everything except that bright slice of pain disappeared. It was like the safety pin I held between my thumb and forefinger was an eraser instead of a miniature weapon.

The other slashes were from Dennis. He had pulled out the leash three days ago when he found the thin slits from the safety pin.

Our dog Pollie had been dead for years, but Dennis kept that worn leather coil in his back pocket nearly all the time.

"You like hurting yourself so much?" he'd barked, holding both of my wrists in the same hand while he grabbed the hem of my shirt to expose the pale skin of my belly. I knew better than to answer him.

Thwack.

"You think you're gonna get some kind of attention at school for that?"

Thwack.

"You gonna bitch to some teacher about how *bad* your life is at home?" He wheezed like he always did when he got worked up. Bunny said he'd gotten too much cement dust in his lungs over the years. I hated the sound.

Thwack.

"I want you to think real hard before you do that again. Trying to make your mother and me look like *we* did something to you."

If he hadn't landed the next blow to my stomach so hard I lost my balance and went to my knees, I might have laughed at the irony of that last statement.

Afterward, he wiped his brow and gave me a hug. Later that night, Bunny came into my room to tell me about ordering the Baskin Robbins cake for my birthday.

I was never quite sure whether or not she could hear what Dennis did when he lost his temper. He definitely wasn't quiet about it. And the house wasn't all that big. Small enough that I had to share a room with the washing machine and dryer upstairs.

I'd never asked Bunny if she knew. Because as long as I didn't ask, I could still tell myself she had no idea it was happening.

And that was better than thinking she heard it and did nothing.

So yeah, I didn't invite Paloma over to the house for my seventeenth birthday.

I should have. Because when I walked through the front door, the house was quiet.

I stopped in the doorway for a few seconds, suddenly anxious about going inside even though I was boiling hot in my sweatshirt.

It wasn't a good quiet.

It was quiet like a cat about to pounce on a mouse.

4

ANDREA

OGDEN, UT

I stood at the entryway but didn't close the door behind me while I shrugged off my backpack and then my red sweatshirt.

I eased my stuff down onto the linoleum and tilted my head to listen, keeping the butterfly earrings Paloma had given me clutched in my hand like a lucky charm. I was dying to try them on. I'd gotten my ears pierced a few years ago, but I wasn't sure whether the holes were still—

Bam.

The sound of metal on metal echoed from the kitchen.

The noise startled me so much, I dropped the earrings. They landed with a quiet clatter, one of them sliding out of sight beneath the side table near the door.

I swallowed, mouth dry, and bent to pick up the lone earring at my feet, unwilling to move any closer to the kitchen. I could search for the other one later.

I knew Bunny wasn't home yet. She worked at the dairy plant until five every weekday, without fail.

Which meant it was Dennis in the kitchen.

I hated when this happened. He was a general contractor, so his work came in waves. Sometimes, he'd be on a job site from sunrise until long after dark, which was fine with me. Other times—the best times—he oversaw jobs in Logan or Provo and was gone for a couple days straight.

But sometimes, like today, he'd get home before noon and start drinking.

Those were the worst days.

I eased the front door shut, my arms popping goosebumps despite the stale, muggy air inside the house.

Bam.

The oven slammed shut in the kitchen, followed by a quieter thump like Dennis had banged his fist against it. "Worthless piece of shit!"

I took a step toward the stairs, pretty sure he hadn't heard me come inside since he hadn't said anything to me yet. If I could make it upstairs to my bedroom without him noticing, there was a good chance he'd keep drinking and maybe settle down on the couch to watch *King of Queens* until Bunny got home.

As excited as I was about that Baskin Robbins cake, I would've gladly chucked it into the trash in a second if I could guarantee he'd do that.

I set my foot on the first carpeted step, careful to place it in the middle where it wouldn't creak.

Thump, thump, thump.

Dennis's footsteps, moving across the kitchen.

Shit. I hustled and took the stairs faster—too fast.

I hit the fifth one just shy of dead center, sending a loud creak into the silence right as his footsteps stopped. I clutched the lone butterfly tighter in my hand.

"Andrea? You sneaking around out there?"

I froze, hoping that if I didn't answer he'd go back to whatever he was making in the kitchen. I could smell the fuggy, burnt odor the oven gave off whenever it heated up, from the food crusted to the bottom. The same way the whole house smelled, but stronger.

"Andrea?" Dennis called again, and the still-raw marks on my arms prickled like a warning.

More footsteps.

I took off, dashing the rest of the way up the stairs.

I was too slow, though.

Out of the corner of my eye, I saw Dennis's bulky frame move into the living room right before I reached the top.

He saw me see him.

"Sneaky," he drawled, but I knew better than to accept the casual tone of his voice. "Here I am, going out of my way to make you an after-school snack for your birthday, and you *ignore me* when I say your name?"

I forced an apologetic smile and shrugged my shoulders like, *I guess I'm just that stupid.* "I—I didn't hear you. I'm sorry, I just needed to get something from my room—"

"You damn well did hear me," he interrupted. The drawl was fading, scraped away by a harder edge. "Do you know what *my* daddy would've done to me if I disrespected him like that?"

When I didn't answer, he snapped, "Get down here. *March.*"

Tears stung my eyes, but not because of his words.

It was because he was reaching for his back pocket. I could already imagine the slap of leather hitting my stomach again, when the bruises were still so new they hadn't even turned yellow at the margins yet.

Also because it was my birthday, and all I wanted was to disappear into my room and admire my new earrings until I could eat those silky purple roses and the creamy rocky road ice cream of the cake from Baskin Robbins.

"Just leave me alone today!" I burst out.

He stared at me in shock as one hand moved toward the pocket where he kept the coiled dog leash. I'd never talked back to him quite like that before.

I knew instantly I'd just made everything much, much worse.

In desperation, I glanced sideways at the portrait of Jesus hanging in the hallway. He wore a white robe and knelt in front of some sparrows at his feet. From where I stood, and the way he was positioned in the painting, it looked like he had his back to me, blissfully unaware of my predicament. He always seemed to be facing away when I needed him. Our family hadn't been to church since I was in elementary school, and it'd been just as long since I'd prayed, but suddenly I found the words I'd memorized as a child running through my head.

Dear Heavenly Father, please protect me.

Dennis blinked, his face turning a deep shade of red, his jaw ticking as he chewed on the words I'd just hurled at him.

Then, faster than you'd think a man his size could run, he bounded up the stairs, taking them two at a time, dog leash now hanging from his right hand.

I froze.

Then, before he reached me, I took off running.

That was a mistake.

Because if I hadn't tried to escape, he might've only added a few more red-and-purple stripes while I cowered in front of him like he wanted, paying the price for my "disobedience."

Instead, he dove forward and darted out a hand to catch my shirt, yanking me back as I lifted my foot to run for my bedroom.

I lost my balance and tilted backward. The butterfly flew out of my hand. For a second, I was sure I was going to fall all the way down those stairs. So I arched my back like a cat, in a desperate attempt to keep that from happening.

That was my next mistake.

Instead of tumbling backward down the stairs like I thought I would, my body slammed sideways. My left temple connected with the sharp, square corner of the banister.

The ugly beige carpet flashed bright red, like an awful fireworks show. The pain welled up with so much force I could barely stand it, then went strangely dull.

I crumpled to the carpet.

With my vision still flashing red, I could only feel, rather than see, Dennis hovering over me. His awful wheeze got louder as he leaned closer.

Blackness curled at the edges of my mind, and I knew that if I didn't fight it, I'd be unconscious in about half a second. Every cell in my body resisted the idea of slipping away into oblivion while Dennis was beside me.

"Andrea," he rasped, flat and low, like maybe I was just faking being hurt.

I tried to blink, to clear the cotton-wrapped pain in my head and the flashes of light behind my eyes. Tried to talk, but the only thing that came out of my mouth was a warm string of saliva and a word that might've been, "Don't."

Dennis blew out a breath, like air going out of a big balloon.

"Goddammit, Andrea," he muttered, sounding suddenly afraid, even tearful.

I thought he was going to put down the dog leash and help me up. That maybe now that I was hurt—hurt bad—all the rage would go out of him, and we'd still get to eat that Baskin Robbins cake tonight when Bunny got home.

That's not what happened, though.

"Why'd you have to go and do that?" he wheezed, anger creeping into his voice, like I'd done something to him.

I tried to answer, but all I could do was moan.

"Hush up. Shh, shh. The more you fuss the worse it'll be," he whispered, and his voice was next to my ear all of a sudden, and that dog leash was snaking around my neck. "You don't gotta suffer much more."

I wanted to scream, but now I couldn't even breathe.

For a few long, agonizing seconds, the pain in my head and the pain in my throat turned up to eleven, and it was so awful I couldn't stand to be in my body anymore.

But then, all at once, my vision cleared and the pain and pressure let go.

I could see.

I could scream.

And I could move.

Like an arrow out of a bow, I scrambled to my feet as fast as I could get them underneath me. "Stop, stop, please, I'll be good!" I begged.

The thing was, though, Dennis didn't even notice.

Because he was still choking that limp, seventeen-year-old girl on the stairs. The girl with an ugly black bruise at her crushed left temple and a line of saliva running down her cheek.

The girl who was me.

5

ANDREA

OGDEN, UT

For a few seconds, I thought I was having an out-of-body experience.

Dennis didn't move a muscle to chase me down the hall. He stayed right where he was, huffing and puffing on the landing, catty-corner to that picture of Jesus.

"Stop it," I screamed again, but he didn't react.

I quit saying it after that because I could see that it was too late.

There wasn't really any blood. But the girl's face—*my* face—had turned an ugly shade of maroon, except for that left temple. It was a bruise so dark it looked black. My chest wasn't rising and falling anymore. And my hands had stopped clawing at Pollie's leash.

I stared a little longer, but the whole thing scared me so much that I did the only thing I could think to do—I ran down the hall and into my bedroom. But when I tried to shimmy past the washing machine in my makeshift room so I could reach the door handle and slam it shut, nothing happened.

I looked down at my hand, where my palm rested lightly on the handle.

I couldn't feel the slick, worn metal.

Because you're dead.

I let go of the doorknob and recoiled into the center of my bedroom as the thought finally forced its way to the front of my mind.

I couldn't be dead. I didn't *feel* dead. But what did being dead feel like?

Less painful than being alive.

Nothing hurt anymore—not physically, anyway. My bedroom, which should have been too hot and stale and smelling of burnt leftovers wafting through the vents—felt and smelled like nothing at all.

The only thing I actually felt was panic. And desperation. And guilt for abandoning the girl on the floor.

I spun in a fast circle around my tiny room, trying and failing to feel the uneven linoleum beneath my feet. The creaky daybed with the faded yellow quilt didn't make a sound when I sat on it.

This couldn't be happening. I couldn't be dead. I just couldn't.

I was only seventeen. And today was my birthday.

A noise from down the hall, followed by footsteps on the stairs, made me jump.

Dennis was on the move again.

A door slammed downstairs—the kitchen door that led to the backyard. What the hell was he doing now?

I didn't want to step into the hallway again, but I couldn't stay away, either.

I braced myself while I walked back through my open bedroom door, all too aware that I couldn't feel the grubby hall carpet beneath my feet with each step. When I reached the landing at the top of the stairs, I stopped moving and made myself look down.

The house had gone completely quiet again, like a moment of silence for the girl on the floor with her lips tinged blue and her choppy auburn hair curling across her forehead at the cowlick.

The lone monarch butterfly earring lay a few feet away from her hand, on the top step, where it had landed.

I knelt beside her, part of me still clinging to hope that this was a vivid nightmare. She looked like me, sure. Same haircut, same clothing I'd been wearing, same tiny slices across her arms. But she was a stranger, too. A 3D version of the girl I'd only ever seen flattened in photos and mirrors.

The hollows in her cheeks were more painfully pronounced than I'd ever realized. She was thin in a way that made me feel silly for ever wishing my pants fit looser around my waist. And she looked so vulnerable lying there that I desperately wanted to protect her from Dennis in a way I'd never been able to do for myself.

And, of course, there was that awful, mottled black bruise at her left temple, and the ugly red indentations from the dog leash still wrapped tight around her neck.

I lay my hand across her throat to cover those marks from view, remembering in sudden, vivid clarity how alive I'd been while he used that leash to snuff me out. *"Hush up. You don't gotta suffer much more,"* he'd said. Like I was some fatally injured animal he'd hit with his car. Like he was offering me a merciful end to my broken life.

The girl's tightly clenched fingers, one of them still hooked beneath that leash, told a different story.

The numb shock and panic, the only things I seemed to be able to feel, began to shift into something else.

When I'd hit my head, Dennis hadn't run for help.

He hadn't called the police, voice shaking with horror and fear, to tell them his daughter had just fallen and needed an ambulance.

He'd knelt and wrapped that dog leash tight around my neck, like it was the very first inclination in his mind.

The back door opened again downstairs, and I froze.

A few seconds later, Dennis appeared at the bottom of the stairs holding a wrinkled gray tarp under one arm.

The rage built inside me like steam in a pressure cooker. "You killed me. You fucking killed me!"

Dennis didn't bat an eye. He just sighed and started up the stairs, wheezing softly like he was already tired of dealing with this mess.

"Get away from me!" I shrieked, but he kept on trudging toward the body.

I glanced at the clock in the entryway downstairs. Four o'clock. Bunny would be home in an hour. What was he going to tell her? Would she call the police?

I wanted the police here *now,* with a ferocity like hunger pangs. The feeling welled up inside of me, pressing and powerful, with nowhere to go.

To my surprise, Dennis paused on the stairs, his hooded, hound-dog eyes suddenly wide.

There *were* sirens in the distance, moving closer and getting louder.

"Shit," Dennis hissed, hesitating like he might run back down the staircase.

I stayed where I was, prickling with desperation. Had a neighbor heard something and called the police?

But just as I started to hope, the sirens faded and disappeared.

My heart sank.

The look of relief on Dennis's sagging face made me want to tear him apart.

Moving with purpose, he bounded the rest of the way up the steps. His left foot landed on the butterfly with a quiet crunch, and he grunted as he picked up the pieces and placed them on top of the tarp he'd spread beside my body.

He stood there staring at me for a few seconds, brow furrowed and his eyes red and glassy. Was he holding back tears? Or was it from the alcohol?

Then he shook his head and cleared his throat. "You were never really ours," he muttered as he squatted and hefted my body onto the dirty, crinkled canvas. Then louder, again, like he was reassuring himself of the words. "You were never really ours."

Of all the things I thought he might say right then, I wasn't expecting that.

He unwrapped the dog leash from around my neck and inspected it. Then, reluctantly, like he hated to part with it, he set it on top of the tarp too. "Shoulda known that if your own family didn't want you, there might be a reason for it."

Never really ours.

Your own family didn't want you.

I suddenly knew exactly what he was talking about, and that surprised me.

The memory thrust itself to the front of my brain, sharp and painful like a long-buried sliver. A memory I'd never even realized I had until now. A memory that didn't even make sense for me to have, since I was only a baby at the time.

Yet there it was. Clear as day, I saw a mental image of our house, newer and cleaner than it was now. Dennis and Bunny, seventeen years younger. And me, an infant in the arms of a middle-aged woman who was saying the words, "*Congratulations, the adoption is final,*" as she handed me over to a smiling Bunny.

"Can't let Bunny see you like this, can we?" Dennis mumbled, yanking me away from the memory.

Then he pulled the tarp over my face.

Everything—and nothing—made sense now.

THREE MONTHS
LATER

6

SABINA

OGDEN, UTAH

August, 2015

While I drove the thirteen hours to Ogden, I tried listening to the radio. But the songs were either annoyingly happy or so gut-wrenchingly sad that I had to pull over for a few minutes until I stopped shaking.

I tried to listen to an audiobook, *Lean UX*. I'd been meaning to read it for work—one of my "personal stretch goals" as a contractor for the Portland-based hospital network who was my biggest client—but it was impossible to follow the thread of the concepts.

I couldn't focus on anything at all.

So, after a while, I just drove in silence, eyes fixed on the road through the wipers that batted raindrops back and forth across the glass.

My mind felt like it was crammed full of snarls of yarn, each a question that had no answer, each a mess that might never be untangled. I reached for them each in turn, picking up the dangling threads again and again to worry them while I drove.

Had Andrea really run away? And if so, why? Happy kids didn't just run away at barely seventeen years old.

If I hadn't chosen a closed adoption when I filed the paperwork with my parents, would things have turned out differently?

Where was she right now? Was she okay?

Would her adoptive parents talk to me? What would they say? I'd only learned their names two weeks ago, when that first letter asking for my DNA arrived and I started Googling Dennis and Bunny Beaumont.

What did I actually think I was going to do when I got to Ogden? Did I really think I'd be able to find her when the police and her own adoptive parents hadn't been able to? Andrea was a functional stranger to me. And this was the first time I'd even been to Utah.

What would happen if I *did* find her? Would she want anything to do with me? Would she even want to speak to me?

I'd planned to stop at some roadside motel for the night when I got tired—in Pendleton, maybe. I'd promised Joel I would. I didn't get tired, though, and I didn't want to stop. Even as the little green numbers on the car dash showed 9:00 p.m., then 11:00 p.m., I kept driving, wired as if I'd chugged half a gallon of coffee over the hours.

Andrea had gone missing three months ago, which meant that I was already beyond late in making this trip.

I stopped just twice—once to refill the car with gas, and again to use the bathroom at a lonely wayside gas station that would've scared the shit out of me on an average day. But it wasn't an average day, and I didn't even hesitate as I unlocked the driver's side door and stepped into the parking lot devoid of light aside from a blinking bulb near one pump.

At the second stop, while I sat in a grimy bathroom stall, I used my phone to book an Airbnb for my stay in Ogden, choosing the first listing that promised automatic booking and check-in, so I'd be able to get inside and crash the second I arrived.

Then I plugged the address into my Maps app and resumed driving.

The first hints of sunrise turned the sky steely gray around 5:00 a.m. as I crossed the border into Utah, and I realized that the thick trees and blackberry brambles lining I-84 had given way to sprawling agricultural fields and mountains in the distance.

I scanned the horizon, eyes roving along the shoulder of the road like I might see a teenage girl with her thumb out, trudging through the dirt with her head down, if I looked closely enough.

When I'd typed *Andrea Beaumont missing person Ogden Utah* into Google two weeks ago, I'd seen her photo for the first time. My baby, all grown up at seventeen years old.

It was her school picture from her junior year, with that generic, marbled blue-and-white background, the hallmark of every cafeteria photoshoot. But it took my breath away. Because my very first thought when I saw the photo was that if I'd bumped into Andrea at the grocery store, I would have known in my bones she was my child. My baby.

It didn't matter that the last time I'd seen her, those cheeks had been round and soft instead of angular and sharp. Teething gums instead of a row of slightly crooked teeth. Fuzzy, nearly bald head instead of choppy auburn hair and bangs curling haphazardly across her forehead from a stubborn cowlick. Her eyes were the same color as mine, honey-amber brown with flecks of green. The shape of our noses—narrow and straight—was identical, and we had matching dimples in our chins.

Everything about the photo made me want to pull her to my chest and reclaim her. Mine, mine, mine.

But each word in the article beneath the photo was a stark reminder she wasn't mine anymore.

Ogden, Utah — A local family is seeking answers after their 17-year-old daughter, Andrea Beaumont, disappeared on her birthday earlier this week. Authorities suspect she may be a runaway, and while her parents acknowledge this possibility, they remain hopeful for answers.

Andrea was last seen at her high school in central Ogden on Friday afternoon. Her mother, Bunny Beaumont, found $200 missing from her wallet shortly after she realized that Andrea was gone. The teenager did not leave a note, adding to the mystery surrounding her disappearance.

"Andrea has always been a headstrong kid," said her father, Dennis Beaumont. "She's had her struggles. We just hope she's safe and knows she can come home when she's ready."

Andrea is described as 5'6" tall, with chin-length auburn hair and hazel eyes. She was last seen wearing a red hoodie and jeans. She may be carrying a black backpack with a blue embroidered butterfly patch on the front.

While police have categorized Andrea as a missing juvenile, they are treating the case seriously given her age and the circumstances of her disappearance. "We're asking anyone who may have seen her or has any information about her whereabouts to come forward," said Detective Monte Barker of the Ogden Police Department.

I'd read that article with a stone in my stomach, trying—and failing—to convince myself that teenagers ran away from home every day.

"In three miles, take Exit 341 for Ogden," the perky voice from my Maps app announced, startling me from the memory.

I flicked my eyes to the phone screen, shocked to see that I'd be arriving at the Ogden Airbnb in seventeen minutes.

My hands suddenly felt slick on the steering wheel, and I had the urge to roll down the window and scream out Andrea's name.

Instead, I kept one eye on the road while I navigated to my phone contacts. I had no idea if the cell phone numbers I'd paid to find on a name-lookup service for Bunny and Dennis Beaumont were correct. And it was way too early for a polite call.

Then again, this wouldn't be a polite call.

I tried Bunny first.

The line rang in my ear as I exited I-15, marked by a bill-board showing a mother and father surrounded by their smiling children beneath the words FAMILIES ARE FOREVER: VISIT TEMPLE SQUARE.

"Hello?" answered a hoarse, female voice, thick with sleep.

I nearly dropped the phone.

"*Hello*," she barked again, louder, clearly annoyed.

I'd woken her up. I couldn't imagine how many calls she'd fielded over the past three months since Andrea disappeared. But I instantly disliked the woman on the other end of the line.

That bristling feeling brought my voice back to me. "Bunny? My name is Sabina," I began, rushing to get the introduction out so she wouldn't hang up. "We don't know each other, but I'm … I'm Andrea's birth mother. I want to help find her. I'm sorry it's so early. I just got to Ogden. I know this is … a lot."

The silence that followed stretched so long I pulled the phone back from my ear to make sure the call hadn't dropped.

"I was hoping we could talk," I prompted, maneuvering the car into a grocery store parking lot, no longer sure where I was headed without the driving directions.

"I should ask my husband," Bunny finally said, sounding less angry and more uncertain.

I pounced. "Yes, I want to talk to him, too. I'm not here to harass you. I … I don't blame you for anything. I just want to know that she's okay," I rambled, willing to say anything if it meant this woman would agree to talk to me.

Another long silence. Then, "Denny's already at a job site. I'm off today, though."

"Oh, thank you," I gushed, even though the words clashed with a brewing distaste for her voice. I tried to shake the feeling off, reminding myself that this woman probably felt the exact same way about me, a pushy stranger calling at 5:00 a.m.

"I'll text you later," she said brusquely, then hung up without a goodbye.

I slowly set the phone in my lap, blinking at the dark screen through blurry eyes and praying she'd actually do it—instead of blocking my number.

I took a steadying breath and looked at the Maps app. The Airbnb was only five minutes away now, mercifully. As the adrenaline from the phone call receded, so did the frantic energy that had been pushing me to drive all night.

I needed sleep. And then I needed to talk to Bunny Beaumont.

Before I put the car back into drive, I pulled up the photo I'd saved to my phone. The one of Andrea, from the news article. The one I'd saved as the wallpaper on the phone's screen.

I tried, for the hundredth time, to tell myself she looked happy. Bright-eyed and spunky, with her lips turned up at the corners. Maybe that smile meant she had a good life with the Beaumonts, the life I'd wanted so desperately to give her.

I knew in my heart that smile didn't mean shit, though. Not with a photographer in the background cajoling her to put on a happy face.

Every woman I'd ever met had learned how to grin with her heart bleeding out into her chest.

7

SABINA

When I got to the Airbnb, I stood bleary-eyed in the entryway, looking around the tiny apartment. There was a bedroom just past the kitchen, but I couldn't bear to think that I was going to sleep for very long, since I'd just arrived.

I told myself I should rest my eyes for long enough to get my fuzzy mind working again. Then I set an alarm on my phone and managed to fall into a mercifully dreamless sleep on the couch in the living room.

It turned out I didn't need the alarm, though. The pent-up adrenaline in my veins popped my eyes open at 8:01 a.m.

I'd missed a call from Joel. But what really drew my attention was a text from Bunny Beaumont. Not a real message. Just an address.

I scrambled to unlock my phone, typed out a reply, then slowly erased it.

Bunny didn't seem like a woman of many words. And I didn't want to get stuck waiting on another text telling me when I could come over. This was an open invitation, as far as I was concerned.

I finally settled on "See you soon" and hit send. Then I plugged the address she'd texted into my Maps app.

My heart pounded so hard in my chest that the app interface went blurry in front of my eyes, but not before I saw that the Beaumont house was only five blocks away from my Airbnb. Ogden wasn't a big city. I already knew that much. But five blocks was pretty damn close.

It felt like a sign.

I *needed* it to be a sign.

Leaving my suitcase where it stood on the floor of the stark, minimalist kitchen at the entryway of the Airbnb, I brewed a cup of coffee and gratefully wolfed down one of the chocolate chip cookies my host had left on the middle of the table with a note that read, "Welcome to our humble home! Enjoy the treats."

I grabbed my car keys where I'd left them on the hook by the front door, then glanced at myself in the hall mirror and raked a hand through my hair. I hesitated as my fingers moved over the cowlick in the middle of my bangs. I'd never given it much thought before, other than to doggedly flatten it out with the straight iron when I blow-dried my hair.

Now I'd think of Andrea every time I saw that stubborn lick of hair.

I swiped furiously at my red-rimmed eyes and rubbed at the mascara stains making my under-eye circles appear even deeper. I looked like shit. But I couldn't imagine that Bunny Beaumont would care. Not when Andrea had been missing for three months.

Yeah, my first impression of her hadn't been great, but I reminded myself that maybe the woman I'd talked with two hours earlier was just—understandably—skeptical of me. She didn't know me from Adam. And if she loved Andrea like I hoped, she'd been through hell for a while now.

All the suspicions I'd ruminated on during the ride up suddenly dissolved into a desperate hope that maybe Bunny Beaumont was every bit as frantic to find Andrea as I was. That I was about to meet someone who understood the unbearably sharp pain that had wrapped itself around every nerve in my body. Another mother who'd cared for my baby for seventeen years.

I applied a fresh layer of tinted lip balm, smoothed my hair one more time, and tried to look less unhinged.

As I got into the car, I called Joel. He answered on the first ring.

"I'm sending you a dossier," he said abruptly when he picked up the phone, without even a hello.

That made my eyes sting all over again. "Thanks, baby."

A "dossier" was what we called the mega-document he made every time we took a vacation together. There had been many, many dossiers over the years. Before Joel and I got married, I tended to fly by the seat of my pants when I traveled, stopping at random, promising-looking restaurants—that were inevitably booked —and gravitating toward whatever tourist trap splashed across the billboards. Not Joel, though. Joel was a diligent Boy Scout, and I'd come to love his ability to suss out the best places to eat and the hidden gems off the beaten path. It was just one of the many things I loved about him.

"If you send me your Airbnb address, I'll add more specifics near your location," Joel said. "But Ogden isn't that big, so I think you'll be good to go. I found you food options, the address for the police station, the three homeless shelters within city limits, and hot spots for some of the unofficial encampments that get used quite a bit—according to Reddit. Apparently there's one near the cemetery that the police are always breaking up. But don't go there at night, okay?" he said, his voice turning soft. "How are you doing?"

I tried to answer, but all I could manage was a snuffle past the lump in my throat. I opened my mouth, trying to tell him how much this gesture meant to me, but all that came out was a sob.

"You don't have to do this on your own, Sabi," he said gently while I cried. "I can be on the next flight. You just say the word."

"No," I said more fiercely than I intended, finding my voice. "You know I want you here. And I can't tell you how much it means that you sent me the dossier. I love you. But I have no idea how long this will take. Your mom can't even walk, Joel. She needs you *there* right now. What I really need is your support, and I already know I have that."

He didn't answer for a few seconds, and I was afraid I'd hurt his feelings. Then, finally he sighed in resignation. From the faint bustle in the background, I could tell he was in the hall of the rehab center with his mom now. "You always have my support. But I'm expecting calls and texts. *Lots* of them. I ... I know I never met Andrea. But she was yours, and that means I love her too. Okay?"

"You're the best human," I whispered, wiping my tears and turning the key in the ignition. "I'm going to meet her adoptive mom right now. I'll fill you in on everything when I'm done there."

It took barely two minutes to pull up at the curb of the address Bunny had texted me.

At first glance, it looked like every other house on the quaint little street in the established neighborhood. A skinny two-story with red brick accents, cracked black shutters and white paint that had seen better days. It sat on a tree-thick lot with tall, crooked elms flanking the perimeter and a canal flowing on one side. There was a detached shed set back from the house that had been painted to look like an old-fashioned barn. The neighborhood had a rural feel, and the acreage across the street was filled with corn. Not suburbia, exactly, but not the countryside either.

As I got out of the car and started down the walkway that led to the front door, a sense of unease hit me so strongly it stopped me in my tracks.

And then, out of the blue, just loud enough that I could hear it above the rustle of the pale green leaves in the elms—I heard a baby crying.

A hiccupping, frantic sound in the distance.

Goosebumps popped across my arms and I shook off the insane thought that had wormed its way to the front of my mind.

I knew I was imagining things, on high alert. Eager for another sign. All babies probably sounded the same when they cried. Like mewling kittens.

But even so, I could've sworn it was my Andrea.

8

ANDREA

When I first laid eyes on the woman getting out of her car in front of Bunny and Dennis's house, I knew who she was immediately.

All it took was one glance at her face to jog the locked memories back into high-definition.

It was like they'd been in a storage box or something, just waiting for me to lift the lid. Some kind of magic that came with being dead, I guess.

The lines around her eyes and the droop of the skin along her jaw were more pronounced than they'd been seventeen years ago. But her kind, bright, hazel eyes were exactly the same. And so was the color of her hair. If I'd still had a heartbeat, it would've burst out of my chest.

If I'd still been able to breathe, my lungs would have stalled.

I picked up my pace and rushed toward her, faster than I'd ever moved while I was alive, not taking my eyes off her for a second until I stood right in front of her on the sidewalk.

And even though I knew for certain that she couldn't see me —because nobody had been able to see me for the past three months since fucking Dennis had fucking murdered me—I held out my arms toward her like I had when I was a tiny baby.

"Mom?" I said, the word coming out like a question as the emotion welled up so big it felt like electricity coming from my fingers and toes. "*Mom*."

Swear to God, she stopped the second I stepped in front of her and said that word.

Until this moment, I'd been wandering around the neighborhood like I usually did while Bunny or Dennis were at home. I wasn't even sure why I kept coming back to their house, except that it was the only home I knew. Or at least, that's what I *thought* until I saw my mom. My *real* mom.

I could hear a baby crying in the distance, and maybe that was why she stopped so abruptly, but the expression on her face was pinched and sad, like she was trying her best not to sob all of a sudden. From the dark circles underneath her red-rimmed eyes, I could tell she'd cried recently.

She stared up at the black-shuttered house and her lips moved, like she was trying to talk herself into walking a little farther up the sidewalk. And that's when I realized that not only was she my mom, but she was here *because* of me, somehow. To find out what had happened to me, maybe.

It made me so happy and so sad at the same time, I wanted to cry too.

The sound of that baby wailing in the distance got louder, and it sort of felt like it was coming from inside my chest, even though that was impossible.

"Mom," I repeated again, like it was the only word I knew, desperate to say it again and again. "I'm right here, Mom. I remember you. I'm … I'm right in front of you."

I reached out for her, gripping her waist in a one-sided hug that didn't even indent the drape in the oversized blue T-shirt she wore.

I was shocked that I remembered her smell, even though I couldn't smell anything at all anymore. Powdery hand cream and a hint of vanilla. I leaned into her, still rattled by how these suddenly clear memories had been hidden away so completely for all my life, until now.

It was as if some door in my mind had suddenly been unlocked and flung open, and I was staring wide-eyed at a room—a whole house—I never knew existed before. Being dead didn't seem to come with any other perks or powers as far as I could tell, but this one was huge.

Prior to this moment, I already knew—from hours of painful eavesdropping on Bunny and Dennis's conversations—that I was adopted. Bunny alternated between crying and fuming, saying that things had never been quite right with me and that I was an ungrateful little shit. Dennis agreed that I'd been "damaged" from the moment I'd arrived as a baby, and insisted that at some point I would return home "with my tail between my legs."

I guess I sort of believed them—the part about me being damaged. That I'd come from somewhere bad and ended up somewhere worse. Until this moment, I'd been imagining my birth mother as some junkie. A nameless, faceless stranger.

She wasn't a stranger, though. Not even close. I remembered being held in her arms, rocked to sleep while I wailed in her ear with an upset tummy. Feeling her warm tears splash down on my mostly bald baby head while her chest shook and she cried along with me.

I wanted to wail all over again as the memories whirled around me. Both of us were crying in almost every single one. It was just because my stomach hurt so much, and I couldn't fall asleep when I was so tired. I couldn't tell her that then, though. All I could do was cry.

Time seemed to stop as I let the memories unfold, suddenly realizing that I could zoom out on what was happening like I was a fly on the wall. That was when I saw the two of us the last time we were alone together in a dim, cramped basement bedroom with the crib in the corner and peeling yellow paint.

"I'm sorry I can't be your mama," she'd said, rubbing her red eyes and tucking a strand of limp hair behind one ear. *"You'll have a better life, with a real mom and dad."*

The memory fast-forwarded, shifting to an older man with curly brown hair and a droopy mustache, who held me in his arms while she signed papers on a kitchen table. *"We're proud of you, Sabina,"* he'd said, even though he was the only one in the room aside from me.

Sabina. That was her name. My real mom's name. And that was the last memory I had of her before she'd sent me away to live with Dennis and Bunny.

The thought made me recoil. I took a big step back on the sidewalk, and some of the love and sadness radiating through me melted into anger.

The baby crying in the distance—here in the present—finally shut up.

"Where are you, baby?" Sabina—I decided maybe I wasn't ready to call her "Mom" yet after all—asked in a barely audible voice, scanning the trees like she might find me among them.

And the truth was, she almost could.

Almost.

Because just half a mile through those trees, I *was* there—my body, at least.

The day Dennis killed me, he'd dragged my tarp-wrapped body into the backyard shed. Then he'd stuffed two-hundred dollars of Bunny's money into the kangaroo pouch of my red hoodie. That night, after Bunny was asleep, he'd returned to the shed and separated my arms, legs and head from my torso, so I'd fit into three separate heavy-duty garbage bags. It was hard to watch that part, but I did it. Because if I didn't see what happened to my remains, nobody would. And that thought was even worse than witnessing the syrupy red-brown blood drip into the tarp beneath the saw blade in the shed, and the crunch of splintering bone.

Dennis had taken those garbage bags to the construction site he was working at—which was just on the other side of the wooded lot behind our house. He'd sealed me beneath a layer of concrete in the early morning hours. A pad for the family's fucking hot tub.

I shook my head and forced the memory away. The sound of the front screen door slamming against the side of the house had just made Sabina jump.

"Go away! Leave us alone," I screamed, whirling around to face the porch, not caring whether it was Dennis or Bunny coming outside. But of course, nobody heard me.

Turned out it was Bunny, wearing her ratty pink robe and *Lion King* slippers. She squinted her puffy, piggy eyes at Sabina and took a sip from her coffee mug, staring for a few seconds in silence.

Sabina lifted her hand hesitantly. "Sorry I didn't text that I was on my way. You're right around the corner from my Airbnb so I just thought …"

Bunny looked around the yard suspiciously, her eyes moving right over me. "You might as well come in, I guess," she finally said, her voice sort of weary and resigned.

I lifted both middle fingers and stared at her with a boiling hatred I'd never dared show while I was alive. "Fuck you, Bunny."

A crow that had been perched in a nearby tree called out so loudly as it flew away that Bunny splashed some of her hot coffee down the front of her robe.

"Shit," she muttered, brushing at the watery brown liquid. And I smiled for the first time in three months at the crow's retreating silhouette.

Then I followed Sabina inside the house.

9

SABINA

The only time I'd ever had an out-of-body experience was when I handed Andrea over to the social worker.

Until now.

It happened again when I first laid eyes on Bunny Beaumont.

All of a sudden, I felt like I'd become a plastic doll who, mercifully, couldn't feel a thing no matter what was happening around me.

I knew as soon as I saw her that I hadn't actually been wrong about my first impression of Andrea's adoptive mother.

She wasn't scary to look at. In fact, she seemed pretty damn unthreatening, standing there on the front porch of the white house in her worn pink robe and slippers that looked like they'd been borrowed from a child. Were those Andrea's slippers? The hair rose on the back of my neck.

For a moment, I tried to tell myself that maybe I was just being judgmental. The rundown house, the shabby clothing, the baby I'd just heard wailing in the distance—combined with the undercurrent of dread I'd felt since I got the letter from the Ogden PD—were making me jump to conclusions.

Then I honed in on Bunny's expression. Her lips were pursed in a tight line, like she was both annoyed and perplexed by my presence. Her round, dark, close-set eyes barely blinked while I walked up the porch toward her in a daze. *Like a shark,* my mind offered.

"Denny isn't going to be happy that I let you come over," she said abruptly when I started to climb the steps. "So you can't stay long. He'll be home in a few minutes." Her lips pressed together so tightly they disappeared while she studied my face, holding the open screen door in one hand and keeping the other on her hip. As I stepped onto the porch and moved closer, I realized that her head was tilted at an angle that mirrored the exact position of the raggedy lion head on her left slipper.

"I'm sorry, I know this is a lot to take in," I began, clawing for a way back inside my body. I couldn't be numb right now. I needed to be sharp and present, needed to get any information I could from her. I hadn't expected a warm welcome, but her demeanor was about as welcoming as a porcupine on high alert. Why was she staring at me like that?

As if in answer to my unspoken question, Bunny cocked her head further to the right and met my eyes, her guarded expression fading for an instant. Her upper lip trembled, and I thought to myself, *She's going to open up.* I leaned forward, eager to hear what she would say.

Bunny leaned back. Her wide eyes narrowed, the guarded expression firmly back in place. I felt the corners of my lips turn down in a frown. Then, to my utter shock, she let out a bitter laugh as she gestured toward the couch behind her in the living room. "You wanna sit? Or …?"

"What's wrong?" I asked, hating the quiver in my voice.

"Sorry. I just … now I know where Andrea got her face."

I took a step back from her and stared, dumbfounded. "Her face?" My hand went to my cheek. Was she saying we looked alike, or—

"Yeah. Denny called it her 'Fuck-you-very-much' face," Bunny said, crossing her arms over her chest.

My stomach recoiled like I'd been punched. Who said something like that about their *child*?

My child. Anger was starting to make my heart beat faster, and all my pent-up emotions threatened to burst out of my mouth, directed toward her. But there was also a warning light blinking at the front of my mind. *Proceed with caution. Stay calm. Keep her talking. Learn everything you can.* I reached one hand up to touch my burning cheek. "I didn't realize I was making a face."

Bunny waved me off and led the way to the living room, where a faded tan La-Z-Boy faced a lumpy couch. "Andrea was the sweetest baby I ever met, but as far as teenagers go ..." She trailed off and fixed me with another hard look, like the rest of that sentence was obvious. "She wasn't *completely* feral. We raised her better than that. But she'd get this look on her face like she smelled rotten eggs and then set her jaw like a horse ready to kick." She tucked the robe tighter around her body and sat down in the recliner.

Her tight-lipped frown was finally gone, but one eyebrow stayed raised just slightly like she was daring me to question what she'd just said.

I stared at her mutely, trying to grab hold of the right words and coming up empty. Never in my wildest dreams had I imagined that this was how my conversation with Andrea's adoptive mother would begin.

Sweat was starting to bead underneath the arms of my T-shirt as I sat down on the couch, if only because standing while listening to this woman was suddenly making me feel unwell. Even though the August morning had been cloudy and unseasonably cool, the house was uncomfortably warm. The air smelled stale, like food caked on an unwashed cast-iron skillet. The carpet in the living room was so worn and stretched that it rose in brown waves at my feet. A murky, dirty ocean. I scanned the walls, looking for photos of Andrea and saw only beige paint.

But in the strangest way, I could *feel* her.

Maybe it was just my desperate longing, my imagination, but that numb, autopilot sensation in my body shifted to that of a quilt tucking me in. Warm and familiar, and just tight enough that I felt suddenly protected.

The feeling was strong enough to snap me out of my shocked stupor and look Bunny Beaumont in the eye. "From what I've heard, teenagers can be challenging," I said, forcing my voice to stay even and measured. "I read the articles where they interviewed you and your husband. Do you really think she ran away?"

Bunny, who had crossed one slipper-clad foot over the other, shot me a sharp look, and I instantly knew that I'd messed up. "What kind of a question is that? Yeah, she ran away. And yeah, I was real broken up about it at first, but I've done a lot of thinking, and now I feel mad as hell. Nothing happened to 'poor missing Andrea.' She was a disrespectful child who never really loved me and then stole all the money out of my wallet on her way out the door." Her lip quivered for the briefest of moments, before she pursed her lips tight again.

The invisible quilt seemed to draw tighter around me in a defensive embrace, and I focused on the feeling as hard as I could. Every word that came out of Bunny Beaumont's mouth was worse than the last. My heart throbbed when I considered what she must have been like to live with. I would've wanted to run, too. Had Bunny told the police what she was telling me? I didn't know much after four minutes inside this house, but I knew that I hated her with every cell in my body.

Still, I stayed the course and tried to regain my facade of composure. From the way Bunny was glaring at me, it was almost like she *wanted* to bait me into storming out of the house. "What can you tell me about the day she left home?" I asked carefully.

Bunny snorted. "Not much. I already told the police this same thing about a hundred times. When I got home around five from the dairy plant, the house was empty. It was her birthday, so I thought she'd be at home, excited about the special cake I spent twenty dollars on. But then I checked my wallet—because I was going to give her a little spending money for her birthday—and realized that all my cash was gone. She must've taken it that morning before she went to school, because I had the wallet with me all day." Her face hardened at the memory. "That's when I knew she ran off. Little brat."

I stayed perfectly still, listening for the truth between the lines of Bunny Beaumont's ugly words. I already knew from the article that Andrea went missing on her birthday, but hearing it made my heart seize up all over again.

"When Denny got home, he went around to the neighbors," Bunny continued. "Nobody had seen her. The last time anybody did see her was at school. Denny got home early from a job site, but there was no sign of her at the house. She never even came home that day." She shrugged and sat up, like she might be preparing to usher me out of the house.

I gripped the waxy microfiber of the old couch and stayed where I was. "Do you have any idea where she might have gone—"

"Zero fucking idea. She thought it was a good idea to run away from home with two hundred dollars and the clothes on her back, so who the hell knows what her next brilliant plan is? Also, not to be rude, but why is this any of your business?" Bunny asked, and those warning bells in the back of my mind started chiming again. "You chose a closed adoption, and I sure as hell did, too. Now you're suddenly texting me at the asscrack of dawn and barging into my home asking me the same questions the police have already asked and acting like you're Nancy Drew? Who the hell do you think you are?"

My mind spun, whipping past the hurt of those words and honing in on the truth beneath them. I was a breath away from being asked to leave. I didn't know why she'd agreed to speak to me at all. Curiosity, maybe? But Bunny Beaumont's curiosity had clearly run dry. I needed to choose my next questions carefully. They might be all I got.

Before I could say a word, though, there was a clattering sound from the back of the house, followed by footsteps.

"That'll be Denny," Bunny said, gesturing behind her. "And he's not gonna be happy to see you."

10

ANDREA

When Dennis came in the back of the house and slammed the door, I stood from where I'd been sitting on the couch next to Sabina, ran into the kitchen, and screamed right in his face. "Get the fuck out of here, you trash-ass piece of dog shit."

I'd started doing that same thing every time I crossed paths with him—hurling insults and swears that got more unhinged every time—and as far as I could tell it had absolutely zero effect. He still walked right through the door with that hollow look in his eyes and steamrolled past me to make himself a sandwich, wheezing softly. But it made me feel better for all the times I'd ever called him "Dad" or felt the slap of that leather leash across my stomach, or froze in terror when I heard his footsteps thumping down the hallway.

It was something, at least.

This time was different, though. I wanted him to walk back out that door with every part of me that was still left. Because the second he entered the conversation, Bunny was going to stop talking. Sabina would be pushed out the door, and then nobody was ever going to find out what had really happened to me. And I just couldn't bear that. In some ways, I felt like I'd hardly existed in the world while I was still alive. To be erased completely now that I was dead was too awful to accept.

So when I screamed at Dennis to get out, panic and rage and anger building inside me like a pressure cooker, I was shocked that he actually stopped in his tracks.

I gawked as his eyes went wide, his mouth puckered tight, and he backtracked into the yard, closing the screen door behind him. Had he heard me somehow?

"Denny?" Bunny called from the living room.

In the few seconds Dennis lingered just outside the screen door on the back steps, I realized what had spooked him—The sound of police sirens, so close by it sounded like they were pulling up to our front yard. Sort of like the day he'd murdered me.

Bunny stood at the back door now. "You coming inside?" she screeched, to no reply.

The panic I'd felt a moment ago surged into excitement. Car doors slammed, and the sirens stopped blaring. This time the police were really here, I was sure of it.

Dennis's face went white as a sheet, and he took another step away from the house, into the weedy yard. "I forgot something in the truck. Hold on," he hissed, just loud enough for Bunny to hear.

Then he turned around and booked it. He didn't run for the truck, though. He made a beeline for the shed—which was where he'd chopped me up. I'd already watched him scour and wash the hand saw and mop the concrete floor, and he'd stuffed the tarp into the garbage bags right alongside my body. So he and I both knew there wasn't anything in there visible to the naked eye. But still, if police cadaver dogs rolled up like I'd seen on *Dateline,* maybe there was a chance the cops would still be able to figure out what he'd done to me.

"Coward," I spat in satisfaction at Dennis's retreating form. Then I darted around the side of the house to look out front, needing to see the police cars with my own eyes.

There was nothing there, though. No police. Not even one car.

I blinked, crestfallen, trying to process what I was—or more accurately *wasn't*—seeing. I was sure I'd heard sirens. And I was really sure, from Dennis's reaction, that he'd heard them too.

I rushed to the shed, to see what Dennis was doing in there.

He stood in the middle of the dimly lit structure, spinning in a slow circle as he scanned the concrete floor, the walls, the tools, probably for any evidence that he'd dismembered his own daughter.

The volcano of anger and despair inside me had subsided a little, but now the pressure started to build again.

I heard another car door slam nearby, followed by the crackle of a radio. I frowned, confused, but satisfied that Dennis still seemed completely panicked.

"Shit, shit, shit," he muttered to himself, eyes glued to the shed door.

And that was when the puzzle pieces clicked for me.

There weren't police cars outside today, just like there hadn't been police cars outside the day Dennis murdered me. The sound of the police sirens, maybe even the baby crying earlier, weren't real.

What was really weird was every time this happened, I could almost feel it. Like those big emotions I had were the steam inside a kettle, making the whistle blow when the pressure got powerful enough. Or, alternately, dissipating when the feelings shifted.

It was like *I* was the one creating those sounds. It made a strange sort of sense. The noises outside had gone silent again, mirroring my anger that had dissolved into confusion.

As Dennis slunk over to the grimy shed window to peer outside, I put my theory to the test and mustered up the emotions that had lit me up a moment earlier.

It was harder than I thought it would be, trying to feel something that strongly on command. So I tried doing what I'd done earlier with Sabina—calling up one of the foggy memories crammed deep in the recesses of my consciousness.

I chose the very first time he'd used that dog leash on me.

I was five. Until now, though, the memory—and plenty more like it—had been murky and difficult to pin down. Not anymore, though.

Like I'd hoped—and feared—the memory came back to me in high-definition the second I latched onto the thread of it.

There I was, on the living room floor with our old dog Pollie, tracing the patterns of color in her fur. She was a beagle mix, with black and brown patches that made her look like several different dogs stitched together. I loved her, even though Bunny complained that she smelled like pee on a good day and a fart-factory on a bad one.

Pollie was sleeping on her side, letting me stroke the swirls of fur on her chest. I was lying on my stomach, wearing my stained Ninja Turtles pajamas with my tangle-haired head tucked against the dog's chest so I could hear her heartbeat. The house was quiet, mid-morning on a Saturday, and my stomach was growling. I knew better than to wake Bunny or Dennis up to make me breakfast though, so I stayed in the living room with Pollie.

I was so absorbed by the dog that I didn't hear Dennis come down the stairs.

The memory panned wide, so I could see the look on his face as his blank eyes moved between me and Pollie, who lifted her head slightly to glare at him.

Part of his mouth contorted into an ugly half-smile as he hesitated where he stood on the landing, scratching his chest through the half-open button down pajamas he wore. Then he darted toward us, into the living room. *"Andrea!"* he boomed as loudly as he could.

I shrieked and scrambled to my feet while Dennis chuckled. But in doing so, I lost my balance and inadvertently slammed a foot against Pollie, who was already so worried that her bladder let loose right on the carpet.

Pollie yelped, and Dennis's laughter soured into a disgusted grunt. "Bad dog," he wheezed, and in two strides toward the door he had her leash off its hook and was swinging.

"No, no, no!" I cried, because it wasn't Pollie's fault, it was his. I didn't say the last part, though. Even at five, I knew better than that.

Dennis cocked his head at me and stopped swinging the leash, and for a half a second I thought he was going to calm down. Make me breakfast, maybe. My stomach gurgled hopefully.

Instead, he started swinging the leash in my direction. "You wanna take her licking for her?"

I stared at him, then Pollie, who was cowering in the corner of the room by the couch.

"No," I whispered in terror. So he shrugged, sidestepped the puddle on the carpet, and started swinging the leash in Pollie's face again, even though I was crying and the dog was whining softly.

I wrapped my arms around my stomach and dug my fingers into the spaces between my ribs, desperately hoping that Bunny would wake up, come downstairs, and put a stop to his temper tantrum like she had a few times before.

Not this time, though. This time I shrieked, "Okay! Okay. I'll take it," before he reached Pollie.

And I did.

As the memory of that first lash rippled through me, I tried to pull myself back into the present, into the shed with Dennis. But it was like scooping up handfuls of water from the ocean. I could only hold onto so much of that emotion when I moved out of it, even though while I was inside that memory, it felt all-encompassing to the point that I was a little disoriented coming back into the shed.

Still, I called up every bit of sadness and horror I could for that little girl in the Ninja Turtles pajamas taking a beating for her dog.

The pressure built, slowly but steadily.

Footsteps thumped on the dirt outside, then faded. And this time, I rushed to the window of the shed to see with my own eyes that the yard was empty.

It was. But the sound was enough to make Dennis—who had his hand on the doorknob—let go and retreat back into the center of the shed, eyes wide and manic, forehead wrinkled. Sweat beaded on his brow.

The reaction was satisfying, but as much as I wanted to stay and fuck with Dennis, I was losing my steam. Like the pressure valve had been ticking a little closer to empty each time I let some out.

I couldn't keep him cornered here forever, though. And besides, I was suddenly afraid that Bunny might've already ushered Sabina out the door.

11

ANDREA

I left Dennis standing in the shed and hurried back into the house.

Another minor perk I'd discovered about being dead—a ghost, I guess—was that I could squeeze through just about any space, no matter how small. Whatever stardust holding me together sort of slunk through any opening.

So that's what I did, slipping under the door crack and through the tear in the screen door.

The living room was empty, but there were heated voices coming from above me.

I flew up the stairs to find that Sabina had somehow convinced Bunny to show her my room. Or what used to be my room, anyway.

The beat-up washer and dryer were still wedged into the far side of the cramped space, their dented yellow bodies touching so that when either of them was running, they clanked together erratically like a psychotic drum solo. I didn't mind that part so much. I'd learned to sleep through it when Bunny popped a load in the dryer late at night. What I hated was the fact that the noise obscured the sound of my bedroom door creaking open when the lights went out. Sometimes, I didn't know he was in my room until I heard him whisper, *"Shh. Don't fuss. The more you fuss the worse it'll be."*

NOELLE W. IHLI

I refused to relive those memories in high-definition.

Once was plenty.

"This isn't a bedroom. This is a laundry room," Sabina said, turning in a half-circle to take in the laundry hanging out of the dryer and a pile of dirty clothes on the floor. "There's not even room for a bed."

"It's not a *laundry room*," Bunny muttered. "Might not be as fancy as whatever you're used to, but the bed fit just fine." She shot a pointed look at Sabina's expensive-looking jeans and pristine sneakers.

I rolled my eyes. My twin bed had been positioned so close to the dryer that I could open and shut its door if I stretched out my arm while lying in bed. Dennis had since moved my bed into the garage.

Bunny had done the same with my clothes, boxing them up haphazardly and shoving them into a corner of the garage with the spiders.

In a lot of ways, it was like I'd never lived in this house at all.

"Where are her things?" Sabina was asking, her voice rising with each word.

The back door slammed downstairs, and Bunny's eyes flicked to the hallway. Her face hardened. "Why the hell is that any business of yours?" She stared at Sabina. "I put them in storage until she comes back. If she wanted them so bad, she shouldn't have run away. I'm not keeping a shrine. What lesson would that teach her?"

Sabina's lower lip trembled, and she pursed her mouth into a tight line like she was trying to hold back what she really wanted to say. "I'm sorry. I didn't mean to accuse you of anything."

"Oh, you should accuse her," I said, like I was part of the conversation.

In the first few days after I died, I'd spent a lot of time listening to conversations between Bunny and Dennis. Mostly to find out if he was going to confess to her or not.

The answer was no. He didn't confess, and she had no idea that I was buried under a cement slab on the other side of the neighborhood. But given that Bunny had spent so little time worrying about my "disappearance" and Dennis had so easily convinced her that I was an ungrateful runaway who was "damaged goods from the start" and "wrong in the head," I hated her almost as much as I hated him by this point. *"We should've held out for a brand new baby like everybody else on that adoption list,"* he'd told her, while they were debating whether to keep my bed and clothes.

From the conversations I'd overheard post mortem, I got the impression that wanting a baby had been a fantasy for Bunny more than Dennis, which he'd indulged. As far as I could tell, Dennis didn't love anything. Not me, not our dog. Not his family. Bunny was the one exception. He loved her.

"Ask her about my friends," I told Sabina desperately as Bunny herded her back into the hallway. She was about to get booted out of the house. I was still surprised Bunny had let her in to begin with, but then again, Bunny didn't know how much there was to hide.

To my delight, Sabina tilted her head in my direction, like she was listening to me. "Who else knew her?" she asked, planting her feet in the doorway of my old bedroom and glancing down the hall at the painting of Jesus and the sparrows. "Can you at least give me some of her friends' names and phone numbers?"

Bunny flicked her eyes from the hallway back to Sabina and waved her hand dismissively. "Andrea was a loner—"

The ever-present embers of rage inside me flared, and something in the laundry room clanked so loud that Bunny nearly jumped out of her skin as she craned her neck looking around.

I was so pleased by that—since I was pretty sure I'd done it with my "ghost juice" as I'd just now decided to call it—that I didn't hear Dennis until he was already up the stairs and halfway down the hall. "Who's this?" he snapped as both Bunny and Sabina whirled around to face him.

Sabina raised her chin and stared at him in silence for a long moment, taking in the dirty blue plaid shirt and the too-tight cargo pants he wore like a uniform on construction sites. His patchy neck beard that trailed past his Adam's apple. The thinning brown hair he combed over the bald spot on his liver-spotted scalp.

There was no mistaking the disgust in Sabina's eyes, and there was no mistaking that Dennis saw it, too.

Finally, she opened her mouth and said, "I'm Andrea's mother." No more apologies about butting in or being my biological mom. Just *"Andrea's mother,"* with a glare that told me she was pissed as hell and fighting back tears.

I moved closer, pretending she knew I was beside her.

Dennis made a sound that might have been a snort or a laugh. "Her *mother*? Well that's pretty damn funny, but I don't care who the fuck you are. I didn't invite you into my house, and from the look on my sweetheart's face, she doesn't want you here anymore, either." He was starting to wheeze with fury.

"You'd better be on your way," Bunny warned, crossing her pink-terry cloth arms across her chest.

Sabina stood a little taller, and her eyes flashed at Dennis.

The resentment I'd felt toward her earlier for giving me to Dennis and Bunny thawed a little, and I reached forward to hold her hand, imagining I could feel her fingers twined with mine.

"Give me the name of one of her friends. *Anyone*. It doesn't matter who. And then I'll leave," she said, planting her feet. "Not before."

I loved her for that with a fierceness that surprised me.

Dennis's nostrils flared so wide, I could see the long black nose hairs he never trimmed. He wasn't used to people—especially women—standing up to him.

"Fuck yes," I whispered. Then I gave Sabina's fingers another squeeze, because her chin was trembling a lot now.

Dennis's hands clenched into fists, like he wished he hadn't thrown that old leather leash away with my dead body.

Nobody moved or spoke for a few agonizing seconds. The tension in that hallway had ratcheted up so high that even being invisible, I was uncomfortable staying where I was.

Then Dennis's eyes changed, like the little wheels in the back of his head had started turning. I could almost read his thoughts.

He didn't want this stranger poking around his home, but he couldn't shove her down the stairs like he'd done to me. At least, not without consequences. And from the smug look he'd had on his face after the police left the day they'd questioned him—right after I "ran away"—he was pretty damn sure he'd covered up my murder completely.

There were no witnesses.

No evidence left behind.

No body.

No murder weapon.

He'd vanished me completely.

"Just tell her where to find Paloma's parents," I demanded, my eyes moving between him and Bunny, trying and failing to call up more of that white-hot emotion I'd been able to wrangle earlier. But I was tired, and it definitely felt like I'd emptied all the steam that would have to build up again before I could use it to conjure any more sounds.

Dennis muttered something under his breath that might have been "Sassy bitch," but to my delight, Bunny did exactly as I'd instructed.

"The busybodies who own the hippie-ass smoothie place a few blocks that way put up missing posters," she said, waving her hands in the wrong direction of the smoothie shop. "Said Andrea was their daughter's friend, but that's bullshit. Pretty sure they just wanted to get on the news. Like I said. Andrea was a loner. She didn't have any real friends."

"Because of you and Dennis," I hissed, but I was thrilled she'd done what I told her to do. Was that another "perk" of being a ghost? Some kind of mind-meld? Or did it only apply to weak idiots like Bunny? I made a mental note to experiment more with that later.

"Desert Greens?" Sabina asked, pulling up the Maps app on her phone and holding it out for both Bunny and Dennis to verify.

Dennis grunted and stomped down the stairs without a reply. When he reached the landing, he yanked open the front door and hollered, "If you aren't out of here in thirty seconds, I'm calling the cops."

"Liar," I spat, wishing with all my heart I had the energy to summon up those sirens again, just to see his face go white as a ghost one more time.

Bunny stayed where she was, blinking at the phone screen Sabina held out. Then she shrugged. "Yeah, that's it."

"We should go," I told Sabina, because there was nothing else to be done here, now that Dennis was back. And when she fell into step beside me, I told myself it was because some part of her really did hear me.

Sabina knelt down to put on her shoes, which she'd removed despite the disgusting state of the house.

Then Sabina's eyes shifted, and she hesitated.

At first, I thought she was going to try to get something more out of Dennis, who stood next to the front door, with arms folded across his chest like the ape he was.

But then I realized she was looking at something—under the entryway table, beside her shoes.

I felt a flutter of anticipation when I realized what she'd caught sight of. "Take it," I whispered.

As if she'd heard me with perfect clarity, Sabina angled her body sideways as she put the second shoe on—and swiped her hand beneath the table before Dennis even realized what she'd done. Sabina didn't say a word to Bunny, who glared down from the top of the stairs. And she didn't lower her eyes when she walked past Dennis out the front door—which abruptly slammed shut behind her.

She got in her car, eyes blazing, right fist clenched tight, jaw set, then hit "Go" on her Maps App to start directions to Desert Greens.

Without looking at the item in her hand, she gently set it on the passenger seat beside a sweatshirt—where I sat riding shotgun beside her.

I looked at her, feeling the invisible pressure valve tick a little closer toward red. Only this time, it wasn't anger moving the needle on the gauge. It was excitement.

Because something was happening now.

Paloma's parents owned the "hippie-ass smoothie place" Sabina would be arriving at in seven minutes, according to the Maps app. And I was pretty sure, from the memories of Paloma I'd re-run and scrutinized over and over again, that she'd been worried about me.

Maybe Paloma had said something to her parents or the police—and maybe she would open up to Sabina now.

Something like hope swelled alongside the excitement. For the first time in three months, I felt like I hadn't simply disappeared into the void forever.

A handful of people still cared that I'd existed once. And maybe, just maybe, Sabina cared enough to keep going until she discovered the truth.

12

SABINA

I drove one block, just far enough that I was definitely out of sight of the Beaumonts' house, then pulled over next to a vacant lot.

The Desert Greens smoothie shop wasn't far away. I wanted to drive straight there. But if I didn't take a few minutes to get a hold of myself, I was going to crash the car.

Something awful had happened in that house. To my Andrea.

I was certain of it now. And that certainty felt like swallowing broken glass.

They'd put my little girl, my precious baby girl, in their laundry room. And I knew in my heart that a cramped, dirty bedroom next to the washing machine was probably the least of what Andrea had endured at the hands of those terrible people.

I wouldn't leave a pet alone with those two. Let alone a child. Why weren't the police scrutinizing Bunny and Dennis more closely? Where was CPS, a search warrant, anything? They'd boxed up all of her *clothes*, for Christ's sake.

It was like they fully expected she'd never return. Huge red flag.

"Call Joel," I told my phone, voice shaking with rage and horror.

Before he'd even said hello, the details of everything I'd just seen and heard were spilling out of my mouth.

"They said she had no friends," I cried. "And they boxed up all her belongings. They did something to her, Joel. I know they did."

They did something to her. The minute those words came out, I wanted to unsay them. Reel in the hope I'd been clinging to like a distant kite. I could feel the thread of that hope about to break from the moment I laid eyes on Bunny Beaumont's sharp, marble-cold pupils.

"I'm so sorry." Joel's voice, sad and low and familiar as my own heartbeat, made me miss him so much I almost begged him to drop everything and come to Utah.

He would have, without hesitation, the second I asked. But I already knew that even the comfort of his embrace couldn't touch the frantic, gnawing despair in my belly.

"This is my fault," I sobbed. "Whatever happened to her is my fault. I loved her, Joel. I didn't want to give her away to anybody. I thought I was doing the right thing. I had no idea. I …"

I put the phone in Speaker mode and set the phone on the dash, lay my head across my hands on the steering wheel, and keened like an animal.

"It's *not* your fault," Joel said, his soft voice turning firmer and sharper than I'd ever heard.

"I don't know how to believe that," I choked. "If I'd just stood up to my parents, if I'd just waited a little longer to think through giving her up for adoption, everything would have been different. She'd be *ours*. She'd be here right now."

"You couldn't have known that any of this would happen. And you were only sixteen," Joel said. "Even younger than Andrea is now. You were a child, Sabi. And even then, you did what you did *because you loved her*. That's all anybody can do, without a crystal ball."

I didn't answer, just squeezed my eyes shut and grabbed the balled-up sweatshirt lying on the passenger seat of the car to muffle the wail that refused to stay trapped inside my throat.

"Listen to me. I'm going to do a deep dive on the Beaumonts' while Mom takes a nap in a little bit," Joel said. "I'll add anything I find to the dossier. Are you headed to that smoothie shop they told you about?"

I wiped my eyes, my nose, on the sweatshirt and sat up straight, blinking into the rays of sunlight streaming through the windshield.

The pockets of sun created a tiny spotlight on the passenger seat, landing on something shiny.

In the middle of that halo of light was that little trinket I'd seen beneath the entryway table in the Beaumonts' house. I'd grabbed it without pausing to think through the ramifications of stealing it, barely realizing what I was doing when it caught my eye. I hadn't even looked at it yet—until now.

"Sabina?" Joel asked, and I realized I hadn't said anything for a few seconds.

"I'm here," I whispered, looking at a tiny monarch butterfly perched in the middle of the passenger seat, wings aloft, as if it had just landed.

The wings were nearly translucent, red and orange with black stripes and outlines that perfectly mimicked a real monarch butterfly. It was made of some kind of plastic. An earring, I realized suddenly, seeing the delicate gold chain and hook attached between the wings.

Did it belong to Bunny? Or could it be—

That's when the quilt-wrapped feeling came back, warmer and tighter than ever around my heart. Along with the words, clear as a bell in the recesses of my mind: *It's mine.*

That thought, abrupt and insistent, whispered through my brain in the first person, confusing me for a fraction of a second. Because I knew without a doubt that the earring wasn't *mine*.

Not mine. Hers, my mind prompted gently. *Andrea's.*

I reached for the little monarch as carefully as I would a real butterfly that might startle and take flight.

"I need to go, baby," I told Joel. "I'll call you back soon, okay? I love you," I whispered, barely listening as he repeated *"I love you"* back to me, then ended the call.

A few minutes earlier, the desperate sadness and rage in my chest felt so big I couldn't bear it a second longer. Now, though? Now, I felt so held and mercifully cocooned inside that invisible quilt, I found myself letting out a shuddering breath, my body shaking involuntarily. The way it did when Joel and I had a rare fight and then reconciled, pulling each other into a tight embrace.

I closed my palm around the sun-warmed plastic wings of the butterfly, shut my eyes, and let the weight of my body sag against the driver's seat.

"Andrea?" I said, my voice breaking on the last syllable. "Is that you, baby?"

I'd never give much thought to the idea of ghosts. The concept had always frightened me. But right now, I needed to believe more than I'd ever needed anything. My gut insisted that Andrea was gone, but it also told me she was still here, too.

The tears slipped down my face from my closed eyes. There was no answer to the question I'd just asked, nothing an observer could have pinpointed. And maybe it *was* just my broken heart or my grief-addled brain, but that quilt-tucked feeling snugged even closer.

I promised myself that no matter what happened in the coming days, I wouldn't ever let myself question what I was feeling right now.

Because I felt her. *I did.*

Not daring to move a muscle for fear the moment would evaporate, I kept my eyes shut. "I love you," I told her, my voice thick through my tears. "I wanted everything for you. I wanted *you.* And I'm so sorry I wasn't there for you when you needed me. I know my apology isn't enough … it's not even close to enough. But I'm here now, and I'm going to fight for you. You're my daughter. You've *always* been my daughter."

13

SABINA

Desert Greens was exactly the oasis the name made it sound like. The adorable little red-brick building was surrounded by wild-looking zinnia beds and set apart from the mass of strip-mall shops to its right by a tiny stream that circulated back to a fountain. The A-frame sign perched by the door read, HELLO, BEAUTIFUL. WELCOME TO YOUR HAPPY PLACE.

There weren't any other cars in the parking spaces directly in front of the shop, and for a second I worried that the place wasn't open yet. It was a quarter to ten a.m. by the time I arrived—after a quick detour back to the Airbnb to dry the tears that had not only turned my eyes puffy but drenched the front of my T-shirt.

A glance in the mirrored reflection of the glass doors reassured me that an OPEN sign hung from the inside handle—and that I'd done a pretty good job with the concealer and blush I'd dabbed on. To my surprise, I almost looked half-decent.

Even more surprising, I felt better. Not good, but better. Like the relief of emptying the contents of your stomach during a bad flu bug. It wouldn't last. I already knew that the churning, gut-wrenching sick feeling would come back. But I'd take whatever relief I could find, for as long as it lasted.

My frantic, grief-addled mind had rallied around one idea, that my daughter needed me.

I felt that in my bones in a way I hadn't before. Not when I opened the letters from Detective Barker, not during all the hours I'd driven through the night, desperate to get to Ogden, Utah. Not even when I set foot in the awful house where Andrea had spent her life. Yesterday, I'd felt like an interloper, a rubbernecker driving toward the scene of a bad accident I had no business inserting myself into.

Not anymore, though.

This was *my* daughter, *my* business. And regardless of how ridiculous it might sound to someone else, I knew she needed me here right now.

The tinkle of a bell announced my arrival as I pushed open the door, breathing in the smell of fresh citrus and taking in the lush, hodgepodge jungle of potted plants that lined the walls on shelves and the floor.

"One second!" a woman's voice called from somewhere beyond the counter.

A blender whirred, and I stepped closer to the counter. To my right was a cork bulletin board, lined with business cards from Ogden Organic Milk Delivery, a woman offering piano lessons, and—

There she was. Andrea.

My Andrea.

Her school photo, on a printed sign with the word MISSING at the top. Beneath her Mona Lisa smile, there was a description of what she was wearing when she disappeared—red hoodie, jeans, and black backpack—along with the number for the Ogden Police Department. BRING ANDREA HOME, read the words beneath the number.

I stared into her wide eyes, darker in black-and-white than they looked in the color version of the photo. Then I glanced to the right, where a whiteboard covered in writing had been hung on the wall beside the bulletin board.

The sound of the blender stopped. Fresh tears sprang to my eyes as I read the messages on the whiteboard.

We love you, Andrea.

You're a beautiful soul and we miss you.

I've never met you, but I can tell you're a good person.

I think we'd be friends.

Sending you good thoughts today.

Through my blurry eyes, I read the note printed on a piece of paper between Andrea's missing poster and the whiteboard. "Leave a kind message for our girl by 2:00 p.m. on Fridays! We'll share them on the Bring Andrea Home Facebook page each week."

There can't possibly be more tears left inside me, I thought, even as they ran down my cheeks, washing away the concealer I'd just applied.

These messages meant that Bunny was wrong. Andrea had friends. Someone who loved her enough to collect these messages and send them out into the ether, hoping they'd pull her back from wherever she'd gone.

"Hey, what can I get you?" a soft, cheerful voice asked.

I whirled around to face the woman behind the counter. Her black hair was streaked with gray, but the bronze skin on her cheeks and the smooth forehead didn't match. I couldn't decide how old she was at first. Her dark brown eyes, set deep and wide with impossibly long curly lashes, studied me with curiosity—and mild concern. "You okay? Sorry if I startled you—"

"Yes, I—I haven't even looked at the menu yet," I rushed, looking up at the neon-lit board behind her like I wasn't desperately wiping snot across my face.

"It's all right," she said gently, looking between me and the whiteboard with a nod. "Take the time you need." She reached for something on the counter then held out a blue dry-erase marker.

"Do you want to leave Andrea a message? I can work on juicing more oranges if you need a minute longer."

I took the marker she held in her outstretched hand. But to my surprise, she didn't walk away to finish what she'd been working on in the back.

Instead, the woman—who wore a name tag that read NADIA—raised her brows a little, studying both me and the picture. "I'm sorry if I'm out of line in saying this, but ... you look just like her."

"Really?" I whispered, knowing I'd replay those words over and over again for the rest of my life. *You look just like her.*

Nadia leaned her elbows onto the counter and nodded. "Really." Her voice was kind when she added, "And I get the feeling you're not really here for a smoothie, are you?"

I shook my head, doing everything I could to hold back more tears. "I know you're at work and I'm interrupting your day, but please ... if you have just a few minutes, I'm hoping you can tell me what you know about ... my daughter." I pointed at the missing poster, fully aware of how many questions that statement would create.

Nadia's eyes went so wide for a brief second that I could see the whites framing her dark pupils. "Oh my goodness," she said, rushing out from behind the counter. And before I knew it, she'd turned the OPEN sign over to CLOSED, flipped the lock on the door, and was leading me by the hand to a nook near the whiteboard, where a cluster of vintage-looking armchairs were scattered around an eclectic array of side tables.

"You're her mother," she breathed, sitting down next to me on a bright, pink-tufted velvet chair.

"Yes. Her biological mother," I clarified quickly. "Bunny and Dennis Beaumont were her—"

"Those people weren't her *anything,*" Nadia snapped, with so much anger in her voice I completely lost the thread of what I'd been about to say next.

I felt my chin tremble. "I was just at their house," I admitted. "I drove here from Oregon last night … I had no idea Andrea was even missing until two weeks ago." I hadn't been planning to share any of this information. It was a lot to take in. But the feeling I got with this woman, in this little oasis that smelled like lemon zest and summer strawberries, was starkly opposite the feeling I'd gotten in the Beaumont home. I felt certain I could trust her, even though she didn't even know my name yet.

Nadia pursed her lips and studied me again, nodding like she understood even the words I'd left unsaid. "They're bad people," she said in a low voice. "My daughter, Paloma … she's talked about Andrea a lot over the past few months. She was worried about her even before she went missing. And now …"

She looked down at her lap and went quiet, and I got the sense that she'd trailed off not because her words had failed her, but because she wasn't sure if I could handle hearing what she wanted to say next.

"Please, tell me everything," I begged. "I know I look like a mess right now,"—I shook my head and gestured to my tear-streaked face with a hollow laugh,—"but I can handle it. My name is Sabina, by the way."

Nadia met my gaze again, and this time there were tears brimming in her eyes. "Sabina." She drew in a deep breath and reached for my hand again, like she needed to steady herself and me, too. "I would want the same if something happened to my Paloma. So I'll tell you what I know."

14

ANDREA

I kept reaching for the words Sabina had said earlier, in the car. *"I'm going to fight for you."*

I'd never seen anybody's eyes blaze like that, on my behalf.

It meant everything.

Tucking the memory away for now, I curled into an empty blue velvet chair beside Paloma's mother and Sabina, not wanting to miss the story Nadia was about to tell. I'd never gotten the chance to meet Nadia, but I really wished I had.

Even more than that, I wished I'd let Paloma be my friend for real. I had no idea she'd been worried about me. No idea she cared so much. We'd only become friends our junior year, when we sat beside each other in nearly every single one of our classes. *"Hey, I think I know you,"* she'd said, turning around at her desk to study me on the first day of World History with Mr. Ewing.

"I think I know you too," I'd replied with a confused look and a laugh, because she did look kind of familiar, but I couldn't say from where. Paloma wasn't one of the ultra-popular kids, but she was pretty, with almond-shaped brown eyes and shiny black hair. And she was always smiling, like some kind of pilot light lit her up from the inside.

Her eyes widened and she asked, "Wait, were you in the Eighteenth Ward a long time ago?"

I almost replied, "What's the Eighteenth Ward," but then I remembered that "ward" was the Mormon word for "church," because almost everybody at Ogden High School was Mormon. I technically was too, even though I'd been like eight years old the last time Dennis and Bunny had taken me to church.

"Yeah, I think maybe? That sounds familiar," I said, and she clapped her hands right as the bell rang and Mr. Ewing told us to stop goofing around and listen to him talk about the Russian czars.

After that day, Paloma smiled and waved at me in the halls. She saved me a seat when we got free-choice days in English. We sometimes passed notes back and forth in class, sharing doodles and being silly, hanging out in the halls while we ate lunch, sending each other memes on Instagram. Paloma was the kind of friend I'd wanted my whole life—the first person who seemed to really take an interest in me as a person—and yet I kept her at arm's length. Whenever she asked if I wanted to hang out after school, I found new excuses until she stopped asking. I told myself that if Paloma knew about my life, my home, beyond the walls of Ogden High School, she'd run the other way. Like the kids in elementary school had when the nickname "And-reek-a" first stuck.

She'd clearly guessed, though. And she'd wanted to be my friend anyway.

Nadia, who had stood to retrieve two containers of juice from the grab-and-go refrigerator set into the wall behind the chairs, let out a sigh and leaned back. She handed one container to Sabina, then nodded to the clock on the wall. "I wish Paloma were here to tell you this herself, but she won't be home until three. You're welcome to come over and talk to her whenever you'd like. I'll give you my phone number before you leave, too. But …" She took a sip of her green juice and looked at Sabina with a pained expression on her face. "I know a few things she doesn't … and that I've only told the police. So maybe this private conversation is better for now."

Sabina nodded, wrapping her hands tightly around the container of "Holy Kale" juice. I scooted closer to her on the edge of my chair, linking my arm through hers, and she relaxed ever so slightly.

Nadia drew a deep breath, then finally dove in. "I started hearing about Andrea at the beginning of the school year, last September. They had a lot of classes together all of a sudden. Paloma said that Andrea was pretty shy and had been teased a lot by the other kids over the years. Paloma was upset about that, and I was proud of her for befriending Andrea. I didn't realize it was Andrea *Beaumont* at that point. Then one day, Paloma mentioned her last name and that her family had been in our ward—our church community—" she clarified, "when both girls were toddlers."

I leaned in closer to Nadia, and so did Sabina.

Nadia shook her head, closing her eyes to remember. "Then I knew exactly who Andrea Beaumont was. Or more accurately, who her parents were. Before all the new construction in this part of Ogden, before the leadership split our ward into two, we all went to church together." She pursed her lips and paused, like she was trying to find the right way to phrase something. Her brows knit together, and her fingers laced around the juice container as she looked Sabina in the eye and said, "I know better than to hate another person. I know better than to judge. But that man ... Dennis Beaumont ... there's something wrong with him."

"What do you mean?" Sabina prompted in a low voice.

Nadia let out a long sigh. "I'll put it like this. In our church, everybody gets a 'calling.' A job. You might be asked to teach the Sunday school classes, or clean the church building, or be the bishop at any time. And when someone gets a calling like bishop, or counselor to the bishop—really important jobs—everybody in the congregation is asked to sustain them, by raising their right hand."

"Like a vote?" Sabina tilted her head slightly.

"No, more like … showing your support. Agreeing that their calling came from God."

Sabina nodded. "Okay, got it."

"When Dennis Beaumont was called to be first counselor in the bishopric—this would've been when Andrea and Paloma were about three years old—I didn't raise my hand to sustain him. I raised my hand in opposition."

Sabina squinted her eyes like she was trying to understand.

I sighed impatiently, wondering why we were taking this side quest into church politics. But, what else was I going to do, other than sit here? So I decided to slip into my memories and see it for myself while Nadia explained it to Sabina.

I wasn't sure how I'd find the thread of the particular memory Nadia was referencing. I was only three at the time, after all. But, then, like I was thumbing through a picture book of all the memories labeled CHURCH hidden in my past, there it was.

I saw Bunny, wearing a green-and-white paisley dress with long sleeves, holding toddler-me on her lap in the pews while I squirmed, trying to get down on the floor so I could play. Church was boring. And so, so long. "Be reverent," she hissed at me. "Look at your daddy."

And there was Dennis, grinning from ear to ear where he sat at the front of the church in a row of seats reserved for speakers and leaders. The bishop stood in front of him at the pulpit microphone, looking down at the congregation.

The bishop cleared his throat. "Brothers and sisters, we have released our beloved Brother Ames from his calling as first counselor in the bishopric. And after much prayer and discussion, we have extended the calling to Brother Beaumont. We now present his name for your sustaining vote."

Three-year-old-me started to squawk, grabbing the collar of Bunny's dress and, when she loosened her grip on me, I giggled and dove under the pew in front of us.

Ghost-me kept watching the scene play out, studying Dennis's big, toothy grin with pure hatred.

"All those in favor," the bishop prompted, "please indicate by the uplifted hand."

Bunny, along with the rest of the congregation, raised their hands in a sea of agreement. I couldn't help but notice that Bunny wore the only real smile in the meeting room, though.

The bishop nodded. "Thank you," he said. "Any opposed, by the same sign."

And that's when I saw Nadia—fourteen years younger than she was now, with her hair in a neat bun and an adorably chubby toddler-Paloma beside her on the pew.

She raised her hand. Tentatively at first, then high enough that there was no mistaking the gesture of opposition.

The bishop's expression didn't change, but his eyes went to Nadia, and nearly every head in the congregation turned to follow his gaze. A few whispers erupted. Some people shifted uncomfortably in their seats.

Nadia was the only one with her hand raised.

She held it up high until the bishop said, "Thank you, Sister. Please find me after the meeting so we can discuss your concerns."

The meeting moved on. Nadia tucked her chin and stared at her fingers, laced in her lap. Her hands were trembling when she reached into her purse to find a book about baby animals for Paloma to thumb through.

When the service was finished, she hefted toddler Paloma onto her hip and hurried to the front of the meeting room.

My three-year-old self stayed with Bunny, who was mutter-ing something about soggy Cheerios and a stain on my dress. To my surprise though, I realized that whatever part of myself was observing the memory could now follow Nadia across the meet-ing room, out the double doors down a long hallway, then into the bishop's office.

The bishop greeted her with a smile and guided her to a chair across from his office desk. The room was small, and the walls were covered in the same weird, hairy wallpaper that covered the rest of the walls in the church. I'd loved to pick at it when we sat in a side pew. The blinds were half-closed, and a portrait of Jesus, arms open wide, hung on the wall behind the bishop.

When Nadia shut the door, his smile disappeared, replaced by a stern look. "Sister Ramos, can we counsel together?"

Nadia nodded, her brows knit together in worry. "Yes. I—I've never opposed anyone's calling before. But I've heard some things that worry me from a few of the young women. Brother Beaumont is too familiar with them. Once, he went into the girls' bathroom during a weekday activity, and he claimed it was just a mistake, but —"

The bishop drew in a deep breath and he shook his head from side to side. "Sister Ramos, I would counsel you to be wary of be-lieving rumors. And I can reassure you that this calling—from the Lord—does not come lightly or at random. Brother Beaumont has been chosen for a reason. To further the work of the Lord—and also to help *him* grow spiritually. At the end of the day, it's our job to sustain him in faith."

A confused expression crept across Nadia's face. "So you're saying it was wrong of me to oppose?"

"Not at all. This gives us an opportunity to counsel together. To remind you that the Lord's ways are not our ways," the bishop said calmly. "I'm not worried about Brother Beaumont. But I would encourage you to search your own heart, Sister Ramos. Heavenly Father commands us to 'judge not.'"

I was so immersed in the memory, I'd almost stopped listening to what Nadia was telling Sabina in the present, while they sat in the velvet-tufted chairs beside me in Desert Greens. When I realized that Nadia was crying, I shook the unsettling memory away fully.

"I wasn't the only one who thought Dennis Beaumont was a wolf in sheep's clothing," she said, wiping her eyes on her sleeve. "But he was just ... I don't know, such a *good* pretend sheep. Always grinning and clapping people on the back after sacrament meeting, and making sanctimonious comments in Sunday school. His wife, Bunny, wasn't exactly well-liked, but their little girl—Andrea—was so darling, and Dennis could be ... well, not exactly charming, but a talker, I guess?"

Sabina drew in a deep breath. "Piece of shit," she seethed, then looked up sharply at Nadia. "Sorry."

Nadia covered her mouth to hide a bubble of laughter. "Call him whatever you want. I haven't even told you about Isabel Palphreyman yet."

EIGHT YEARS
EARLIER

15

ISABEL PALPHREYMAN

June, 2007

There are only six women mentioned by name in *The Book of Mormon*: Mary, Abish, Sarah, Sariah, Eve, and Isabel.

I got Isabel. The "harlot."

When I complained about it to my mother, after some particularly merciless teasing in Sunday school one week, she snapped, "It's a pretty name, Isabel. Don't be crass."

Over time, I realized that the real reason I got stuck with the name was that my parents were scraping the bottom of the barrel, doggedly sticking to their *Book-of-Mormon* theme while figuring they'd get a boy before they ran out of girls' names. We already had a Mary—my mother. And Sariah, Abish, and Eve. my three older sisters. Sarah was the last remaining name aside from Isabel, and that was too close to Sariah.

In the end, no boys came shooting down the pipeline from heaven, so I got the name Isabel.

When I was eleven years old, my Sunday school teacher, Brother Beaumont, had put a stop to the teasing about my name when the other kids started up again during class. He got so stern with the boys that one of them actually started to cry.

I was so grateful for that, I felt bad for all the times I thought he was ugly, with his greasy combover and soft wheezing breath.

Back then, he was just another suit-wearing man who went to our church and had a wife and a little girl named Andrea.

But all that changed the summer I turned sixteen.

By that point, Brother Beaumont wasn't the Sunday school teacher anymore. He'd been serving as the first counselor in the bishopric, which meant he was in charge of interviewing the incoming "Laurels," the name for the group of sixteen-year-old girls that gathered during the third hour of church each Sunday for "Young Women's." The interview was basically a check-in, to see whether I was staying pure and obedient.

I was so nervous for my interview that after I walked the four blocks to the church from my house, I slipped into the bathroom to wipe my face and armpits with damp paper towels, trying to cool the prickles of sweat and red splotches on my skin. It wasn't that Brother Beaumont made me nervous, exactly. It was because I'd gotten my first boyfriend earlier that year—Archer. I was a sophomore and he was a senior, and he was the most beautiful boy I'd ever laid eyes on.

Archer and I hadn't gone "all the way" or anything, but I was becoming increasingly sure that our makeout sessions fell under the category of "heavy necking and petting," which I'd only just learned the meaning of during a "chastity chat" lesson in Young Women's.

Sister Klein, my leader in Mia Maids—the age group of girls before Laurels—had read our class a verse from *The Book of Mormon*, Alma Chapter 39, her voice full of emotion and her eyes getting red and misty. That scripture had been stuck in my head on repeat.

"'These things are an abomination in the sight of the Lord … above all sins save it be the shedding of innocent blood or denying the Holy Ghost.'"

"These things" included necking and petting, Sister Klein explained. And necking and petting meant kissing and touching. Sure, an innocent peck was fine. Like the kind you might give your mom or dad. But if you added "desire" and touching into the equation? *Then* you were necking and petting.

That realization made my stomach lurch. Not only had I been kissing Archer with a whole lot of desire, but I hadn't pushed his hand away when he slipped it under my bra behind the school portables after school, either. In fact, I kissed him harder than ever.

Sister Klein had looked each of us dead in the eye and added, "Girls, as daughters of your Heavenly Father there is nothing more important than your virtue. Keep yourselves pure. Keep yourselves chaste. You would never deny the Holy Ghost or shed innocent blood. So if you're telling yourselves it's not a big deal to mess around with a boy, the Prophet Alma is warning you to think again."

By the time I forced myself to walk back to the church foyer, Brother Beaumont had already finished with his other interview, and was standing in his office doorway, looking around. Someone had turned the lights off in the hallway, since it was a Tuesday night and nobody else was at the church except for me, Brother Beaumont, and the bishop—who had his door closed across the hall for another interview.

"Sister Palphreyman," Brother Beaumont said when he saw me, "you've certainly grown up over the last three years." He gestured for me to come inside his office, which was weirdly tiny—about the size of my bathroom at home. I avoided his eyes, sat down in the green-cushioned chair facing his desk, and stared at the walls. Like the rest of the church building, they were covered in a scratchy, textured wallpaper that had coarse little hairs poking out of it demanding to be picked at.

I clasped my hands in front of me to hide the fact that they were shaking. Was I going to be honest about what I'd done with Archer? I pretended not to see his outstretched arm, trying to shake my hand, and kept my head down, sitting in the straight-backed chair facing his.

From my Mia Maid's interview with the bishop two years earlier, I knew the questions Brother Beaumont was about to ask me.

He'd start with, "Do you pay a full and honest tithe to the church?" That was a softball. I'd always paid ten percent of all my babysitting money.

Then would come the question I'd been dreading. "Sister Palphreyman, are there any sins you haven't repented of that need to be confessed?"

Keeping my eyes lowered, I listened as he situated himself in his chair and arranged some of the papers on his desk.

"I barely recognize you from that gangly thing I had in my Sunday school class."

I tried to laugh, but what came out was a painful-sounding squeak.

Brother Beaumont was quiet for a second. Then he said, "I'm getting the feeling you might be a little nervous for this interview?"

I nodded, because I was afraid that if I spoke, I'd start crying.

He sighed heavily and scooted his wheeled chair out from behind his desk, close enough that our knees were only a couple of inches apart. And then, in a soft voice that made the hair on the back of my neck bristle, he said, "Sister Palphreyman, do you trust your church leaders?"

I hadn't been expecting that question, but the answer was easy. "Yes," I said without hesitating.

He nodded approvingly. "I want you to think really hard before you answer this next question then, okay?"

"Okay." As long as it wasn't about necking and petting, I would know the answer.

He looked me dead in the eye then asked, "Sister Palphreyman, do you trust your church leaders enough to give you a kiss?"

I stared back at him, dumbfounded, my stomach clenched like a fist. What kind of question was that? Was this a test? There was no way I wanted to kiss Brother Beaumont or any of the old men in leadership positions in the church.

From the way he was staring at me intently, waiting, I knew the right answer though.

I couldn't find my voice, so I gave a tiny nod of my head instead.

He grinned, then reached one hand into his desk and pulled out something tiny and silver.

A Hershey's Kiss.

"Very good," he said, handing me the candy.

The fist in my stomach relaxed, and I smiled from pure relief. It had been a test, and I had passed. And for a second, I'd forgotten all about Archer.

But the relief was short-lived.

Brother Beaumont leaned forward, close enough that I could smell his sour breath. "Now, the Spirit is prompting me to jump right into the difficult questions in our interview. I think you have some things to get off your chest. Am I right about that?"

I made that tiny nod again, terrified that he might be able to see directly into my soul. Ever since I was little, I'd been taught that the bishop and his counselors were stand-ins for Heavenly Father. They might be your next door neighbor, or your friend's dad one minute, and a stand-in for God the very next.

"Do you masturbate, Sister Palphreyman?" he asked, cocking his head and making his voice stern as he scooted even closer.

I shook my head no, definitely not. I'd been asked this question in past interviews, and based on what I understood from our lessons in Mia Maids, it was mostly a thing that boys did.

"Have you ever had romantic or sexual feelings for someone of the same gender?" he tried, and I wondered why—if he could see into my soul—he wasn't just asking me the right question first.

"No," I said firmly, feeling my cheeks get hot and wishing he'd move his chair farther away from mine. The stench of whatever he'd eaten for dinner—fish, maybe—was coming off him in waves, and that wheeze was starting to creep into his voice. It made me want to tuck my nose into the corner of my dress sleeve.

"Have you engaged in necking, heavy petting, or inappropriate touching of any kind?"

My mouth was so dry I could barely swallow, let alone speak. The Hershey's Kiss was melting in my hand where I held the silver foil tight.

"Isabel means 'harlot,'" taunted the voices of those boys from my Sunday school class.

"Yes," I whispered.

And that's when Brother Beaumont slowly reached out a hand and put it on my knee.

Was this another test?

I held my breath, because his face was now only inches away from mine. "I'm proud of you for being brave enough to tell me that," he said, searching my face. "And this happened with your boyfriend—Archer, right? The older boy?"

How did he know that? Had Sister Klein told him? One of the other girls in Young Women's? My parents? I wanted to ask him to move his hand off my knee. I wanted to take back what I'd just confessed. Instead, I just nodded.

Then I averted my eyes and fixed them on the small, frosted-glass window above his left shoulder and tried not to breathe, thinking, *This is a test. It'll be over soon.*

"What exactly have you done with Archer?" he prompted.

When I didn't respond, he added, "It's important for you to make a full accounting of your sins for the repentance process to work."

My lungs burned for oxygen, and I finally drew in a gasping breath that made my stomach heave.

"We … my boyfriend … Archer and me … have been kissing. He touched my—" I couldn't finish the sentence, because my stomach hurt so bad and because tears were pouring down my cheeks and into my mouth. I let the Hershey's Kiss fall beneath my seat, since otherwise the chocolate was going to start melting on my dress.

"That's right. You're doing just fine, Sister Palphreyman. Sometimes repentance isn't pretty," he said, that rank hot breath still right in my face. "Touched your what?"

I gestured to my chest, too scared and sick and embarrassed to say the words.

His eyes stayed fixed on the front of my dress. Then slowly, like he was hoping I might not even notice what he was doing, he slid one hand from my knee to the middle of my thigh.

I drew back, recoiling against my chair, and finally looked him in the face.

And what I saw scared me so much that I forgot all about what I'd done with Archer on the empty tennis courts.

Brother Beaumont's eyes looked different than they had when I first came into the room for the interview. Emptier, darker, and wider. Like each iris had fallen into its own black hole.

I turned my head ever so slightly to gauge the distance to his office door. Was the bishop still next door? If I screamed, would he hear me through the wall?

Like he could see inside my head, Brother Beaumont gripped my leg tighter and leaned closer. "If you trust your church leaders, the repentance process—"

But I was done with trust.

Like the back of my legs were spring-loaded, I leapt to my feet in one quick motion, arching my body to avoid both of his hands as they tried to grab my dress.

Run, run, run, my mind screamed. *Run, Isabel, run.*

16

ISABEL

I ran all the way home from the church building, my sandaled feet slapping the pavement and my maxi dress billowing out around me as I tore through the quiet streets in the gray half-dark of our neighborhood.

For those glorious four blocks, I allowed my mind to go blank, letting my feet do the racing. Just gulping air into my lungs again and again while the wind dried the tears streaming down my face.

It was only when my legs stopped pumping and I stood in front of our house that my mind began to churn.

The relief that I'd gotten out of that office without something awful happening evaporated as a whirlwind of terrifying thoughts took its place. What was I going to tell my parents? The questions he'd asked me? That he'd touched my leg? That didn't sound that bad. Had it actually been that bad?

The first inklings of shame threaded through my fear.

I sat down on the porch steps and forced my breathing to calm while I steeled my resolve. I had to tell my parents what had happened. What Brother Beaumont had done wasn't right, being that close to me, touching my leg like that during an interview.

Unless it really was just another test, like the Hershey's Kiss? Was this the same kind of thing? Had I failed?

I shook my head. *No.* Everything about that interview had been wrong.

I drew in another steadying breath and balled my hands into fists. I could hear the faint sound of the TV playing in the living room, which meant that my mom and sisters were cuddled on the couch watching *Downton Abbey.* My dad would be in his office reading, since *Downton Abbey* was a "girls show."

I didn't want my sisters to know what had happened, didn't want them to see the tears on my face. I felt confused and embarrassed just telling my parents. So I decided I would knock on Dad's office door and say I needed to tell him something important. Then he would go into the living room to get Mom, and the three of us would talk in his office.

I would start with the Hershey's Kiss then tell them everything that had happened with Brother Beaumont at the interview— minus the details about me and Archer, who they already disliked since he wasn't a member of the church.

They'd hug me while I cried, and then we'd call the bishop together to tell him what had happened.

Brother Beaumont would be released from his calling as first counselor to the bishop, maybe even get disfellowshipped or excommunicated from the church. I could still go into Laurels and forget about what had happened in that office.

Everything would be okay. And I'd never let Archer do much else besides kiss me.

I stood up from the porch on shaky knees and, before I could talk myself out of it, walked to the front door and twisted the knob.

The smell of the rolls Mom had baked for dinner and the sound of my sisters laughing at something on the TV made me feel like crying all over again, but in a good way.

Dad's office door, just down the hall and to the left past the front entryway, was closed. As I walked toward it, I heard the muffled sound of his voice, a pause, then another muffled sentence. He must be on a phone call.

I kept moving toward the living room. I'd find Mom first, instead.

But when I poked my head around the wall, I saw Sarah, Abish, and Eve tucked under a blanket, turned away from me, watching TV. No Mom.

I backed up a few steps and started upstairs, figuring she was in her bedroom.

Then I heard the faint sound of her voice, coming from down the hallway.

I turned and stared at Dad's closed office door. Why were both of them in there right now? That wasn't normal. Not with the door shut.

Before I could wonder about it any longer, the office door swung inward, casting a triangle of orange into the dimly lit hallway.

My dad's face, usually all smiles and crinkled brown eyes, stared back at me like a stranger, solemn and worried. He rubbed a hand over the gray and white stubble peppering his jaw. "Isabel, please come in here and talk with us."

For the second time that night, my mouth felt so dry it might as well have been filled with sand.

His expression was so sad that I had the fleeting thought that someone had died—my friend Ruby, or my grandma? Was our cat Pepper okay?

Shaking with fresh fear, I walked toward him with halting steps and entered to see Mom standing beside his desk, her eyes on the floor.

"What's wrong?" I burst out, unable to bear the silence any longer. From the look on their faces, whatever had happened was worse than what Brother Beaumont had done.

My dad gestured to his Blackberry, lying a few feet away on the desk. "Brother Beaumont just called to tell us about your interview."

It felt like I'd been zapped by an electric fence.

Even my ears were suddenly numb and zinging. I couldn't breathe. I couldn't move. It was all I could do to stand upright, staring at my parents' crumpled expressions.

Brother Beaumont had called them? That didn't make sense.

"He told us what happened in your interview," Dad said in a strained voice that made me think he was trying not to cry. "How … upset you got when he said he'd have to tell us about you and Archer."

I felt my jaw droop open a little, like I was some kind of cartoon character. This wasn't right. This wasn't what we were supposed to be talking about. A current of shame and rage and horror zipped through me in an unending circuit.

Brother Beaumont wasn't supposed to tell them *anything* I confessed.

Brother Beaumont had touched my thigh.

Brother Beaumont was lying.

My parents believed him.

Mom took a step toward me, wringing her hands in front of her. The tears that had been welling up in her eyes finally spilled down her cheeks. "Oh, Isabel. I'm so disappointed in you. Brother Beaumont said you ran out of the interview and threatened to 'make him regret it' if he called us." She made a little hiccuping sound through her tears. "But he *had* to tell us what you confessed. Archer is eighteen, so if you were … if you two were intimate—"

Intimate. The word made me want to throw up.

"That's *not* what happened." My voice came out shrill, and even to my own ears the words sounded unconvincing, untruthful. "Brother Beaumont put his hand on my knee and—"

Dad cleared his throat. "Do you know what statutory rape is, Isabel?"

I didn't. But I knew the word "rape," so it had to be something awful. I wanted to curl up on the floor and die right there. "No," I whispered. "But …"

The tears were falling so fast, my throat closing so tight, I couldn't finish.

My dad's eyes were helpless and sad when he glanced at my mom, then back at me. "It means that we should really be calling the police right now." He sighed. "But that kind of charge can ruin someone's life. We're calling Archer's parents instead—for now. If it's not already clear, the two of you are no longer allowed to see each other."

Mom was nodding, her fingers laced in front of her heaving chest like she was praying. Maybe she was. "Should we drive her back to the church, so she can apologize to Brother—"

"No!" The word sliced through my raw throat, louder than I'd planned.

My parents stared at me in shock. I realized, suddenly, that the TV had gone silent in the living room, which meant my sisters were likely listening in the hall.

"Go to your room, Isabel," Mom said, her voice quivering. "Now."

And for the second time that night, I turned and ran through an open office doorway as fast as I could.

17

ISABEL

2007–2012

For a month after that awful interview with Brother Beaumont, I wasn't allowed to take the sacrament—the bread and water meant to represent the blood and body of Jesus.

I wasn't "worthy."

And everyone—my new classmates in Laurels, my Young Women's leaders, my sisters—knew it. Nobody even had to tell them. I wasn't dating Archer anymore, and I wasn't taking the sacrament. There were only so many reasons that happened.

When my parents finally explained to me what statutory rape was that night, I swore up and down that me and Archer had never gone that far. He told his parents the same thing. Brother Beaumont had been lying.

Nobody believed us.

They believed Brother Beaumont, who sat on the pulpit next to the bishop on Sundays, looking down at me with his shark-black gaze while *he* took the sacrament.

I refused to look back at him, except during the prayer when everyone's eyes were supposed to stay shut. Then I lifted my chin and imagined my eyes were lasers, cutting through his sunburned turkey neck until his liver-spotted head fell onto his shoulders.

It was the only time I felt any kind of relief from the pain in my chest. My heart was broken. And instead of healing, it festered.

Over the next three years, things only got worse.

When I wasn't angry, I felt numb. And when I didn't feel angry or numb, I felt desperately and completely alone.

Isabel the harlot. Nobody said it to my face anymore, teasing. Now they whispered it behind my back.

Everything that had felt safe and comforting and real before felt wrong now. Church, my friends in Laurels, even my sisters. The way they looked at me, talked to me, even walked past me in the hall, changed after what happened that night with Brother Beaumont.

My grades turned from A's and B's to D's and F's.

The deadline to apply for college at BYU came and went.

I spent more and more time alone in my room, putting in headphones and listening to music nobody else could hear, but blasting it so loud that my ears rang in the silence afterward.

When I turned nineteen and graduated from high school, I refused to go to church anymore.

By that point, Brother Beaumont was long gone. We had a new bishop with new counselors, and the Beaumonts had moved to a different neighborhood. But I still saw his shadow everywhere I went.

My refusal to go to church was the final straw for my parents.

"If you're going to live under our roof, you'll make righteous choices, Isabel," my Dad said, standing at the foot of my bed and looking at my mom for confirmation.

She nodded, resolved.

I stared at them both dully, refusing to show any hint of the panic I felt on the inside. I didn't have a job. I didn't have friends. I didn't have anywhere else to live.

When Dad left the room, Mom sat next to me and gently removed the headphones I'd shoved back over my ears. To my surprise, there were tears in her eyes. "Izzy, I've been praying for you every night for the past three years. I don't know how to help you anymore. But God does, and I'm just going to have to trust Him. Because … well, even if Brother Beaumont did what you said …" She trailed off and shook her head, like this was too much to consider, then continued. "Even if that really happened, you need to forgive him. This bitterness and anger is coming from Satan, not Heavenly Father. Let it go, Isabel. Come back to us."

It was only years of practice that kept the tears from welling up in my eyes.

I looked at the wall and refused to say anything else until she finally shook her head and went back downstairs with Dad.

I moved out a few weeks later, responding to an ad I'd found on Craigslist from a woman promising a one-bedroom apartment in exchange for daily house cleaning.

It wasn't a woman who met me in the Walmart parking lot and took me to the rundown eight-plex near the cemetery, though. It was a man in a beat up Dodge Charger who barely looked at me as he tossed my duffel in the trunk.

And it wasn't house cleaning.

The apartment was nothing like the pictures—filthy carpet, a couch that smelled like mildew, a mattress on the floor with no sheets and a door that didn't lock all the way. The two "managers" who greeted me said that the cleaning gig had "fallen through." But I could still stay. They offered me cash to be "friendly" to a man who would be coming by later that night. Just one, they said. Just once.

I stammered out a terrified "okay." I didn't know what else to do. And unlike that day with Brother Beaumont, I couldn't think of anywhere to run.

So I just made myself as numb as I could and got through it. To my surprise, it wasn't as bad as I expected. And I earned a little money, too.

But it wasn't just once, of course.

And that's how, for the next two years, I became a harlot for real.

Isabel the harlot, Isabel the harlot, I sometimes chanted in my head while I did what I had to do. It was something else to focus on besides the endless array of men whose eyes reminded me of Dennis Beaumont.

I cut my long blonde hair short and dyed it pale blue. Anything to distance myself from the person I'd been before. I tried sips of the cheap red wine some of the other girls in the eight-plex offered me and discovered that it packed the cavity in my chest with just enough gauze that I fell asleep without dreaming of anything that made me cry.

I considered trying the "goodfellas" a couple of the girls offered in exchange for my tips—tiny white pills that guaranteed a peaceful night's sleep—but stopped short because I was scared that if I let myself feel that good, I'd only want more.

Then one Friday night in the middle of winter, everything got worse.

It started with a knock on the door.

Most of the time, the knock that told me a client was waiting—sent to my apartment by one of the managers—was three short raps.

This time, it was two short raps, then two raps with long pauses in between.

I opened up anyway. Any time before 10:00 p.m., we had to open up to clients. That was the rule.

And there he was.

It was like he'd stepped right out of my nightmares and into the corridor of my rundown one-bedroom apartment with the door that didn't always lock properly. Same bald, liver-spotted head and greasy combover. Same scraggly beard. Same half-smile. Only this time, he wasn't wearing a suit. He was wearing faded brown coveralls and work boots caked in snow and mud, like he'd just come from a job site.

Brother Beaumont.

He looked as surprised to see me as I did to see him.

"Isabel Palphreyman," he said in wonder, his breath puffing white from the freezing air, taking in my blue hair and letting his eyes travel from my eyes down my body. "I always wondered what happened to you."

He took a step forward.

I tried to shut the door in his face.

I could deal with being a harlot for everybody else. But not for him. *Never* for him.

"No," I called out, "somebody help me!" I leaned into the door with all my might, hoping my voice would echo through the stairwell, that one of the other girls would come out of their apartment, that one of the Johns would come out of the "office" downstairs and investigate what was going on.

But everybody—including me—was used to the occasional scuffle. The odd scream. The raised voices.

Some of the clients liked it rough. The other girls knew better than to interfere. And besides, most of us were either asleep or out of our heads when we weren't servicing. It was a cold night. The only thing you'd get from sticking your nose in someone else's business was goosebumps and a cussing out.

He leaned his shoulder, then his hip, hard into the flimsy door so I couldn't slam it shut, grabbing for my bare arm.

His touch burned like acid. Just like I remembered.

I gave up trying to blockade the door and ran through the apartment away from him, even though I knew there was nowhere to go.

18

SABINA

OGDEN, UTAH

2015

I was shaking with rage by the time Nadia finished telling me about the "rumors" she'd heard about Isabel Palphreyman.

She sat back in her chair, eyes troubled. "Isabel was a really nice girl. Kind, and very polite. Back when we were still in the Eighteenth Ward, she babysat Paloma a couple of times and brought a whole bag full of coloring books and toys with her." She wiped at another tear working its way down her chin. "From what I understand, after what happened with Dennis Beaumont, everything sort of fell apart for her. She left home and lost contact with her parents a few years after it happened."

"No wonder," I muttered. I'd mangled my juice container's spout so badly, picking at the flexible plastic, that little droplets of pale green leaked down the side and onto my hand. "So nobody believed her at the time? And he stayed on as some kind of priest?"

Nadia nodded, staring down at her laced fingers. "I don't think anybody—aside from Isabel's parents and the bishop—even knew about it. I didn't hear the story until years later, long after we'd moved out of that ward. I met up with an old friend from the

Eighteenth Ward who knew the Palphreymans pretty well, and she told me what she knew."

"That's incredibly fucked up," I seethed, voice shaking, no longer caring whether Nadia was bothered by my swearing. "Especially after what you told them about the bathroom thing when they made him a counselor? How did they ignore so many red flags?"

Nadia bit her lip and was silent for a few seconds, like she wanted to keep the words inside. "I heard he stopped going to church a while back. There was a rumor he got disfellowshipped. I don't know the details."

"What does that mean?" I asked, tired of all the church lingo, horrified by what I was learning about Dennis Beaumont but desperate to hear every detail all the same. "Like he was excommunicated?"

"No … it just means he did something the church leaders took seriously. So he couldn't hold callings anymore. Or take the sacrament."

I blinked at her, stunned. "Hold on. He wasn't allowed to eat the *bread and wine* anymore? What about the police? Why didn't anybody call the police?"

Nadia kept her eyes on the floor. "Well, we use water, not wine. But I have no idea. Like I said, I don't know the details. I can understand how upset you must—"

"I'm not upset, I'm furious. This is sickening. This bastard was preying on girls that whole time, and nobody even—"

"If it was anything like what happened with Isabel, there probably wasn't proof. Just Andrea's word against someone else's."

I slammed my hand down on the side table, nearly toppling Nadia's juice container and making her flinch. "That's bullshit, and you know it. I'm sorry, but people get arrested for less every day. Someone should have contacted the police. Have you told them what you heard about Isabel? Why the hell haven't they arrested him or searched his house? He did something to Andrea, I know he did."

I could no longer pretend that Andrea was simply hiding in an unsearched corner of Ogden like a lost puppy, scared and waiting to be found.

And that realization made my hands shake with fresh grief, mingling with the old like a bursting dam.

"I share your anger, and I told them everything I knew when they interviewed me," Nadia said in a low voice. "And everything I suspected. I gave them the bishop's name, the Palphreymans' names. I begged them to search his house. Paloma told them everything she knows, too."

"So why haven't they arrested him?" I cried in a voice just shy of a scream.

"I asked the same thing a few weeks ago," Nadia said. "The detective assigned to the case told me he can't get a search warrant on suspicion—he needs probable cause. From what I understand, they have nothing to contradict Dennis and Bunny's claim that Andrea ran away from home. No witnesses, nothing."

"There has to be some witness, something they're overlooking." I squeezed my eyes shut in despair. Nadia was right. If the police had any sort of lead that would secure a warrant, surely they would have done it by now.

Nadia sighed heavily. "Last year, Paloma told one of their teachers about some bruises she'd seen on Andrea's back when she leaned over at her desk ... The teacher probably wasn't supposed to tell Paloma the outcome of that report, but when she asked him about it, he told her that he'd contacted CPS. They interviewed Andrea at school and concluded there wasn't any evidence that she was being abused at home. She told them she bruised easily and had a rowdy puppy."

A memory of the baby I'd held in my arms, the delicate skin of her tear-stained cheeks pressed against mine, flashed to the forefront of my brain. The idea that he might have bruised that perfect skin made me want to curl up on the floor and howl.

"What the *fuck* is wrong with everyone?" I demanded instead, my voice full of splinters, as I held Nadia's gaze.

The picture that was forming of my daughter's life in Ogden was growing worse by the minute.

Nadia flinched again and moved away from me ever so slightly, like I was a snake about to strike. She didn't look away, though.

We stared at each other, my heart thundering in my ears, and for a minute I was sure she was going to ask me to leave Desert Greens. She didn't have to tell me any of this. Regret trickled through the anger pulsing in my veins. I'd been polite to the point of pandering with Bunny, and here I was practically screaming at this woman who had closed her business for the morning to tell me everything she knew. "I'm sorry," I whispered, choking on a fresh wave of tears. "I shouldn't have yelled. You and your daughter at least tried to help Andrea. No one else has done anything."

"You're not wrong to be angry," Nadia said, her voice small. "And I'm not defending anybody's actions. I can't stop thinking about what I should have done differently, what might have happened if … if I'd confronted Dennis Beaumont myself." She drew in a shuddering breath. "The church leaders handled things wrong. I keep thinking that maybe if Isabel Palphreyman or her parents had gone to the police back when all of that happened, instead of going to the bishop …"

I drew in a sharp breath, her words suddenly sparking an idea. "Hang on," I said, pulling out my phone to do a quick Google search. "This happened eight years ago, give or take? I doubt that's past the statute of limitations for sexual assault." An answer popped up on my screen. Isabel's assault was well within the statute of limitations. My heart beat faster. "Even if Isabel's parents and the bishop didn't believe her back then, Isabel could *still* go to the police now. And maybe that would be enough for a search warrant. Do you know how we could get in touch with Isabel—"

Nadia looked up at me and shook her head sadly. "That's another heartbreaking story."

19

ISABEL

OGDEN, UTAH

2012

Dennis Beaumont was faster than he looked.

And what happened that day in my apartment was worse than I could've imagined.

"Little tease," he wheezed, pushing me down on the carpet. "You've always been a little tease, haven't you Sister Palphreyman? You did the same thing all those years ago." He laughed. "And here you are literally *selling yourself,* and yet you tease? I see right through you."

I went deadweight beneath his rough hands and dirty finger-nails. I couldn't run. I couldn't fight. All there was left to do was freeze—and disappear inside myself until it was over.

When he finally stood, I stayed on the ground, so still and quiet that he prodded me with his foot. "Playing possum now? That's no way to give a man his money's worth."

My stomach lurched, but I kept my eyes shut and my body perfectly still, praying he'd walk back out the apartment door and leave me where I lay.

After a few seconds he shuffled around above me, his faint shadow passing back and forth across my face. Then I heard a strange sound. A shutter-click.

That made my eyes pop open.

He stood above me, holding his phone out in front of him as he snapped a photo of my half-naked body.

"I bet your parents wonder what you're up to these days. Maybe I'll send them a little anonymous tip," he drawled.

"No," I begged, finding my voice as the shame, unbearably hot, unfroze me. "Please don't."

"Well, then next time, you better be a little friendlier," he said with a half-smile.

I met his hollow-dark eyes in horror. The flickering blue-white glow of the fluorescent lights bounced off his shiny head and turned the sparse, dirty blond hair that ringed his scalp a sort of sickly green shade. It looked like he'd stepped directly out of a nightmare.

I wished to God it was a nightmare.

* * *

That night, I packed my few things with shaking hands and slipped into the frostbitten December.

I didn't tell the "apartment managers" I was leaving, even though I knew they'd be furious when they found out. Which meant I didn't even pick up the money they owed me for my last clients that day.

I didn't have a plan. I didn't have anywhere to go. All I cared about was making sure that Dennis Beaumont couldn't find or touch me ever again.

The only person I said any sort of goodbye to was a girl named Rita, who stepped into the breezeway on the ground floor of the eight-plex to smoke just as I was tiptoeing down the stairs.

She eyed my blue backpack with the word IZZY stitched across the front pocket—a nickname that I'd tried on for a hot second when I was twelve. It was stuffed with my clothes and around two hundred dollars in cash—everything I'd managed to save over the past two years. The rest of the money had gone to rent and the so-called managers.

"Where ya headed, hon?" Rita asked, leaning back against the wall and tapping the ash from her cigarette as she snuggled deeper into her oversized black hoodie.

I shrugged. Her tone was kind, not prying. But the last thing I wanted was to tell anybody where to find me. "I just can't stay here anymore," I mumbled.

I made the mistake of meeting her gaze for half a second, and she narrowed her eyes in concern.

He'd bitten the top of my lip—and my left cheek. I'd glanced in the mirror before I fled, and the skin on that side of my face had swollen up so much, it looked almost comical. Like I'd gotten a whole bunch of filler on just one side of my face and forgotten about the other. But there were bruises starting to bloom amid the swelling, in the faint bite-pattern of human teeth.

"Shit. You wanna come inside? Talk for a sec?" Rita prodded, gesturing to her door. She sounded almost apologetic, like the state I was in was her fault or something.

I hesitated. It was eleven o'clock, past the time the manager would send clients knocking. Did I want to talk this through instead of rushing into the freezing dark?

No. I wasn't safe here. Not that I ever had been. But every cell in my body knew it now.

I shook my head, hoping the layers of clothing I was wearing would hide the fact that I was shaking. "I really just need to go."

"Here," she said, thrusting her hands into the pocket of her hoodie and pulling out a baggie. "Get a good night's sleep at least, hon."

I hesitated, then took the baggie of little white "goodfellas." "Thanks. Don't say anything to the managers, okay?"

"Didn't see a thing," Rita said softly, staring into the darkness beyond the eight-plex. "Take care of yourself, okay?"

I tucked my chin into my hodgepodge layered clothing and hurried into the night without responding, because I was already crying again. I walked fast down the eerily silent streets, passing the pitch-black cemetery on my left, not stopping until I reached the underpass that connected with I-84.

It wasn't very far from the eight-plex. Maybe a mile and a half, but far enough. It was the only place I knew I could reach by foot that would give me some kind of shelter where I could huddle up in my layers of dirty clothing and too-small winter coat for the night.

I thought about finding a payphone, but what was the point?

Calling the police was out of the question. If I admitted what I was doing when Dennis found me, they'd arrest me—and everyone else there—for prostitution. "Out of the frying pan and into the fire" as my dad would have said.

I thought briefly about calling my parents.

Did they miss me? Did my sisters still love me? Had they shut me out of their memories like I imagined they had? Were my mom and dad's faces as stony and angry as the day I'd left home? They had no idea how far I'd fallen since then.

If they heard my voice on the phone, would they tell me they loved me, beg me to come back to a warm bed and dinner? Or would there be a long, guarded silence?

Would they finally believe me about Dennis Beaumont if I told them what had just happened? Or would they be so disgusted by what I'd become that they'd hang up the call then and there?

I looked down at my dirty, shapeless clothes and hefted the backpack stuffed with the meager money I'd earned selling my body. Then I reached up to touch my bruised tear-stained face and choppy, five-dollar-box-dyed blue hair.

My mom and dad hadn't believed me back when I was wearing my Sunday best, with a prayer in my heart and my long blonde hair tied back in a bow.

They absolutely wouldn't believe me now.

I slowed my steps as the shape of the highway and the underpass came into view, silhouetted against the sky so cloudy it was devoid of stars.

Even though it was getting late, the distant hum of cars droned out of view above me on I-84, headed north toward Tremonton, or south toward Salt Lake.

The narrow road running beneath the underpass was quiet and empty, though. A couple of lights flickered along the recesses of the hulking cement walls of the huge concrete structure. Small fires illuminated the walls of drooping tarps. A few figures hunched alongside shadows that slowly took shape into a shopping cart, garbage bags, and sleeping bags.

My body shook more violently as I moved closer, taking in the smell of wet pavement, cigarette smoke, and human waste.

But as I got near enough to make out some of the people scattered along the walls of the underpass, I forced myself to take a steadying breath. Nobody looked my way. Nobody sprang from the shadows to stab me. Nobody paid much attention to me at all, which made my stomach unclench the tiniest bit.

One woman with gray hair framing her face like a frizzy halo in the firelight waved at me tentatively.

I waved back and set my backpack down in an open patch of dirt and weeds a short distance away from her.

I didn't feel safe, exactly. But I felt safer than I had an hour ago. And that was something.

There was no telling how long I would be able to stay here, but that was a problem for tomorrow. From the snatches of conversation I'd overheard in the breezeway, I knew that some of the other girls had spent time here before they came to the eight-plex. The cops trolled it regularly to tear down any encampments that got too visible or too sprawling, but they turned a blind eye if you could keep yourself inconspicuous and tucked away. It wasn't worth their time to hassle you if you stayed light on your feet.

The road beneath the underpass wasn't busy, and most cars passing by had simply gotten off the wrong exit and were turning around to get back on the highway. Only a few people used this road to reach the Ogden cemetery.

Between the shelter from the underpass and my layers of clothing, I was almost comfortable. After a moment's hesitation, I curled myself into a ball in the dirt on the other side of the old woman. However, when I closed my eyes, trying to let sleep pull me under, the memory of Dennis Beaumont's figure standing over my body, snapping a photo, was waiting.

A heavy truck sped across the highway above, making the cement wall behind my back rumble a little. I stifled a sob by clamping down my jaw, sending my lip and cheek throbbing again.

I'd never felt so broken, so dirty, so used-up.

The feeling got so big and unbearable, pushing down on my chest so tightly that it felt like the night itself was trying to swallow me whole. Like this underpass was its jawbone.

I was alone, I was hurt, I was ruined, I was worthless.

I wasn't even a harlot anymore. Just a piece of trash.

My hand moved to the pocket of my coat.

I took out the baggie of little white pills.

Then I popped one into my mouth and closed my eyes, begging for the sleep Rita had promised.

20

ISABEL

OGDEN, UTAH

2012

The sun came out the next morning.

It was winter weak, faint between the wind-spun clouds, but there all the same.

I knew it appeared like this every day, but as I opened my eyes and blinked into the warm rays stretching fingers of light toward my spot of frozen ground in the shadows, the sunlight felt like a small miracle.

Maybe it was just the last lingering effects of the goodfella I'd swallowed a few hours before. But it felt like the sun was emerging from its hiding place just for me. Like if I squinted hard enough, I might see Jesus, smiling the way He did in the picture books my mother read to me when I was little.

I sat my frozen body upright and surveyed the underpass, eyes landing to the left, on the older woman's figure. She'd fallen asleep beside the tiny fire she'd made, a rumpled sleeping bag wrapped around her shoulders.

She's not a piece of trash, my mind whispered. *So maybe I'm not either.*

I swallowed past the lump in my throat, drew in a big breath, and reached into my pocket to touch the bag of goodfellas.

I couldn't quite bring myself to toss them into the garbage yet. However, I made myself a promise that I wasn't going to reach for another pill tonight, either.

* * *

Over the next few days, I kept my promise. I traded some of my cash for a sleeping bag that smelled like old cheese but was actually pretty warm, a tiny camp stove, a lighter, and a water bottle.

The old lady, whose name I didn't know—she didn't know mine either, we didn't ask—let me walk with her a few blocks to a food pantry that handed out free meals twice a day. It was next to a discount bakery, which sold stuff like barely expired mini-donuts and cheap loaves of bread. I was terrified to leave the shelter I'd found at the underpass and walk around in the daylight, but I tucked a sweatshirt around my neck like a thick scarf, drew my hood up over my head to cover my distinctive hair, and told myself that nobody who saw me would recognize me.

The walls of the underpass made a decent shelter from the elements, and I was pretty warm in the sleeping bag at night, even if it did stink. So I didn't bother trying to trade for a tent. And it was a good thing I didn't, because just three days after I arrived, two police cars with flashing lights showed up and started tearing down shelters.

I was ready when it happened. I grabbed my sleeping bag— which doubled as a carrier for most of my clothes—shoved the camp stove into my backpack, and booked it along the sidewalk. I followed a few paces behind Art Guy—a dude pushing a shopping cart full of paintings he toted down the street every morning—and Crow Lady, a woman who seemed intent on befriending the big black birds that swooped by the underpass all day, teasing the pigeons and picking at foil wrappers and debris.

The old woman and a couple of other folks who had tents and tarps draped up on cardboard boxes and pallets stayed where they were, with their things. I could hear some of them yelling at the police as I hurried away, head tucked into my sweatshirt and coat.

I wanted to make sure the old woman was okay, but I was too scared to do anything other than shuffle away from the underpass.

When the flashing red-and-blue lights finally moved on and I dared to return, the people who had stayed behind with their shelters were gone, along with their things.

That made me cry for the first time since running away from the eight-plex. But I told myself that the old woman would be okay. The way she'd smiled and waved at me from her shelter the night I showed up, then so kindly showed me the way to the food bank without me even asking, made me think she was pretty good at not just surviving but holding on tight to the best parts of herself while she did it.

I decided I wanted to learn how to do that, too.

I fell asleep thinking about that very thing that night, the warmth of it making me sigh in a way even the goodfellas hadn't.

While I slept, I dreamed that I was home. Not at the house I grew up in, not the pink bedspread with white hearts in the room I shared with Abish. Not the cold, creaky apartment where a knock on the door made my stomach clench every time. But my *own* home, with the kind of thick, soft carpet I loved, bright green plants crawling along the windowsills on long delicate legs, and windows letting in lots of glorious, warm sunlight.

I was standing on that carpet with my bare feet so happy and satisfied when something in the real world woke me up.

My battered lip and cheek—still healing—were suddenly on fire again. It took a second to realize it was because somebody was pressing a hand over them, tight.

And they were jamming a knee so hard against my chest that I couldn't make a sound, let alone breathe.

I couldn't see clearly, not just because it was dark but because of the way he was smashing my head into my sleeping bag with his hand.

I didn't need to see him, though. His voice and his breath, wheezing and hot and rancid, were seared into my memory.

How the hell had he found me?

"I came by your place tonight," he rasped. "Imagine my surprise when I heard you'd up and ran away."

I twisted my hips, desperately trying to kick my legs out of the sleeping bag so I could strike at him, but he leaned even harder onto my chest.

I couldn't breathe. I couldn't even pull in a sliver of breath.

"I guess I shouldn't be surprised. We both know how you like to tease me," he added. "Shh. Don't fuss. The more you fuss, the worse it'll be."

I told myself that the second he shifted his weight, the second the pressure on my chest lessened and let the air rush back into my lungs, I would scream.

But the pressure didn't stop.

The dark outline of the smashed-up sleeping bag in front of my face started to go fuzzy at the edges, and I wished more than anything that I'd reported him to the police, even if it got me in trouble or locked up.

I wished that I'd found that payphone and called my parents, even if they still didn't believe me. Even if they hung up on me.

Because as the pain in my chest had turned so sharp I was sure I couldn't bear it another second without losing consciousness, I knew I'd lost my chance.

Not the chance to be believed. Just the chance that, when they found my body, somebody might look twice in Dennis Beaumont's direction.

He pressed his chapped lips to my ear. "My little harlot," he whispered. "No more running."

That was the last thing I heard before my vision went black.

21

ISABEL

OGDEN, UTAH

2015

I ran my fingers over the faded black letters stitched onto the dirty blue backpack that was shoved in the corner of the tarp shelter: IZZY.

I was a little surprised that Crow Lady had kept the filthy backpack going on three years now. The zipper was broken, the front pocket had a hole wide enough that it was basically unusable, and at one point a mouse had babies in the main pouch when the backpack sat slumped in the temporary shelter for a few days during a snowstorm. But I guess a backpack was a backpack.

For a while, I told myself it was because Crow Lady cared about me, cared about what had happened to me, even though we'd only spoken once, when I offered her a sleeve of mini-donuts on a particularly frigid winter night in exchange for letting me share her fire for a while.

But today, Art Guy noticed it on the ground beside her while he was walking past and proved me wrong.

"Is that your name? Izzy?" he asked Crow Lady, pausing to adjust the art supplies he held in both hands.

She looked up from the *Ogden Living* magazine she'd grabbed from the stacks outside the library that were there for the homeless—or anybody else—to take for free. "Nah." She hesitated then added, "I'm Marlie. I took the backpack when that blue-haired girl left. You remember her from a few years ago?"

Not died, *Left.*

That upset me so much, I spoke for the first time in a while. It was hard to see the point of speaking, since nobody could hear me anymore. However, I made an exception because I really thought that Crow Lady—Marlie—knew I was dead. "You saw the police take my body away," I cried in protest.

That wasn't totally true, though, I realized. Marlie had poked her head out of her makeshift shelter briefly when the police showed up at the underpass to take my corpse away, but she'd turned away just as quickly, busying herself with taking down the shelter and hustling along so they wouldn't try to pin her for camping.

Nobody wanted to mess with the police or draw attention to their shelter. Not when they could help it.

I was positive that Art Guy—I still had no idea of his real name—knew what had happened to me, though. He was the one who'd flagged the cop car down on his way to the corner with his art three years earlier. *"Hey. There's a girl lying on top of her sleeping bag at the edge of the underpass. It's cold out ... so something's not right. She's got blue hair,"* he'd said gruffly, juggling the canvases and acrylic paints in his full arms. Then he went on his way to the corner and set up his art.

Now, both Marlie and Art Guy tilted their heads and made a *hmm* sound, clearly trying to remember.

"She wasn't here very long, but her blue hair sure was pretty," Marlie prompted, her fingers absently folding and unfolding the page of an article called "Best Easter Brunches in North

Utah." She screwed up her mouth in concentration. "You remember her, right?"

"Yeah … that girl's dead," Art Guy said matter-of-factly, like he was commenting on the half-scrubbed off graffiti sprayed across the wall behind Marlie. "You didn't know that?"

Marlie's mouth puckered into a tight O, and she set the magazine down on the concrete beside her. "How do *you* know she's dead?"

"She was lying on top of her sleeping bag early one morning. I saw her while I was walking to the corner. She was passed out—or at least I thought she was." He shuffled from one foot to the other, like he was uncomfortable retelling this story. "I mean … she didn't look good, but I didn't want anybody to see me leaning over an unconscious girl, either. So I told the police to check it out. They always drove past my corner at least a couple times a day. The cops came back the next week to ask me if I knew anything about her, because apparently she was dead. Overdose. They found some pills on her."

"An overdose." Those words made me want to scream as much as the first time I'd heard them.

It *wasn't* an overdose. Not even close.

Marlie let out a sigh and picked her magazine back up off the ground, scanning the bird that had just landed in the gravel by the road. "Well damn," she said softly. "I thought she just went somewhere else, since it was getting real cold." Her eyes went misty for a quick second. Then she nodded at Art Guy's armful of canvases. "I've got more magazines in my tent. You want any for painting ideas?"

I watched, dumbfounded, as Art Guy waved her off and went on his way.

Marlie went back to reading *Ogden Living*.

That was it.

I shouldn't have expected anything else.

It was honestly shocking that Art Guy and Marlie were still here at all. All of the other people I'd seen at the underpass over the last three years were long gone now. At least these two were familiar faces. But it made me feel extra stupid for hanging out with them near the cemetery all these years like the ghost I was, convincing myself that Marlie had kept my backpack to remember me by.

I'd found my way home once—just once—wandering the streets until I recognized familiar landmarks. My mother was in the front yard, pruning roses and laughing with a neighbor.

She looked happier, lighter, than the last time I'd seen her. I was pretty sure she had no idea I was dead, and neither did anybody else. And that idea hurt so much that I turned around and walked right back to the underpass, deciding I'd stay there until the police, or my family, or anyone really, was finally interested in figuring out what had really happened to me.

I knew deep down that wouldn't happen, though.

They thought they knew what had become of me.

Dennis had made sure of it. Once I was dead, he'd searched my pockets—maybe rummaging for ID—and found the goodfellas instead. He'd shoved his dirty fingers inside my slack mouth and placed two pills under my tongue. Then he'd pried open my balled-up fists so I was holding the bag of leftovers.

That's how the police officer had found me.

As soon as he did, I watched the certainty settle on his expression. I was just another junkie who'd taken one too many of those little white pills to get through a winter's night.

"Another damn fentanyl overdose," one of the officers who found me told his partner, lip curling in a grimace. *"Doesn't take much."*

He had no idea that several of my ribs were fractured beneath the skin on my chest.

He didn't look closely enough at the faint, nearly healed bruising on my face to recognize the subtle pattern of human teeth on my lip and cheek.

He didn't see the need to recommend a rape kit, DNA testing of the dried spittle sprayed across my left cheek, or a full autopsy.

And nobody would go looking for Dennis Beaumont.

After the police officers found me and covered my body with a sheet, some EMTs had put me on their gurney and slid me into an ambulance in the early morning hours. I'd ridden with them to a morgue—just a few hours from the underpass where I'd spent my last living hours.

I watched while a police officer took my pale, rigid hand, pressed each of my fingers into an ink pad, then carefully rolled them onto a piece of paper.

Then I listened in disbelief as the medical examiner spoke briefly with the officer who had picked up my body, and performed an exam that was quicker than the required physical I'd gotten when I played basketball in sixth grade. "All those 'fentanyl kills' billboards are sure helping," she muttered under her breath when she saw the bag of goodfellas still clutched tight in my rigid fingers. "Cause of death consistent with scene," she scribbled in her notes.

I stayed in that morgue for thirty days after that—the exact length of time the county was required to hold an "unidentified decedent."

It hurt that nobody was looking for me. And it hurt that nobody ever walked through those steel gray doors to claim me. But why would they? My prints weren't in the system. I'd never had a job that required it, and I'd never been arrested. I was over eighteen, so I wasn't a missing minor. And *I* was the one who'd left home and cut off contact with my family. Nobody was out there trying to track me down. Besides, the photo they put up on the Ogden City Police Facebook page in an attempt to identify the "Jane Doe" with blue hair and sunken cheeks looked nothing like the old me. I saw the photo on the mortician's computer one day, along with the official cause of death listed as OVERDOSE.

For thirty days, I stayed with my refrigerated, naked body in the lower level of the morgue with the other ghosts and their bodies.

At the end of the thirty days, the medical examiner released my body to the nearby cemetery—even closer to the underpass— where a funeral director assigned me to burial plot 1002.

There were a lot of other ghosts at the funeral home.

I didn't realize they were dead at first glance.

They looked just like the living people I saw moving around the funeral home. They weren't see-through, and they didn't have glowing red eyes or floating hair, like the ghosts in the scary movies I'd seen.

They just looked like normal people. Solid and opaque and real. Only instead of striding across the room back and forth with purpose like the funeral home employees, they wandered aimlessly, hunched in corners, and screamed or cried—unheard—when family members or friends arrived.

A couple of them met my eye. One teenage boy wearing a tuxedo and bowtie waved at me tentatively.

I waved back at him then looked away. Besides that interaction, we mostly kept to ourselves, the same way everybody had at the underpass encampments.

The next day, they put my body in the ground, where it had been ever since. There was no funeral. Just the sound of the backhoe scraping away at the earth, a wooden casket thudding into the hole they'd made, and dirt piled back on top.

The evening of my burial, I walked the mile to the underpass encampment and found Marlie with my backpack in her shelter.

I'd kept close to her ever since.

Every day for the past three years, I'd walked back and forth between the underpass and the cemetery to walk the grounds. I told myself it was because I was bored. Sometimes I even made a game of trying to tell the living mourners apart from the ghosts who clustered around the headstones or ambled aimlessly through the green grass pathways.

It was pretty much impossible to tell the difference—even the men and women wearing pioneer-type clothing. The first time I saw a woman wearing a billowing crinoline skirt and bonnet, flanked by two teenage girls in head-to-toe collared dresses, I'd raised my hand to wave at them, figuring they had to be dead. But all three looked right through me, and a few seconds later the mother pointed to a gravestone and said, "That's your Great, Great, Great Aunt Caroline." A few minutes later, a whole carload of pioneers pulled into the parking lot and joined them, holding armfuls of flowers and carefully placing them on graves. They weren't dead. They were just doing some kind of church activity.

After that, I pretty much ignored the other people in the cemetery.

I kept taking my daily walks, though. Because deep down, I hoped that one day I'd see my mom or dad or sisters. At some point, surely someone would realize I was dead and come to put my name on the grave marker instead of the words "Jane Doe, found January 10th, 2012," alongside a laminated copy of that same photo they'd put on the Facebook page.

Maybe they'd even bring me flowers, like they did for the pioneers.

Sometimes I toyed with the idea of going back home again. But it felt wrong.

I knew that if I did, I'd be a ghost on a whole new level. Both invisible *and* forgotten. Besides, I didn't want to be there for the moment they learned that I'd been found on the side of the road, at a homeless encampment, with a baggie full of drugs clutched in my fingers.

Yeah, they would grieve me. But there would be no surprise in their eyes when they heard the police report about my supposed cause of death. And they'd cringe when they saw the photo the police had posted on their Facebook page, trying to identify me, with my blonde curls long gone and my cheeks turned hollow and gaunt.

I didn't want to see the disgust in their expressions. Sometimes it was better to wonder than to know. So I'd stayed at the underpass with Marlie and Art Guy, thinking that after enough time had passed, someone would recognize my photo on that Facebook page and come claim me.

But the months had turned into years.

And nobody ever came.

22

ANDREA

OGDEN, UTAH

2015

Sabina had pages full of notes in her phone by the time she was finished talking to Nadia at Desert Greens.

I wished so badly I could join the conversation. If I could say even one sentence, I'd be able to tell them exactly where to find my body.

But of course, I couldn't do that. All I could do was listen and watch—and muster up mostly useless, haphazard sounds once in a while when the pressure of my emotions ballooned big enough.

At one point, I made the bell—which was sitting silent at the counter—ding twice. Sabina and Nadia had both startled, then continued talking.

At another point, I was pretty sure I manufactured the ruckus of some dogs fighting outside. I couldn't be sure it was the "ghost juice" that'd done it, but it happened right when Nadia said that, from what she understood, Isabel's family didn't really consider her a missing person—even though they had no way to contact their daughter and hadn't heard from her in years.

In other words, she was just another missing girl that nobody really cared to find.

That was when I slipped back into the memory of being at church with Nadia and Paloma the day Dennis had been sustained as first counselor to the bishop. Only this time, I scanned the pews looking for Isabel Palphreyman.

I wasn't sure how I'd expected to recognize her. Isabel had been quite a bit older than me. A teenager, while I was a toddler scurrying around under the pews.

I floated through the memory anyway, searching the rows of families wearing their Sunday best while the speaker—newly minted First Counselor Dennis Beaumont—rambled on at the pulpit.

I wanted to scream at him to shut up. But that wouldn't do any good, so instead, I walked up and down the pews, tuning out the sound of his grating voice.

My gaze finally landed on a family sitting near the front and smiling up at Dennis. A mother, father, and three teenage girls. I wasn't sure if I'd recognize them, but another memory—of Bunny calling the father "Brother Palphreyman" once in passing—layered on top of this one, and I knew I had the right family.

They all looked so shiny and clean. Perfect, almost, like they'd just been unboxed. The girls and their mother had matching wavy blonde hair, peaches-and-cream complexion, a spray of freckles, and light brown eyes. The women even wore matching pastel dresses in different colors.

"Is that you, Isabel?" I asked one of the nearly identical girls —she was maybe fifteen years old. I wasn't expecting a response. This was just a memory, after all. Not a real experience.

To my surprise, the girl raised her eyebrows and made an abrupt squeak.

I froze. Could she actually hear me?

Then the mother, a woman wearing a blue floral dress with a smocked collar, cut her eyes toward her daughters. "Shh. Listen to the speaker," she whisper-hissed, fixing her gaze on her daughters and nodding toward stupid Dennis. "Isabel, I saw that. Hand me the string."

The girl I'd tried speaking to gave her mother, then her younger sister—*Isabel*—an annoyed look. "I wasn't doing *anything*. She was the one tickling—"

"Shh," hissed their mother and held out her hand.

Isabel smirked but obligingly parted with the tiny thread she'd been using to tickle her sister's elbow. Then she sighed and looked up at Dennis with a bored expression.

I took a step closer to her, wishing I'd had a chance to befriend her in real life. Or at least talk to her. "I'm sorry about what happened to you," I told her inside the bubble of the memory.

I studied her bored expression a moment longer, suddenly remembering that Dennis hadn't hurt her yet. That wouldn't happen for another couple of years. "I'm sorry about what he'll do to you," I corrected myself. Then I reached out and touched her arm.

Isabel blinked rapidly, like I'd startled her awake. Then she stood up in the pew and stared right back at me.

I gaped at her.

This time, her mother and sister had absolutely no reaction whatsoever.

She looked me dead in the eye. "Who are you?" she asked incredulously.

Still stunned, I managed to stutter, "I'm Andrea. That little girl." I pointed to my toddler self, who was only half-visible across the aisle in a diffcrent pew, crawling around at Bunny's feet.

Isabel glanced between me and the pudgy girl wearing a dirty dress. Then at her family in the pew. Then up at the pulpit, where her eyes darkened.

The memory abruptly felt thick and heavy. Like the air right before a storm when the clouds are set to break loose with rain and lightning.

And then, just like that, Isabel blinked, sat back down in the pew beside her sister, and went back to staring up at Dennis with a bored look on her face.

What the hell just happened? It was the first time anybody had acknowledged me in months. And the feeling made me want to sob—if I still had eyes that could shed tears.

"Wait, please talk to me again," I begged.

But even when I stood right next to her, waving a hand in front of her and repeating those words, she stared through me.

Overwhelmed, I wrenched myself away from the memory to make sure Sabina hadn't left the smoothie shop without me yet.

It was a good thing I did.

Sabina wasn't leaving, but the clock above the velvet chairs where Nadia and Sabina sat showed that it was almost three in the afternoon. There were now two empty acai bowls on the table in front of the two women. Nadia wasn't talking about Isabel Palphreyman anymore. She was showing Sabina the Facebook page she and Paloma had set up so people could send nice messages to me, encouraging me to come home.

I wanted to read all of the messages before she put her phone away, but I was still rattled from what had just happened. Had Isabel really been talking to *me*? I was sure she had. And how was it possible that much time had gone by in the present? It felt like I'd only been "surfing" the memory for fifteen minutes at most.

I was beginning to get the sense that maybe time moved a little differently when I got wrapped up in a memory, especially when I started wandering beyond the borders of what I'd seen originally.

A sharp knock on the glass door startled me so much I jumped. If I'd still been alive, I would have knocked over the table and the chairs.

The bell—sitting untouched on the counter—made a dinging sound.

Sabina turned her head toward the bell and stared at it for a long moment while Nadia hustled to open the door.

On the other side of the glass was a girl wearing a familiar backpack slung over one arm.

A fizzy, warm feeling spread through me, and I grinned. "Paloma!"

Paloma wasn't smiling, though. She was looking between her mother and Sabina with a guarded expression.

"Who are you?" she demanded, the second Nadia unlocked the door and ushered her inside.

"Paloma!" Nadia exclaimed, cheeks reddening. "This is Sabina. She's Andrea's birth mother."

Paloma's stony expression softened in confusion, but only for a moment. She studied Sabina's face, and I just knew she was thinking about how similar we looked. She nodded warily then let the backpack drop to the ground at her feet where it made a muted thud. "Okay. So why do you have that in your car?" she asked, eyes fixed on Sabina.

Sabina tilted her head to the side in confusion. "Have what in my car?" I knew I was probably mirroring the same expression. Paloma was sweet, even-keeled. I'd never heard her talk to anyone like this. She was clearly angry, maybe even scared.

It took me a second to realize what Paloma was talking about, even though I'd been waiting for someone to put the pieces together.

It hit me right as Paloma blurted it out. "That monarch butterfly earring," she said, still glancing between Sabina and Nadia, her voice betraying a hint of a wobble. "I was wondering whose car was next to my mom's, since the sign on the door was turned to closed. And when I peeked inside the car, I saw what was sitting on the passenger seat."

Sabina's eyes widened and she shook her head back and forth like she was trying to decide on the right words to explain how she'd gotten the earring. She finally decided on the truth, and I loved her for it. "It was under a table at the Beaumonts' house," she admitted. "I went there to try to talk to them this morning … and I took it."

Paloma's expression suddenly shifted from suspicious to teary-eyed and frantic. "I *knew* they did something to her," she said, voice shaking. "That proves it, doesn't it, Mom?" She turned to Nadia, her long brown hair falling across her face as she put her hands to her cheeks. "Those are the earrings I gave Andrea for her birthday. The ones I made her."

"Yes!" I exclaimed. "Yes, tell them, Paloma."

"What?" Sabina asked, standing. "Help me understand?"

Paloma wrapped her arms around herself and glanced at Sabina. "I gave those earrings to Andrea the morning she 'disappeared.'" She made little air quotes with her fingers then kept going, talking fast now. "In one of the articles I read, Dennis said that Andrea never got home from school that day. He finished a job early, so *he* was at the house. He said he never saw her that day after she went to school in the morning. But he *lied*. If those earrings were in the house, she definitely *did* come home from school that afternoon. We have to tell the police."

Sabina looked like she wanted to leap out of her skin. "Yes, *yes,* maybe then they can get a search warrant. Let's go." She grabbed her purse from the chair. I followed close behind.

Nadia gently placed her hands on her daughter's shoulders, giving her an incredulous look. "Hold on. Are you sure about the earrings?" she asked.

Paloma nodded vigorously, eyes on the floor. "Yeah. I'm sure." She looked sideways at Sabina. "I put my initials on the inside wing. If we take it to the police, I can show you."

Sabina was already halfway out the door, with me on her heels.

"Hang on, I'm coming with you," called Nadia, hurrying around the counter to grab her keys. "I've got the detective's number in my phone, I'll call and let him know we're on our way."

Sabina shot her a grateful smile.

So did I.

It was finally happening.

This time, the police sirens drawing closer and closer to the Beaumonts' house would be real.

23

SABINA

I didn't touch the earring again, afraid I'd already fucked up by touching it—and, well, stealing it—in the first place.

But if I hadn't snatched the tiny object from underneath the table, I never would have realized what it was, and Paloma never would have seen it in my car. Which meant she never would have had a chance to tell me that she'd given it to Andrea the morning she went missing.

It was the best of my bad choices.

At least, that's what I told myself while I watched Detective Monte Barker use gloves to gently retrieve the butterfly from the seat of my car and bag it—after verifying Paloma's tiny initials on the underside of the right wing.

Detective Barker was younger than I'd expected. Mid-thirties, with a clean-shaven baby face, bright blue eyes, white-blond hair, and a trendy haircut—shaved on the sides and neatly parted deep to the left. When I saw him, I realized I'd been bracing for a grizzled small-town detective with a gray mustache, arthritic hands, and a scowl. Or maybe a Barney Fife type.

Instead, he seemed intelligent and kind. Sweet, even. I expected him to berate me for taking the earring, for going inside the Beaumont home at all, for inserting myself into this investigation without permission. He didn't do any of that, though.

He greeted Paloma and Nadia by name—he'd clearly spoken with them more than once. And when I shook his hand and told him who I was, he nodded slowly and squeezed my hand. Like he understood why I was here.

After he'd collected the earring from my car, he ushered us inside the police station and directed the three of us to separate interview rooms.

I was questioned first, walking him through everything Bunny Beaumont had told me and describing what I'd seen in the house—including the piss-poor excuse for Andrea's bedroom and the fact that they'd already put all of her belongings into storage.

I told him about finding the earring at the last second before Dennis Beaumont insisted I leave, and then about the stories Nadia relayed to me about Isabel Palphreyman, about Paloma seeing the earring in my car when she got home from school.

He didn't say much. Just asked questions every so often. Nodded for me to continue.

Mostly, he let me talk.

When I ran out of words, I reached for the question that had been burning inside me since I laid eyes on the Beaumont home that morning.

"This is enough to search their house, right?" I demanded in a small voice, exhaustion and desperation creeping into my tone. "He did something to her. I know he did." The fluorescent lights buzzing overhead were too bright, the sound of ringing phones and the creak of the plastic chair too mundane for the conversation taking place in this cramped room.

Detective Barker let out a slow, careful breath. His eyes flicked to the camera in the corner of the room with its blinking red light. "I understand your frustration, Ms. Turpin. I really do. But it's not that simple. And as much as I wish I could share more details of the direction this investigation is headed, I can't. Right now, I'm merely asking questions. No answers in return, unfortunately."

He sighed again, and I got the feeling he was weighing his words very carefully. "I'm not saying the earring means nothing. It might be very significant. We won't know either way until we test it for prints and DNA, and review everybody's statements. But I can tell you that from a defense lawyer's perspective, the earring would be the first piece of evidence on the chopping block. It's a chain-of-command nightmare. Who's to say where or how you got it? Who's to say y*ou* didn't plant it at the Beaumonts' house?"

"I didn't—I wouldn't—" I was starting to feel physically ill.

He held up a hand. "I'm not accusing you of anything, Ms. Turpin. But I'm telling you why I can't go kicking down doors right this second. If I walked into a judge's office today and asked for an arrest warrant, they'd laugh me out of the room. And a defense lawyer with half a brain would have the Beaumonts out of here within the hour."

"This *proves* Dennis was lying, though. It proves that Andrea came home after school that afternoon. You've got three people willing to testify that Paloma gave her those earrings for her birthday, the morning she disappeared—"

"Ms. Turpin." His voice had an edge to it when he interrupted me this time. "I'm looking at all the possibilities, and I'll certainly consider this new information. But again, all I can tell you right now is that we will use the statements and any potential evidence you've provided in whatever ways the legal system will allow."

I folded my arms tightly against my stomach and closed my eyes, so tired and overwhelmed by grief and frustration that I wanted to lay my head down on the scarred tabletop and fall asleep then and there.

"Ms. Turpin," Detective Barker said gently, then waited until I met his gaze. "If something violent happened to your daughter, I want the person responsible for it behind bars. Believe me, I do. And right now, that promise is the best thing I can offer you."

For a moment, neither of us said anything. I stared back at him, trying to memorize the sincerity in those baby-blue eyes.

Then I walked out of the police station to wait in my car, eyes fixed on the bright orange clouds above the horizon as the sun sank lower and lower.

The quilt-wrapped feeling was conspicuously absent, replaced by a hollowness in my chest.

While I stared at the sky, I tried to tell myself it had been less than twenty-four hours since I'd gotten here. That in all reality, I'd accomplished a lot during that tiny amount of time. I'd made contact with the Beaumonts. I'd found Paloma and Nadia. And I'd discovered a clue that confirmed my suspicions about Bunny and Dennis Beaumont.

They were liars at best. And at worst?

I shut my eyes and watched the after-image of the blazing clouds fizzle into spots of yellow and green, then darkness behind my eyelids.

With every minute that passed, I was more sure that the worst had happened to my baby.

That Andrea wasn't missing.

She was dead.

It was the intuition that had been growing by the minute, sending roots through my system since I first heard Bunny's voice on the phone. A horrible knowing, crowding out those last little bits of desperate hope that Andrea really was a missing person. That maybe she'd lived a terrible childhood and had run away for good reason, but that she was still out there somewhere waiting to be found by someone who would love her like she'd always deserved to be loved.

When Nadia and Paloma emerged from the police station an hour later, I saw the same realization in their stricken expressions, too.

They looked as hollowed-out as I felt. Paloma, especially. Her mascara had dripped down her face along with her tears, smeared into black streaks across her cheeks.

In her red-rimmed eyes I saw that realization that Andrea probably wouldn't be reading any of the kind messages on the Facebook page she and Nadia had created, urging Andrea to come home.

I fully believed Detective Barker when he said a judge would probably laugh him out of his office if he asked for an arrest warrant right now. But at this point, I'd bet just about anything that Dennis Beaumont had been the one to make Andrea disappear, no matter what a judge thought.

"We'll talk again soon," Nadia promised when we exchanged phone numbers. She wrapped me up in a hug, but there was no more urgency in her voice.

Paloma turned away without saying goodbye and got inside the passenger seat of Nadia's Toyota.

I gave them a feeble wave, then returned to my car and pulled out my phone. I had a missed call and a couple of texts from Joel, asking me to call him.

I knew that if I returned his call right now, I'd either be a crying mess for the dozenth time in a few hours, or I'd snap at him. Not because he deserved it, but because the stew of anger and horror and sadness in my stomach was churning so hard, and I'd used up every bit of my social niceties trying not to explode on the strangers I'd spent the day with.

I love you. Tsunami. Talk in the morning? I typed out.

Tsunami was the code word we'd used since the first year we were married. It basically meant that one of us was too overwhelmed to connect without melting down. A disaster that needed time for the waves to recede.

The text bubbles appeared almost immediately.

Then, *I love you too. Hang on.* Alongside a photo of a life preserver.

I clung to that message like the lifeline it was, all the way back to the Airbnb.

24

ANDREA

I hadn't realized how high I'd gotten my hopes until they rained down on me.

The police weren't going to be able to do a damn thing about that earring.

I'd listened in on Sabina's, Nadia's, and Paloma's interviews. I'd watched Detective Barker's face while he made notes and recorded them all. And as Paloma and Nadia headed for the parking lot, I lingered in his office just long enough to watch him shove the notes across his desk and tell a fellow detective, "My gut says they're right. I think Dennis Beaumont killed her. But we've got no body, no witnesses, no evidence of foul play, and that earring is the first piece of evidence that *might* have gotten me a search warrant. But given that the bio-mom took it from the house … there's no way." He raked his hands through the long blond hair on top of his head, mussing up the perfect flip of his part.

I stared at him for a long few seconds. Long enough to read that his disappointment and frustration were genuine. Long enough for me to decide I liked him.

"You're right," I murmured. I'd only crossed paths with Detective Barker once before today, when he came to interview Bunny and Dennis at their house, the day after I "went missing." Back then, he'd been all polite smiles and handshakes and, "It's a pleasure to meet you, Mr. and Mrs. Beaumont. I'm so sorry for what you're going through." But seeing the genuine emotion on his face now, and the way he'd talked to Sabina, I was starting to wonder if he'd been putting on an act for Bunny and Dennis.

It made me feel the tiniest bit more hopeful.

But only the tiniest bit.

I already knew they weren't going to find blood on that earring. The earring had gone skittering beneath the entryway table *before* he laid hands on me that day.

The other earring, wrapped up in a tarp with my body—and just as broken—was where all the evidence lay. Under a layer of concrete, a short walk from my house.

It might as well have been in China, though. Because I didn't see how they were ever going to find me now.

When Sabina got back to the Airbnb, she didn't bother ordering food or turning on the TV. She didn't even turn on any lights when she walked through the front door, or brush her teeth. She just undressed down to a tank top and her underwear and curled up in the fetal position in bed.

I lay down right next to her in the crook of her arm, pretending she knew she was holding me.

I wanted to see if I could make some kind of noise happen again, like I had before with the sirens and the wailing baby and the dogs barking outside Desert Greens. Something to let her know I was here with her. But when I tried to find that pressure valve of emotion, I came up empty. I was all tapped out. She was too, and so maybe it was better that I didn't disturb her anyway.

As Sabina's breathing turned steady in sleep, I reached back into my memories until I found one I hadn't explored yet, from back before Sabina gave me up for adoption.

I'd been about six months old when I went to live with Bunny and Dennis. Which meant there were six months' worth of memories with Sabina I could unwrap like presents until I ran out. It was actually a lot more memories than it sounded like, since if my math was right, it added up to about four thousand hours. I'd already decided I would savor them all, as slowly as possible, until they ran dry. Even the sad ones. Even the ones where the house was dark and we were only sleeping.

Reaching for random memories in my subconscious—ones that had been locked away and forgotten before I died—really did feel like picking out gifts from beneath the Christmas tree. Tightly wrapped, glinting surprises that offered no hints at what was inside. The paper might be tattered, but inside was something to be cherished—like the earrings Paloma had given me. Or the box might be shaped like the new sweatshirt you wanted, so you got your hopes up, but really it was a cheap package of socks. That was mostly my experience with Christmas in Bunny and Dennis's house. However, I'd seen enough TV to know that Christmas morning was usually a little more exciting for other kids.

Tonight, curled up beside Sabina, I chose a memory that felt gold-tinged, hoping it was a good one.

I saw sixteen-year-old Sabina gripping the handles of a rickety stroller she pushed down the neighborhood sidewalk, trying to get the front wheels raised up onto the curb. In the seat of the stroller, baby-me leaned backward as the stroller wheels came up, and locked eyes with Sabina.

The tipping motion of the stroller was making me smile, a gummy grin that crinkled my cheeks from ear to ear.

I basked in the memory of what it was like to be that baby. The feeling of a diaper strap digging into my delicate skin, the sunlight bright in my eyes, the world tilting backward, Sabina's familiar face above me. I loved my mom. I loved being outside in the cool, sunny morning. For once, my tummy didn't hurt.

When I zoomed out a little, examining the memory like an observer, I studied Sabina's face. Her expression was fixed in concentration as she maneuvered the stroller up the curb. Her bleary eyes swept across both sides of the street, and she seemed to shrink into her jacket as she hurried along the sidewalk, like she didn't want anybody to see her out for a walk. Her dark auburn hair was damp and uncombed, and her skin was pink and clean like she'd just gotten out of the shower.

She didn't see me smile at her or hold out my arms to be held. Her gaze was fixed on the end of the street, where the sidewalk veered toward a park. Baby-me fussed a little in the stroller, wanting her to tip me backward again, frustrated that I couldn't do anything about the diaper strap digging into my thigh.

Sabina kept hurrying toward that park, making little "shh, shh, shh" noises while she did, trying to make me stop fussing.

Then the sound of scurrying footsteps and something crashing through the hedge to our right made her stop. "Oh!" she said in surprise.

Both of us turned to see a giant, tabby-striped cat with a huge tail saunter out of the bushes in front of my stroller. It meowed happily, a loud creaky exclamation, and pushed its face into my lap like a dog.

This time, Sabina saw my smile.

I cooed at the cat, grabbing for the thick fur at its neck and trying to take hold of its ears with my clumsy fingers. When it shook free of my grasp and put its paws up on my stroller, I let out a little bubble of delighted laughter.

It was the first time I'd done that—laughed—and I liked it so much I did it again.

Sabina's tired face broke into a grin, and she knelt beside me and the cat, who started up a lawn-mower-loud purr. "You love the kitty, baby? Sweet girl," she whispered, gently squeezing the chilly bare toes of my left foot, where I'd kicked off my sock at the start of our stroller walk. Then she took off her jacket and tucked it around my legs, even though it was cold enough that goosebumps prickled across her own bare arms.

I smiled again, cooing and reaching for the cat that had wisely moved beyond my grasp so that Sabina could scratch the downy fur beneath its chin.

I rewound that part of the memory again and again, zooming in on Sabina's hazel eyes while she looked back at me and said, "Sweet girl," then so carefully tucked the jacket around my bare foot so I'd be warm enough.

When I zoomed back from that moment, I could see an unleashed dog trotting through the yard on the other side of the hedge, set to crash through it—and that fleeting bubble of happiness.

I finally let the memory continue, watching as the dog started barking furiously, the cat's tail fluffed out to twice its size while it hissed and raced away, and Sabina shouting to leave us alone.

Baby-me wailed, startled by the dog and unable to hide my frustration at the irritating diaper strap. Sabina's face puckered, and she darted her eyes from the distant park sign to the stretch of sidewalk we'd just traveled.

Lips pursed, chin tucked and trembling slightly, she turned the stroller around in defeat. Like that dog had been yet one more sign from the universe that this wasn't working.

I drew back from the memory, returning to the dark, quiet room where I lay tucked up next to Sabina.

She rolled to her other side, away from me, sighing in her sleep.

I stood and stepped away from the bed, suddenly wondering if I was disturbing her.

"Sweet girl," Sabina whispered, clear as a bell. "Come back."

25

SABINA

When I woke up, sunlight was pouring through the slats of the shutters in the window at eye-level across from the bed.

I hadn't set an alarm, sure that my body clock would pop me out of bed in the morning the way it had every time I tried to rest yesterday. But from the slant of the sunlight streaming into the bedroom, I might have missed morning altogether.

Instead of panicking about the time I'd lost, like I would have yesterday, I lay perfectly still, intent on memorizing every part of the vivid dreams that had played through my mind all night long.

I was afraid that if I moved and woke myself fully, I'd forget some of the details.

My throat hurt when I tried to swallow, and my eyes were gummed-up and gritty like I'd been crying all night.

I suspected I had, but not the tears of anger or despair that had turned my eyes red and puffy after talking to the Beaumonts— and after visiting the police station with Nadia and Paloma. The ache in my chest today was softer, tender. Full of longing and love.

I'd dreamed of Andrea all night. Memories that had gone fuzzy and vague over the past seventeen years had turned suddenly clear and precise, like a movie.

And, much like rewatching a beloved movie, I noticed things I'd never seen before despite the familiarity. The intense look of adoration in my baby's eyes when she flicked them away from the kitty to meet my gaze. A little squeal of delight when I tipped her back in the stroller while I struggled to navigate the curb. The way she sighed when her pink toes, cold from kicking off her sock, were tucked into the palm of my warm hand.

Those tiny, precious memories had been so elusive the first time I lived them. Beautiful moments tucked inside all of the awful, painful ones: sleepless nights, panic, and heartache. I'd all but missed them, because they contradicted what I believed at the time. A belief I'd carried with me for seventeen years, even though it sounded so juvenile and I could barely put words to it: I'd always been sure that my baby had hated me.

It felt like she'd rejected me as a mother from the moment she came screaming into the world in the middle of the night. As if she sensed my incompetence and immaturity from the first time I held her, when the nurse snapped at me to support her head. She'd cried so much, been such a difficult baby, and I'd been so exhausted and stressed that I'd seen everything through the lens of my own desperation.

I closed my eyes and spoke the words in my heart out loud, because the heavy ache in my chest confirmed with each beat that this was the only way she'd ever hear them. And the stubborn barnacles of hope insisted that she *could* hear them.

"I always thought you didn't want me for a mom," I whispered. "But you did. You loved me." My voice hitched on the last words and the soggy patch of pillow beneath my cheek turned warm again. "I guess you probably thought the same thing about me. That I didn't want to be your mom. But I did. And I loved you." I corrected myself. "I *love* you."

The quilt-wrapped feeling returned.

Until this moment, the idea of being haunted had never once crossed my mind as a good thing.

Now I found myself wishing for it with every part of my heart.

And I realized, while I lay there in the sunlight with my eyes closed tight and my heart locked on the idea that my daughter was somehow nearby, that it felt less like I was wrapped up inside a blanket and more like *I* was stitched together with it.

Maybe I always had been. Two worn cotton squares in a cosmic quilt.

I suddenly realized that it was the same way I felt about Joel, connected to him despite the eight hundred miles between us right now.

After a few minutes, I finally opened my eyes and sat up in bed, reaching for my phone on the nightstand. The first thing I saw was a novel-length text message from Nadia.

Didn't sleep much last night. Yesterday was so heartbreaking and discouraging, but I'm so glad I met you. What you're doing for your daughter is a beautiful thing. Paloma and I talked for a long time, and we decided to make some changes to the Facebook page dedicated to Andrea. We've been holding out so much hope that she's still out there somewhere, but yesterday felt like a wake-up call. I hope you don't find the changes we made upsetting.

This morning, we asked all the local businesses that were willing to put up Andrea's missing poster three months ago to re-place it with a new poster. You'll see what I mean when you look at the site.

I also managed to track down a number for Isabel Palphrey-man's mom ... it was an upsetting conversation. She hasn't heard from Isabel in years and doesn't have a way to contact her anymore. She insisted it was Isabel's choice. When I brought up Dennis Beaumont and asked if she knew about Andrea going missing, she asked me not to call again. When I told her what I'd just posted on our Facebook page, she hung up on me.

Heart beating fast and waking me up fully, I closed the text thread with Nadia, opened the Facebook app on my phone, and tried to navigate to the BRING ANDREA BEAUMONT HOME Facebook page.

That name didn't appear in my search bar. Confused, I thumbed over to my history—where I found it. The name had been changed to JUSTICE FOR ANDREA BEAUMONT.

My skin tingled with electric chills.

The page description had been updated, too. It was no longer a request for messages of hope and love. It was a call to the community to help us find out exactly what had happened to Andrea.

Based on new information we cannot share fully at this time, we no longer believe that Andrea Beaumont is a missing person. It is with heavy hearts that we ask you to share this updated poster and help us find justice for Andrea Beaumont.

Was the "new information" Nadia mentioned the earring I'd found? I wasn't sure exactly what she was referring to, but I didn't really care. Andrea *wasn't* a missing person. My gut screamed that it was true.

Beneath the text was a pinned post with the updated missing poster.

JUSTICE FOR ANDREA
Somebody Knows Something
Andrea Beaumont, 17, was last seen alive on April 11, 2015. If you have ANY information—no matter how small—that could

help her friends or family uncover the truth, please come forward.
Help us bring justice to Andrea Beaumont.

I read the words on the missing poster twice, contrasting them with the poster I'd seen in Nadia's shop the day before. This was no longer a request for help finding a missing girl. And there was no mistaking the subtext of the words *last seen alive.* This was a direct clap-back to Dennis Beaumont's bullshit story about Andrea running away from home.

I exhaled slowly, realizing I'd been holding my breath. The updated missing poster had been uploaded three hours ago and already had a few shares. Unable to stop myself, I read through the handful of comments beneath it.

The first was from a profile with the name THE SALTY SHEEP PUB. It was a photo of the updated missing poster hanging on a mirror in what appeared to be a bathroom. I tapped on the photo to make it bigger and realized that it hung on the mirror alongside another poster that read, "GET HOME SAFE. On a date that isn't going well? Somebody bothering you? Ask for Andrea at the bar. We've got your back."

I inhaled sharply, scanning faster to read The Salty Sheep's comment beneath the photo. "Done. I never believed she was 'missing' from the start. Which is why we've had this posted in the women's restroom for a while now. Maybe it's some comfort knowing her name is helping other women stay safe. #justiceforandrea #askforandrea."

Two more businesses, Flute and Fox and Beehive Brewing, had commented in the same thread, saying they planned to follow suit.

A burst of pride and gratitude swelled alongside the ache in my chest. "Thank you," I whispered. It meant more than I expected to read these words from strangers.

I was about to close out of the page when I realized that there was a second post pinned beneath the updated missing poster—a photo of a smiling blue-eyed, blonde-haired teenage girl. The caption beneath it made my heart thud even faster.

Can you help us get in touch with Isabel Palphreyman? We believe she may have helpful information about Andrea's case.

I stared into the girl's eyes and shook my head, understanding now why Nadia's conversation with Isabel's mother might have gone off the rails.

None of that mattered, though. What mattered was that there were comments underneath the post with possible sightings and SHARED notifications.

This was a movement. These were threads that might lead to answers, search warrants, arrests, a way to bring my daughter back to me in whatever way that might still be possible.

As I moved into the kitchen to make coffee, hoping to take the fuzzy edge off my whirring brain, the words from the updated missing poster repeated in my head like drum beats. *Somebody knows something.*

26

ANDREA

While Sabina sipped her coffee, she texted Nadia to thank her and Paloma for the updated page and the new posters, promising to stay in touch with anything she learned. Then she called her husband Joel to tell him about what had happened at the police station yesterday, and everything she'd learned about Isabel Palphreyman, the Beaumonts, and the butterfly earring.

I told myself she put the call on speakerphone so I'd be able to hear too—even though I could've easily listened in by pressing my ear close to the phone while I sat beside her, invisible.

With the phone face-up on the shiny oak table between us, Sabina drinking coffee from a "Ski Utah" mug, and both of us sitting in chairs side by side, I could pretend for a few minutes that the two of us were just a mother and daughter calling home.

For the first time, I let myself believe that she really might sense me here with her.

That feeling, all by itself, made being dead less lonely. I was pretty sure Sabina had been able to see at least some of the memories I'd drifted through the night before, after she'd whispered the words, *"Sweet girl."* And then this morning, when she woke up, she'd spoken directly to me for the second time.

In a lot of ways, that feeling was better than anything I'd experienced while I was alive.

It made me wonder whether there was more to the whole "life after death" thing after all.

I'd never thought very much about heaven or hell or anything to do with death. What seventeen-year-old did? But I'd sort of figured that if there was anything to it, all of the mysteries of the universe would unravel the second I crossed over.

That hadn't happened. But the more I paid attention, the more those mysteries opened up to me like puzzle boxes.

It made some of the grief and loss the tiniest bit lighter.

It wouldn't bring back the years that Dennis had taken from me or the now-dashed possibilities that maybe I could have found my way back to Sabina in the living world and met her for real. But it was something.

"Can I call you back in a little bit? Mom needs lunch and her afternoon meds," Joel said as Sabina took the last sip of her coffee.

Sabina shook her head. "No, you don't need to do that. I'm going to take a look at the dossier you sent me and start following more rabbit trails, see what else I can find. I'm really hoping some tips come in from the new missing posters Nadia put up."

"Okay … but Sabina?" Joel let the half-finished sentence hang in the air for a few seconds, and she tilted her head at the phone screen, waiting. "Be careful, okay? This could turn ugly. If you're right about this guy, he's done some awful things and has a lot of reasons to make sure his secrets stay hidden."

She nodded slowly, and I was glad to see the somber expression that meant she wasn't writing him off for being worried. Joel was right. Dennis was dangerous—and we were only a few blocks away from his house. If he felt cornered, he wouldn't go down without a fight.

As Joel and Sabina said their goodbyes, I studied the tiny thumbnail photo of him displayed on Sabina's screen. The smiling man with short dark brown hair, a deep dimple in his left cheek, and wire-rimmed glasses glinting in the sun and making it impossible for me to tell his eye color.

I'd already pieced together that Joel wasn't my biological dad. But the way he talked to Sabina, his voice full of warmth and kindness, made me wish he was. I'd already decided that when Sabina went home, I would follow her to Oregon. Even if my body still lay undiscovered beneath a layer of cement in Ogden, Utah.

For one thing, I was pretty sure she wasn't going to leave without answers. But most of all, I wanted to be where she was. Sit beside her and Joel at the table for dinner, tuck myself into a spare bedroom, walk down the beach by their house in Neskowin that Joel had mentioned on the call.

Haunt them, pretty much. But I didn't think they'd mind.

* * *

Sabina spent the next two hours at the kitchen table combing through the dossier Joel had created, copying and pasting the information into a new document of places to visit, people to speak with, leads to follow, questions to ask Nadia and Paloma. The lists included my school, my teachers, my classmates, and anybody she might be able to find from our old church. She hesitated over the homeless shelters and food pantries that Joel had flagged in his dossier, then ultimately skipped them.

I didn't blame her. I wasn't in any of those places.

I was in the ground.

I watched in fascination as she worked, brow furrowed and fingers tapping on the keyboard while she created a game plan and organized her thoughts, only pausing when a new text chimed from Nadia. The new missing posters had been shared more than fifty times. And comments of support were flooding in from old classmates who remembered me, even a few church members who recalled Isabel Palphreyman. Nobody knew her whereabouts, but Nadia was hopeful that the right person would see the Facebook page soon.

After Sabina read that text, she turned her attention to the Facebook page, scrolling back in time to three months earlier, when Nadia and Paloma had first created it.

I rested my arms on her shoulders, not wanting to miss a second of this since I couldn't exactly jump on the computer and cyber-stalk it myself.

The page had shared the first news article where Bunny and Dennis had been interviewed, claiming I'd run away from home. Then there was a post asking the community to help bring me home, prompting everyone to leave messages of love and encouragement.

Sabina slowly scrolled up the page, methodically opening the comment threads on each post, making the occasional note about anyone who seemed to leave a particularly heartfelt or personal message.

She stopped on one post that had gotten a lot of attention and comments.

"Oh shit," I whispered gleefully. It had been written by a neighbor, whose name I barely recognized. I'd only seen her a handful of times in passing, but apparently she had paid more attention to me than I'd realized.

"Holy shit," Sabina whispered, in a near echo.

To Andrea, if you're reading this: I hope more than anything you come home. You were such a lovely girl. You kept to yourself, but you were always kind, and I always got the impression you had a good heart. Maybe this isn't the place to say so, but nobody is saying it so I'm going to: I don't think you're coming back. It hurts my heart to make this accusation, but I've met Dennis and Bunny Beaumont. I wouldn't trust a dog with them, let alone a child. The police should be doing a better job investigating their BS story about their daughter "running away."

Beneath it were comments ranging from shock to agreement to "this isn't the place for speculation like that."

And then there was the comment that had gotten the most reactions:

STFU Keyboard Karens, trying to ruin the reputation of her poor parents. You should be ashamed of yourselves. Pretty sure I saw her in line at the soup kitchen a few weeks ago. Looked strung out.

"What the hell?" Sabina clicked on the commenter's name—Jenny Johnson—and revealed a generic-looking profile that had zero friends. The photo was a cutesy image of two dogs, a German Shepherd and a corgi, sitting in a bathtub full of bubbles.

I moved in closer, bristling. I was pretty sure I'd seen that photo before, but where? My memory opened its vault at lightning speed, and I found it as quickly as I thought to ask the question. The photo was from a calendar called Dog Days, and the image was from April of this year. Dennis had given Bunny that calendar for Christmas. She'd flipped through the photos that morning, exclaiming at the cute dogs, but we'd never actually hung it up on the wall. Instead, it had been tucked in the junk drawer.

My memories whirled, sorting. That wasn't the last time I'd seen the image of those dogs, though. I'd also seen it that day Sabina showed up at the house. On the workbench in Dennis's shop.

"Jenny Johnson is Dennis," I practically screamed.

Sabina narrowed her eyes as she studied the photo of "Jenny," then clicked back to the main page and kept scanning through the posts and comments on JUSTICE FOR ANDREA. When she got to the latest post—the one about the new missing poster—she drew in a quiet gasp.

Like Nadia had said, there were a lot of shares, and a lot of comments. But the one that drew my eye first was Jenny Johnson. She had copied and pasted the exact same comment from months earlier, about supposedly seeing me "strung out" at the soup kitchen.

Sabina scowled, then wrote, "Jenny Johnson. Fake profile?" on her notes.

"Damn right it's fake," I huffed, ready to rage. "It's Dennis."

At first I thought the phone trilling was another one of my sound tricks—based on the anger flooding through me. But no, Sabina's phone really was lighting up.

It was an 801 number. Utah.

"Hello?" Sabina said distractedly, finishing up the note she was making in the document. I leaned closer to hear the caller on the other end.

"Ms. Turpin, this is Detective Barker."

I leaned so close I was practically wedged between Sabina's chin and the phone. Had they arrested Dennis? Was the earring our ace in the hole after all?

Sabina was clearly thinking the same thing, because she closed the computer and sat up abruptly, hurrying to put the call on speaker phone. "Oh, hi, yes! I didn't recognize the number. What's happening? Did you arrest him?" She squeezed her eyes shut and held her breath like she was willing it to be a yes.

Detective Barker sighed. "I'm calling to inform you that a temporary restraining order has been filed against you."

Sabina's eyes popped open, and she fumbled with the phone she was holding out in front of her, nearly dropping it. "Wait, *what*?"

"You are legally required to stay at least one hundred feet away from Dennis and Bunny Beaumont, and their residence. They submitted the request for a protective order yesterday, shortly after I spoke to you. The judge just approved it. They have footage from a doorbell camera that shows you stepping into their yard, looking around their property. Both Bunny and Dennis sent in statements that you refused to leave their home when asked, and that you made threatening statements."

Sabina stared at the wall, her chest heaving. "You have got to be fucking kidding me! I wasn't 'looking around their property.' I took maybe one or two steps off the sidewalk into the weeds when I saw Bunny standing on the porch? And I didn't make any threats. That's bullshit. Bunny invited me inside to talk, and I left their house when Dennis got home and asked me to," she snapped.

"I understand your frustration, but the footage he submitted clearly shows you standing in their yard, peering around. And from what they told me, you just rented an Airbnb a few blocks away from their house?"

"I wasn't 'peering around,' and I had no idea the Airbnb was by their house when I rented it. Ogden is *not* that big—"

"I understand, Ms. Turpin. But the video they sent in can reasonably be interpreted as stalking, and the Beaumonts are within their legal right to—"

"Dennis Beaumont is a *murderer*," Sabina interrupted, seething.

There was some kind of commotion from the house next door, like a load of bricks had just hit the cement, and I wondered if it was real or if the anger pulsing through me had created the cacophony.

I didn't bother to look out the window and check. I was too mad.

"I understand this is frustrating, but I'm legally bound to uphold this order. If you go within a hundred feet of the Beaumonts or their property again, they can—and probably will—call the police."

Sabina clenched her jaw tight. "Fine."

Detective Barker let out another pained-sounding sigh. "I need verbal confirmation that you understand the protective order, Ms. Turpin."

"Oh, I understand," Sabina bit out. Then she hung up the phone before he could reply.

For a few minutes, she sat at the table with her eyes closed, inhaling and exhaling in a slow, steady pattern that somehow made me feel calmer too.

"I see you, Jenny Johnson," she finally whispered. Then she stood, scooped her laptop under one arm, grabbed the keys to the car, and stomped outside.

I had no idea where we were headed, but I was definitely not going to stay behind. All I knew was that wherever Sabina went, I was going, too.

27

SABINA

I had absolutely no idea where I was going.

All I knew was that I needed to get out of the house and blow off some of the rage making my hands shake on the steering wheel. I probably needed to eat, too. Between sleeping late, combing through the Facebook page, and doing a deep-dive into Joel's dossier, it was nearly dinnertime, and the only thing I'd eaten all day was the last of the chocolate chip cookies from the welcome plate at the Airbnb.

If I didn't eat something and take a minute to clear my head, I was going to drive straight back to the Beaumonts' and start a screaming match—in violation of the restraining order.

That wouldn't help me or Andrea, though. Dennis Beaumont, on the other hand? It would help him. As Joel would say, "Never wrestle with a pig because you'll get dirty and the pig likes it."

I ended up in the parking lot of the Salty Sheep, mostly because its name had stuck in my mind, but also because it felt like a safe place to tuck myself away and lick my wounds.

Before I sat down at the bar to order food, I slipped into the restroom to see for myself what the restaurant owner had posted on the Facebook page. I saw it the second I walked into the empty bathroom. The JUSTICE FOR ANDREA poster, taped right in the middle of the long mirror in the women's restroom, hanging alongside a printed sign urging anyone who needed help or felt unsafe to use her name at the bar as code for "I need help."

I'd already seen the photo, so I wasn't quite expecting the rush of love and gratitude when I saw it in person. The anger that made me see red just a few minutes earlier didn't magically drain away. But it felt less chaotic, less likely to send me flying at Dennis Beaumont.

"That's my girl," I murmured, staring at my own reflection hovering just above my daughter's face, her wide eyes a carbon copy of mine.

While I nursed a glass of pinot gris and waited for my food at the bar—something called a "Sheeple Sandwich," a pub favorite— I texted Nadia to tell her about the restraining order, and to ask what she thought about "Jenny Johnson."

She replied almost immediately.

Are you kidding me???? That's outrageous. But you know what? It means he's/they're scared of you. We're onto something. And Jenny Johnson is a total fake. I almost banned 'her' from the page at one point, because she keeps copying and pasting that same message about supposedly seeing Andrea at the soup kitchen. But I sort of want to see what else she might say? It definitely might be Dennis, or Bunny.

When I looked up from the text, the bartender, a woman with a curly ponytail and a collared teal polo with a sheep on the lapel, returned with my sandwich. "There ya go, babe. Enjoy."

My mouth watered at the sight of the lamb sandwich piled high with caramelized onions and chimichurri. "Thank you, that looks so good." I was even hungrier than I'd realized. On a whim as she walked away, I added, "Hey, I saw the sign in your bathroom. Do people really 'Ask for Andrea'?" I didn't want to tell her who I was, but I couldn't stop myself from asking, either.

She paused mid-pivot, then turned to face me. "Yeah, a handful of times. I wish we'd done something like that sooner. Sometimes I can spot the girls who need a little help. They're shrinking in their seat while their date—usually some dude who thinks he's hot shit in a trucker hat—gets louder, grabbier. But last week, a woman sitting right over there," she pointed, "was slurring like she was already drunk, even though I knew I'd only served her one Coors. Asked me if 'Andrea' was working tonight when I closed their tab." The bartender's eyes turned steely. "If she hadn't said that, I would've let her date take her home to sober up. But I made up some BS excuse about how she'd left her purse in the bathroom, so she needed to come with me—and you know what? Her Tinder date was gone when we came back. Turns out he'd roofied her."

I fought back tears. "Oh, wow," I managed, keeping my eyes on the sandwich so she wouldn't notice.

"Yeah. We gotta help each other out. There's too many creeps out there." The bartender leaned back against the bar top. "That girl on the missing poster? I think about her a lot. She was just seventeen years old ..." She lowered her voice and glanced at me, like she was trying to decide whether to continue.

"Do you know much about her?" I prompted, picking up the sandwich and taking a nibble. "This tastes as good as it looks, by the way."

She nodded but didn't smile. Instead she lowered her voice and said, "I probably shouldn't say this, and it'll sound crazy, but when I saw the photos in the news articles about Andrea, I realized that her dad had come in here once, a few years ago. I never forget a face. He strutted in and plopped down at the bar like he was gracing me with his presence. And when I brought his drink over, I noticed that there was something red smeared on his top lip. Like ... like blood. When I pointed it out, he wiped it off and gave me this weird smile." She grimaced and shook her head. "I mean, obviously that was way before his daughter went missing, but what the hell? I told the police about it when I saw the story about his daughter in the news, but I have no idea if they thought it was important or not. No one ever followed up with me. I personally think he killed her."

The beautiful, perfect lamb sandwich suddenly tasted like cardboard in my mouth, but I forced myself to chew and swallow anyway. How many other people in this tiny community had had a brush like that with Dennis Beaumont? How many had relayed that experience to the police? And how many, like the Palphreymans, had simply moved on with their lives and tried to forget because the truth was too awful to consider?

The police clearly hadn't acted on the bartender's information—at least, not yet. I told myself that, like Detective Barker had said during my interview, he couldn't exactly go kicking down doors until the police had a case built and evidence to arrest him. But the red flags surrounding Dennis Beaumont kept mounting—and those were just the ones I knew about.

When I finished my meal, I headed back into the parking lot of the restaurant and stood for a few minutes, blinking into the sunlight making its way toward the horizon. The temperature had risen over ninety, warmer than it ever got on the Oregon Coast in August, and the air smelled like a heady mix of grilled meat and fresh peaches, the delicate scent wafting on the breeze from the orchards sprawling on the other side of the road.

I took another step toward the car, unsure where I was headed next. It was a little late to start making cold calls, but with the long summer days, I still had a couple of hours until it got dark. So where should I go?

I pulled my phone out of my pocket to study the map I had polka-dotted with pins: the Beaumonts' house, my Airbnb, Andrea's school, a list of food banks and soup kitchens, and the popular homeless encampments Joel had noted from his deep dive on Reddit.

Most of the soup kitchens and encampments were a few miles away, nearly in Layton. I probably couldn't reach them before darkness fell. But there was a small triangle of pins nearby, only a mile away from the Salty Sheep.

I zoomed in on the area that marked a soup kitchen and a couple of known encampments. If I left now, I could reach them before dark. But what did I really expect to find there? And what was I looking for? Would the soup kitchen still be open?

I closed my eyes and breathed in that strange but tantalizing smell of ripe fruit and grilling meat. Maybe it didn't matter if I knew exactly what I was looking for. I hadn't expected that the bartender in the Salty Sheep would have a story to tell about Dennis. Or that I would connect with Nadia and Paloma like I had from stopping by Desert Greens.

Maybe I'd find more than I was expecting, wherever I went next.

I was learning fast that Ogden was a small world. In some ways, even smaller than tiny Neskowin. While there was no doubt this bustling community had a much larger population than my tiny town of barely two hundred, the people here seemed connected to each other in ways the coastal community wasn't. So many of them had attended church together at one point or another. Maybe that was it. Regardless, it was becoming apparent that if I kept exploring, kept asking for Andrea in my own way, I would find more threads to follow.

And with that in mind, I set off.

28

ANDREA

Watching Sabina eat the lamb sandwich at the Salty Sheep made me feel jealous and sulky.

It wasn't because I felt hungry. Not hungry like while I was alive, anyway. It was more like a longing for the experience of eating something so good it made you sigh. That had only happened a handful of times during my life. Bunny didn't like to cook, so most of our meals consisted of Dino Nuggets or Chef Boyardee. Dennis could actually cook—simple stuff like grilled cheese and spaghetti, at least—but he only did it on the days he got a gleam in his eye and I knew he was going to make me pay for the meal later.

The lunches I brought to school had been beans and rice, which wouldn't have been that bad if I didn't have to eat them every single day. Bunny had gotten ten gigantic dry-packed #10 cans of each, back in the days when we were Mormon and she volunteered at the Cannery. She refused to buy more lunch supplies until they ran out. So each week on Sunday, I made myself a pot of both, and tried out different combinations of expired seasonings I found in the cabinets in an attempt to make them taste like something else.

I'd nearly made it through all ten cans by the time Dennis killed me.

That's what I was focused on while Sabina drove away from the Salty Sheep. Would I have liked sushi? What about filet mignon, tiramisu, risotto? All the fancy things I saw people eat on TV? I stared out the window, not sure where Sabina's Maps app was taking us, lost in the list of things I'd never get to experience. It wasn't just food. What about my first kiss? A boyfriend? A place of my own, my first job, college, traveling somewhere outside of stupid Ogden, Utah, learning how to ski or ride a horse or play the guitar?

"What the hell?" Sabina muttered, and I suddenly realized that the car's "check engine" light was flashing in time to a strange, high-pitched whistling sound. She pulled off the main road and into a neighborhood, where she stopped the car and turned it off. Then she got out her phone and Googled "whistling noise check engine light."

"Sorry," I said half-heartedly, shaking away the depressing thoughts that were making the pressure valve tick toward red—and probably causing the sound and the light. This party trick was interesting, but it was losing its appeal quickly. What did it really matter if I could manufacture random sounds and maybe a flashing light or two?

Restless, I scanned the neighborhood of little brick houses that all looked basically alike aside from the knick-knacky junk in the front yards. Nothing looked familiar. I was about to turn around to see what Sabina was Googling, when something familiar did catch my eye.

A boxy white sedan was idling maybe two blocks behind us.

The windshield was tinted dark enough that I couldn't see the driver inside. But an alarm bell started to clang in my mind as I studied the license plate number—a feat I never could've pulled off at this distance while I was alive—then flipped back through my memories to compare it.

I didn't have to go very far. The last time I'd seen that car was when my body was stowed in its trunk, separated into trash bags that Dennis had driven to the construction site under cover of darkness.

"Shit," I whispered. The license plate was a perfect match.

Sabina was turning the key in the ignition again, gaze focused on the place where the check-engine light had been flashing a second ago.

I forced my panic away, not wanting her to think the car was breaking down, but all the while my mind was spinning. Dennis following Sabina? *He* was the one who'd asked for a protective order—and now he was tailing *her*?

He was keeping tabs on her. Nadia was right—he *was* scared of what she might dig up.

The realization both thrilled and terrified me. I wanted Sabina to find out the truth more than anything, but not if it put her in Dennis's crosshairs. What would he do if she got too close to answers?

"Look behind you," I begged her, needing her to know what I knew. "Dennis is following you."

She wasn't paying a shred of attention, though. Just sighing with relief at the fact that the check-engine light had gone dark, eyes flicking back to the Maps app she'd pulled up to take us to our next destination, four minutes away.

I kept my eyes on the white Honda Accord.

It stayed where it was while Sabina made a U-turn and drove right past it, following the Maps app back to the main road.

But as she made a left turn out of the neighborhood, I caught a glimpse of the Accord as it made a U-turn to follow her.

"Turn around, notice the car," I told her, raising my voice to a near yell. I knew better than to think the message would go through, though. I'd already learned that my verbal instructions were way less reliable than my ability to drum up random sounds when my emotions got high. At one point while she ate her sandwich at the Salty Sheep, I'd laid out the story of exactly what Dennis had done with my body. She'd continued eating, which told me she definitely did not hear the words I was saying about how he'd separated my legs from my torso.

At one point, Sabina flicked her eyes to the rearview mirror, but the Accord was two cars behind us.

She looked slightly on edge, but she clearly had no idea he was following us.

"Shit," I whispered again as the Maps app lady chirped, "In five hundred feet, your destination is on the left." Where were we going, anyway?

Sabina tapped the brakes and eased the car to the side of the road, where a sign beside a white brick building displayed the words OGDEN FOOD MINISTRY—along with its hours. It had been closed for about forty minutes. Sabina sighed heavily, put the car in park, and picked up her phone from its holder. I kept my eyes on the Accord. It stayed right behind us, pulling over on the other side of the street.

After a few moments, Sabina drove away from the food bank. The Accord followed.

I hoped we were going back to the Airbnb. Instead, Sabina followed the driving directions for a few more blocks and stopped the car again.

I tore my gaze away from the Accord and looked around wildly, trying to figure out where we were and why we were stopping again. The empty, two-lane road that snaked beneath the underpass was flanked by weedy gravel on either side. Bits of trash fluttered in the breeze, flashing in the early evening sunlight like some kind of warning signal. The light cut off abruptly into shadow where the hulking concrete covered the road.

This must be one of the encampments Sabina had on her list.

"Stay in the car! What are you doing? I'm not here. I've never even seen this place before," I hissed at Sabina, grabbing her forearm and hanging on like it would accomplish anything.

Sabina hesitated, then removed the key from the ignition and stepped out of the car. I kept my fingers laced around her arm, and she tugged me along like an invisible balloon.

Above us, the highway thrummed in a steady heartbeat, but down here the street was devoid of traffic. A grocery cart missing one of its front wheels sat parked in the gravel by the base of one support pillar, and beyond that was what looked like faded blankets and maybe a dust-caked sweatshirt. There were peanuts, of all things, scattered near the back wheels. Some old, rain-damaged magazines flapped in its basket like feeble birds. A cluster of blue and red graffiti that looked like someone had once tried to scrub it away shouted from the eaves of the concrete underpass, hulking above the shopping cart.

Sabina's eyes, wide and blinking, fixed on those things in turn as she took a tentative step toward the underpass, squinting into the shadows.

I kept my eyes on the Accord, which still hadn't moved. I could feel my terror bubbling up, but I didn't try to tamp it down. "Come on," I hissed, just as the sound of a slamming car door cut through the steady roar of traffic like a gunshot.

Sabina whirled around in the direction of the Accord. For a few seconds, her eyes lingered on it.

"Yes, good! Now get out of here! He's in the white car," I cried, so damn proud that I'd managed to make the right sound this time.

Then something rustled beneath the underpass a few feet away, and Sabina forgot all about the sound of the car door and spun back toward the shadows.

I was about to make a mad dash for Dennis's car—maybe try to get the sound of police sirens to play again in hopes he'd drive away—when I saw something that stopped me.

A young woman emerged from the darkness near the shopping cart. She wore a hoodie pulled up over her head, with the strings tied so tight you could just see her eyes and nose. She was pretty—and about my age—give or take a few years. I couldn't really tell.

The girl didn't give Sabina more than a passing glance as she approached. But when her head swiveled toward me, her big pale brown eyes narrowed.

I stared at her in an impolite way I'd never done while alive. Because what did it matter? She wasn't really looking *at* me, just *through* me.

The girl didn't walk by us, though. And she didn't say a word to Sabina—who was still creeping toward the underpass seemingly oblivious to the woman's presence.

"Who are you?" the girl murmured, and I knew the second the words left her mouth that she was somehow, impossibly, speaking to *me*.

29

ANDREA

I was so stunned, I didn't even answer her at first.

The girl frowned, then sighed like she was feeling wistful about something, and kept moving.

I shook myself out of the stupor and called after her. "Wait, are you actually talking to me?"

It had been so long since anyone had looked directly at me, spoken to me. It sort of made me want to cry.

The girl stopped walking then bobbed her head up and down. "Yep."

"But …" I said stupidly. "So you're …"

"Dead? Yeah, I'm pretty damn dead. Now answer my question. Who are you?" she demanded, looking me up and down while she crossed her arms across her chest.

The way she said it put my guard right up. Why did it matter who I was? I hesitated, still blown away by how alive she looked. If she hadn't started this conversation, I would've assumed she had every bit as much of a heartbeat as Sabina. I suddenly felt stupid for assuming that I was the only ghost on the planet—and that everybody I saw walking around was alive.

Another question mark lit up in my mind. What had tipped her off that I was dead?

I felt a burst of annoyance that she was talking to me at all. I needed to keep eyes on Dennis and stay with Sabina—who was chatting with somebody beneath the underpass now.

"I gotta go," I said, moving to follow Sabina. The novelty of meeting another dead girl had worn off about as quickly as the novelty of being dead.

"Wait," she called, all the suspicion gone from her voice. She was suddenly paying attention to me, her eyes fixed on mine. "Hold on a sec. It's just—I know this is going to sound insane, but I dreamed about you."

I wasn't planning on stopping again. For one thing, Sabina was having a full-on conversation that I was missing, and for another, the Accord wasn't stopped anymore. It was inching along the side of the road toward us, the sound of its engine lost in the traffic zooming past overhead.

"You dream?" I asked, incredulously. As far as I was aware, I hadn't slept once since I'd been dead. Not like before, anyway. More like zoning out through memories until Sabina woke up.

"Yeah. I mean, sort of," she said in a rush, gesturing with her hands. "It was a memory of when I was in church. And you came up to me and said my name."

A strange sense of familiarity spread through me. And when I studied her eyes a little more closely, I realized I'd seen them before.

"It was super weird. The memory was all normal, and then all of a sudden you were there, saying my name and touching my arm. And then you were gone." She untied the string on her hoodie, revealing short, rumpled blue hair.

"Holy shit," I whispered, finally connecting the dots. "You're … you're Isabel? Isabel Palphreyman?" With her blue hair, sunken cheeks, and thin face, she barely looked anything like the girl I'd seen in my memory. But those eyes …

"Yeah," she said, smiling tentatively like she could hardly believe the words that had just come out of my mouth. I could hardly believe them, either. "And you are …"

"I'm Andrea," I whispered. "I went to your church when I was really little."

I watched the words hit her like darts. The smile vanished from her lips as quickly as it had appeared. "Oh my God," she breathed, voice shaking. "You're Andrea … Beaumont? Dennis's daughter—"

"He's not my dad," I cut her off with more venom than I'd intended. "They adopted me."

She blinked in surprise but didn't question what I'd told her. I shifted to keep one eye on the white Accord, which was still creeping steadily toward us. It was maybe a block away now, across the street from Sabina's car. I could just make out the shape of the driver's bulky frame through the tinted windshield.

Dennis. There was no way he'd do something to Sabina in broad daylight, would he?

He killed you at 3:30 in the afternoon came the chorus from the back of my mind.

Wailing sirens played in the distance—my favorite sound trick—and the Accord stopped moving. The silhouette in the driver's seat twisted his body around to look at the road behind him, but the sound of sirens was already fading.

There wasn't time to ask Isabel all the questions burning a hole in my heart. And I could tell by the way her eyes were fixed on me that she had just as many to ask me. But right now wasn't the time. I just needed to know one thing before I dragged her along with me.

"Did Dennis … ?" I asked, unsure how to finish the thought, feeling queasy in a way that made zero sense given that I couldn't vomit and didn't have a stomach anymore.

Her eyes went steely, and she didn't prompt me to complete my sentence. "Yeah. He did something to me. He killed me." There was so much pain in her voice, it made me wince. Then she whispered, "You too?"

I nodded, and for the first time she followed my gaze when it drifted back to the white Accord.

"Who's in that car?" she asked warily. "And who's that woman talking to Marlie?" She gestured between the Accord and the underpass.

"Dennis is in the car," I muttered, and she recoiled like I'd slapped her. "And that ... that's Sabina. My real mom," I said pointing at her back. "She's trying to find out what happened to me —and you, too."

Isabel gave me a bewildered look like I was speaking French, but she just said, "Oh."

"I'll be right back, okay?" I said, already rushing away from her, toward the Accord. "I just want to put eyes on Dennis. Can you go listen in on Sabina's conversation?"

Without waiting for a response, I flew across the sidewalk until I stood beside the tinted driver's side window. It was cracked down an inch, like Dennis was trying to listen in on what Sabina was saying. But with the traffic droning past on the interstate overhead, there was no way he could hear.

He looked pissed, eyes narrowed and honed on Sabina's back, just visible near the first pillar of the underpass.

At first glance, there was nothing suspicious inside that car. A couple of Crown Burger wrappers on the passenger seat, the fuzzy blue dice hanging from the rearview mirror. And of course, Dennis himself. He shifted in the driver's seat and sucked air between his teeth in a weird, strangled whistle while he kept his eyes on Sabina.

Then I looked down at Dennis's phone, lying face-up at an angle in one of the cup holders.

Its screen glowed pale yellow, and when I weaseled myself through the crack in the window to get a closer look, I saw that it was some kind of GPS app.

A red dot pulsed in the center of the screen.

It was labeled with the word BITCH.

He'd put a tracker on her car.

And that wasn't all. Now that I was inside the Accord, I could see something poking out from beneath the passenger's seat.

An open package of zip ties.

Were those meant for Sabina? How long had Dennis been following us? When had he put the tracker on Sabina's car? What was he planning to do? I didn't want to find out the answer to any of those questions.

Waves of horror and anger pulsed through me, and I racked my brain for a way to harness the searing emotion. The sirens were getting old—what else would make him drive away right now?

I remembered how the check-engine light had come on in Sabina's car. Could I do something like that again?

I imagined the pent-up emotion like a tank full of helium. Then I pictured exactly what I wanted to happen, clear as the memories I saw in my mind's eye.

For a moment, nothing happened.

And then the sound of a familiar ringtone. Three short chimes, then a long one.

The GPS tracking app on Dennis's phone screen disappeared, replaced by an incoming call. "What the hell?" Dennis choked out.

ANDREA, read the caller name on the screen—along with my number. That phone had been in an evidence locker since the day I disappeared. And Dennis knew it.

I wanted to squeal with excitement at what I'd just done, but I was too afraid the pressure cooker of emotion would run out of steam or that I'd lose my focus.

With a shaking hand, Dennis answered the call.

I concentrated harder than I ever had, latched onto the memory I wanted to forget most, and hoped like hell.

It worked.

There was a moan, then a scuffling sound on the other end of the line. Dennis's face went white, and he dropped the phone back onto the passenger seat with a quiet thud, chest heaving like he was about to have a heart attack.

I wished he would.

The phone's speaker spit out the sound of a choked, strangled gasp that made me want to cry. Then dead air and silence.

I had replayed the exact soundtrack of my death.

The call dropped, but not before Dennis had jammed the car into drive, sending the tires screeching on the asphalt back the way he'd come.

I stood there until I was sure he wasn't coming back, feeling both powerful and drained at the same time.

He wouldn't be gone for long. And I didn't know what I was going to do when he came back. But dammit if I wouldn't find a way to haunt him in every way I could, if it meant keeping Sabina safe.

30

SABINA

I wasn't sure what to expect when I approached the skinny woman with a low ponytail, humming to herself while she rummaged through a grocery bag of what looked like pastries.

The air beneath the underpass suddenly felt tense—and more shadows shifted along the walls. The woman looked up at me, her eyes wide and frightened when she realized I wasn't just walking past. I was approaching her.

The moment felt like a scene right before a jump scare in a horror movie, but strangely, I didn't feel afraid. Actually, I felt like I had when I'd moved some cobwebby planter pots into the garage and discovered a nest of terrified baby mice inside one of them. Like I was this bumbling interloper who'd just ruined their meager safe place.

"Don't be scared," I said to the woman in a rush, holding out my hands palm-up. "I'm—I was just hoping to talk to someone who lives around here."

She quickly glanced at her plastic bag, at the dirty asphalt-colored tarp tucked into a crack in the cement wall and supported on two crooked, collapsible poles. One yank and the whole thing looked like it would tumble, and maybe that was the point. This shelter was clearly made to move at a moment's notice. And given the way the woman was rising up on the balls of her feet and leaning away from me, she might be preparing to do exactly that.

"Are you a cop? Because if you are, you have to tell me," she said in a high-pitched rush, reaching beneath the tarp and stuffing a tattered sleeping bag under one arm. "I'm not camped here, I don't live here, I'm just resting in the shade for a few minutes." She pointed at the cart and magazines. "See, that's my cart, I'm not camping or anything. Just resting."

I took a step back, not wanting to spook her any more than I already had. "No, no, I'm not a cop. I promise. I'm just looking for somebody … a missing girl. And I was wondering if you've seen her?"

Before she could say no or rush away, I pulled my phone from my back pocket and flashed the screen forward to reveal the smiling photo of Isabel Palphreyman that Nadia had posted on the Facebook page.

The woman's shoulders sagged with relief, and she set the bag of pastries down on the dirt at the entrance to her shelter and ambled toward me. "Sure, I'll take a look. Can't promise you anything, though. Some people don't wanna be found, and I'm not a snitch."

"Of course, yes, thanks," I said, my own shoulders relaxing.

A flapping of wings behind me, next to the shopping cart with one wheel, made the woman stop just before she reached me. "Ohhh, Jasper!" she cooed at the crow that had landed on the handle of the shopping cart and was staring at her expectantly. She turned back to her shelter. "Hold on a minute, I haven't seen Jasper in days," she tittered, grabbing something from inside her sleeping bag and then a half-eaten donut from her bag.

I watched in fascination as she approached the bird with slow, even steps. It blinked at her but made no move to fly away. When she got within about three feet, she laid the donut and a shiny dime on the dirt at her feet, then sat down and waited.

The crow—Jasper—made a mewing sound like a kitten, bobbed his head, and spread his glossy black wings. Then, to my amazement, he flew the short distance toward her, picked at the donut to tear off a few crumbs, then scooped up the dime in his beak and flapped away.

"You're like Snow White," I marveled, and she flashed me a grin so wide her eyes nearly disappeared behind her crows' feet.

"Damn right," she said. Then beckoned for my phone. "Now, let's see this girl."

I held my breath while her big brown eyes narrowed, studying the photo for long enough that I knew she wasn't just giving it a passing glance. In the image, Isabel stood on a rocky lakeshore, her long blonde hair shimmering in the sun, her sun-kissed cheeks turned up in a brilliant smile.

"Have you seen her?" I asked, unsure if I saw a flicker of recognition or if it was just wishful thinking.

She frowned and shook her head. "Hard to say … but I don't think so. I'd remember somebody young and pretty like that. Hell, she looks like she could be on the cover of one of my magazines with that hair." She pointed to the stack in the grocery cart, where the pages were fluttering in the breeze that had picked up.

"How about this girl?" I asked, flipping to the photo I'd saved of Andrea. I hadn't planned on asking, but I was already here, so why not?

This time, the woman shook her head quickly. "Nope. Haven't seen her, either."

I bit back my disappointment and forced a smile. "That's okay. Is there anybody else here I should ask?" I gestured to the other side of the underpass, where a handful of other shadows were tucked along the walls.

She shrugged. "If you want. But I've been down here longest of anybody," she admitted. "I only said what I said earlier because I thought you might be a plainclothes."

The wind started picking up harder now, blowing the dirt at our feet in tiny dust devils that made her shelter rock back and forth. The sun was moving fast toward the horizon, and the temperature had dropped enough that I wished I had a sweatshirt.

I decided that I would cross to the other side of the underpass and show Isabel's photo around as quickly as I could, and then it was probably time to head back to the Airbnb. I was brave enough to be here during the day, but terrified to find out what the underpass was like at night—no matter how unthreatening these people might seem. Plus, the feeling of being scrutinized by unseen eyes kept making the hair on the back of my neck rise, even though I knew they were likely just curious looks and that I was the uninvited intruder here.

"Thank you for your help—I'm so sorry, I didn't even ask your name or introduce myself," I said. "I'm Sabina."

"Marlie," she said after a moment's hesitation. Then, wistfully, "Hope you find those girls. They're lucky somebody's looking for them."

"Thanks," I said, past the knot in my throat as I started moving toward the nearest shadowy figure, maybe twenty yards away on the same side of the underpass.

I had taken no more than a few steps before the wind blustered through the underpass with a violent rush that momentarily blocked out the sound of traffic overhead.

I stumbled back toward Marlie, shielding my eyes from the storm of grit and wrappers that pelted my skin. She yelped in surprise and dove to grab hold of the corner of her shelter. It was too late though, and there was a muted snapping sound as the tarp billowed up in the wind like a sail, yanking free of one of its bungees before slapping against a pillar and crumpling in a heap.

"Shit," Marlie said angrily as the gust of wind died back down. Behind me, there were more mutters of annoyance as people picked up belongings that had gone flying.

"Let me help you," I said, grabbing hold of one pole and half of the tarp that had fallen in on her shelter while she grabbed the other side.

As we lifted the dirty tarp back into place, I couldn't help but take a closer look inside at the sleeping bag and rumpled clothing.

Nothing stood out—at first.

Then my eyes stopped on a dark lump with a faded, lighter-colored patch in its center. There was a word written on that patch that I couldn't quite make out.

I leaned a little closer, realizing that the lump was a back-pack.

"Hey," Marlie was saying, and I could tell from the bristle in her voice that I wasn't being subtle at all about what I was doing. But I didn't care.

Because there, in handwritten letters on the patch sewn to the backpack, was the word IZZY.

31

ANDREA

I gawked at Isabel in amazement. "You're like Storm from the X-Men."

She grinned, and it was the first time I'd seen her smile. Her eyes stayed on Sabina and Marlie—who Isabel called Crow Lady. "Yeah, I guess so. I didn't mean to make it *quite* that crazy. I just didn't want her to leave before she found that." She pointed to the faded blue backpack Marlie was pulling out of the tarp shelter.

I nodded, and we both went quiet, not wanting to miss a second of this moment.

Both Sabina and Isabel wore about the same expression—wary hope and disbelief.

Sabina's voice trembled when she said, "Where did you get that backpack?"

Marlie's eyes went so wide you could see the whites on the top and bottom. "A girl who was here a few years back … but she didn't … but … Her mouth dropped open, and it was almost like I could see the puzzle pieces click into place. Same way they were clicking into place for me.

Sabina pulled her phone from her pocket once more. "Do you think you could look at the photo again? I'm wondering if maybe Izzy is short for Isabel."

Isabel herself just watched, eyes shining and hands laced in front of her like she was praying. Maybe she was. I could feel the desperation coming off her like an electric current. She'd been waiting for this moment—waiting to be found—a lot longer than I had. "Yes, that's me," she whispered, moving close to Marlie's ear as she studied the photo of the blue-eyed, blonde-haired girl in the photo that looked almost nothing like the gaunt, blue-haired woman who stood beside me.

"Holy shit," Marlie murmured. "Izzy, Isabel. I think you're right. She didn't look anything like that photo though. Had real short, blue hair when I met her. And she was a lot skinnier. Barely the same girl." She leaned closer to Sabina's phone. "But dammit, yes, that might just be her."

"Oh my god. Okay, tell me everything you know, please," Sabina said, flipping to a notes app in her phone. The steady breeze dropped as fast as it had ratcheted into a brief storm a moment earlier, and the air turned as still and expectant as the look on Isabel's face.

"She's dead," Marlie said, her voice a raspy whisper. "An overdose. At least, that's what Otto—the guy who sells art on the corner—told me."

Sabina clenched her jaw and winced, like she'd been bracing for this blow but it hurt all the same.

Marlie kept going. "I—I didn't find out until just a few days ago. I thought she just sort of up and left. People do that here. You share a meal one day, and they're gone the next." Her lips curled into a guarded half-smile and she shrugged.

Isabel rolled her eyes and frowned, but there wasn't any real anger there. "Yeah, right … I just ditched my backpack full of cash and left …"

Sabina looked west, where the sun had fully settled behind the horizon, turning the far end of the underpass a murky orange and blue. "Is there anything else you can tell me about her? Anything at all?"

Marlie screwed up her face in concentration. "Not really. We didn't talk much but she seemed real nervous, always looking over her shoulder."

Sabina pursed her lips and nodded at the backpack. "The police will want that," she said carefully. "I hate to send them here, but ... her family doesn't even know she's dead. They need to know what happened to their daughter."

I was expecting Isabel to be sort of happy about this—about her family learning what had happened to her—but instead, her expression turned stormy again, and the breeze kicked up sharply. Without thinking too much about it, I stepped closer and took her hand.

When I did, the shock was like stepping into a cold pool.

A wave of emotion that wasn't my own—sadness, longing, resentment, anger—pulled me under. The feelings were accompanied by flashes of memories, like a messed-up slideshow of angry, disappointed faces I recognized as Mr. and Mrs. Palphreyman. And I knew right then that I had even more in common with Isabel than I thought.

I kept hold of her hand until the waves got softer. Then the two of us followed Sabina back to the car in silence while Sabina dialed Detective Barker. Marlie must've agreed to it, because she was on her feet, quickly disassembling her shelter and carefully placing the tarp and poles into the shopping cart alongside the hodgepodge of magazines.

When she was finished taking down the shelter, she shifted nervously from foot to foot, glancing at Isabel's backpack lying in the dirt a few feet away. "You sure I gotta talk to them?" she called to Sabina, her voice high and nervous. "I already told you everything I know."

"Yes, please," Sabina said, hurrying back across the gravel until she stood beside Marlie. "Just tell them exactly what you told me. That you didn't realize the backpack was important—or that her name was Isabel Palphreyman. Then you can go."

Marlie cocked her head, glanced at the shopping cart full of her tarp, sleeping bag, and clothes, and I thought I saw the tiniest smirk on her lips, like she was thinking *Go where?*

The sky turned a dusky purple while we waited for the police to arrive. Sabina texted Joel that she had news about Isabel Palphreyman and promised she'd call him soon—but didn't mention the underpass. I kept looking around for the white Accord, but there was no sign of Dennis. I found myself wishing I hadn't scared him away. Maybe the police would have caught sight of him —stalking the woman he'd filed a restraining order against.

Isabel didn't say much while we stood there beside Sabina in the gathering dark. Just stared at her backpack and kept her arms folded around her middle like she was trying to wrap herself up in a hug.

When the unmarked car pulled up alongside us five minutes later, Sabina let out a breath in relief and hurried toward the headlights. Marlie cringed and set her mouth in a line, fingers clutching the shopping cart's faded red handle, like she was ready to run.

She didn't run, though. Voice shaking, she repeated exactly what she'd told Sabina—then hurried down the street the second Detective Barker said she could go.

He bagged the backpack, same as he'd done with the earring, and gave Sabina a strange look. One part grudging admiration, one part confusion. He worked his jaw like he was chewing on whatever words he was thinking about saying, then finally settled on, "Thanks. I'll make sure this gets processed." Then, "What made you come here tonight?"

Sabina raised an eyebrow, like she was trying to assess whether he was accusing her of something or not. After a beat, she shrugged. "Jenny Johnson. Name ring a bell? She's in Nadia's Facebook group. Claimed she saw Andrea at a soup kitchen. I'd been meaning to check out some of the popular encampments anyway, and then I started wondering … maybe there was a reason 'Jenny'"—she made air quotes with her fingers—"had this area on her mind."

Detective Barker didn't reply, but I thought I saw something flicker in his blue eyes. Instead, he lifted his chin in the direction Marlie had hurried off. "Is that your car down the block? I can walk you there. I'd strongly recommend you get back home. This isn't the safest area."

A fresh gust of wind sent a spray of dirt across his clean black pants, and Isabel muttered, "You think?"

Sabina let out a sigh but didn't protest when Detective Barker fell into step beside her, swatting at the dusty film now sprayed across his pants.

When Isabel didn't follow, I turned to face her. "Come on. You're not staying here, right?" A ripple of panic snaked through me at the idea that she might say no.

She glanced back at the underpass, which looked every bit as scary as I imagined it would be at night. I still couldn't believe she'd lived here. The laundry room-bedroom I slept in at Bunny and Dennis's house wasn't great, but it was the Sheraton compared to this.

I reached for her hand, the way I had earlier, and she let me take it. And, just like before, I knew in an instant what was going through her mind. Fear, that she'd be walking away from her view of the cemetery. Distress, that she was leaving the familiar place she'd haunted for the last three years. Despair that even though the police knew she was dead now, nobody would ever really know what happened to her.

"Sabina won't let anyone forget us," I insisted, letting go of her hand before I got lost in the threads of memories that lurked in the shadow of all that emotion. Sabina was already getting back into the car, and the last thing we needed was to lose her.

"Come on," I called to Isabel, rushing ahead.

Before I got into Sabina's car, I peered beneath the vehicle and did a quick scan of the underside. There, like I suspected, I saw a tiny black square that looked slightly out of place from the rest of the vehicle. "Bastard," I muttered, slamming my hand as hard as I could against the tracker—which of course did absolutely nothing.

The engine rumbled to life as I slipped through the tiny opening between the passenger-side window and its frame.

To my relief, Isabel was right behind me. I remembered thinking that I wished I'd gotten the chance to be her friend.

Maybe that was still possible.

We were silent for a few minutes while Sabina drove in the direction of the Airbnb, gaining speed through the quiet streets.

"I like your mom," Isabel said wistfully after a few minutes. Then she held out her hand. "I think we can like … show each other stuff this way. Do you want … do you want to know what he …" She trailed off, but I knew what she was asking, and I recognized the somber, eager hope I heard in her voice.

The idea that somebody, anybody, would know exactly what I'd gone through made me feel less alone than I had since I took my last breath.

"Yeah," I said, nodding somberly. "I'll show you what happened to me, too."

32

ISABEL

A phrase from *The Book of Mormon* kept echoing through my mind
while I held Andrea's hand tight in mind and saw the awful things
Dennis Beaumont had done to her.

"They see as they are seen."

I'd memorized it for a scripture mastery contest in church one
year when I was eleven.

The verse was talking about people in heaven, and I'd wondered what it meant at the time.

I was pretty sure I understood now, even though I hadn't seen
any sign of heaven.

Just like my own memories—impossibly vivid and clear ever
since I'd died—the scenes Andrea showed me were more immersive than any movie. Really, it felt like I was right there beside her.
But as the first memory unfolded, I quickly realized that it wasn't
just visual. In a strange way, I could feel everything she felt, too.
Right down to the smells and sensations.

Her fragile hope as she traced the delicate wings of a hand-
made monarch butterfly earring, clinging to the token of friendship
like a lifeline.

Her irritation, then fear, when she realized Dennis had come
home early on her birthday. The scratchy carpet prickling beneath

her feet, the stale smell of the old house turning suffocating as she realized that she was alone with him there.

Her terror when he chased her up the stairs. The panic as his footsteps moved faster behind her, as his hand grabbed hold of her arm.

Her pain, when her head hit the banister—hard enough to send static bursting behind her eyes. Hard enough that for a moment, everything went dark. But not hard enough to kill her.

Her agony as he wrapped the dog leash around her neck and pulled it so tight that even the labored, ragged breaths drawing in and out of her lungs stopped short, and her heart kicked into overdrive.

Her disbelief, when she realized that she was standing beside her own body. That her own father had just taken her life rather than try to save it. Those awful words he'd said to her—the same words he'd said to me—while she gasped her last breaths. *Shh. Don't fuss. The more you fuss, the worse it'll be.*

Her rage as he chopped her body into pieces and put them in garbage bags, then lied to the police while she walked his hallways as a ghost.

Then, finally back to fragile hope—when she saw Sabina, her birth mother, standing at the edge of the Beaumonts' front yard.

I wasn't nearly prepared for the intensity of what I felt and saw. The raw, aching awfulness of it. This was the closest I'd ever come to walking a mile in someone else's shoes.

It took everything in me not to let go of her hand as some of the worst memories swallowed both of us whole. But at the same time, I knew without a doubt—because I could feel it—that it meant the world to her to be seen. *Really seen.* So I stayed there with her in the car on the dark driveway, hands clasped tight while a tsunami of memories pulled us under again and again, only vaguely aware that Sabina had long since gone inside the Airbnb.

When the memory of Sabina faded and Andrea finally drew back her hand from mine, I shook my head in horror and amazement. Outside, the stars flashed bright in the clear sky while the wind howled around us, whipping the dark silhouettes of trees tucked beyond the reach of porch lights. It felt like the memories had passed between us in a few minutes, but it was clear that hours had elapsed.

Throughout the neighborhood, the dogs were howling with the wind like a weird, tuneless chorus. I listened to their strange symphony, imagining that Andrea and I were the conductors. And maybe we were. All down the street in both directions porch lights were blinking on and off. One man a few doors down peeked his head out through the orange glow of an open window and yelled, "Shut up, you filthy animals!"

Some of the dogs went quiet in response.

Then one broke into a long, soulful wail that sounded like the world's loudest, worst violin solo. The man shouted back a string of expletives—which were solidly outlasted by the howl—and then he slammed the window shut.

Andrea's serious expression dissolved into a tentative grin, and she covered her mouth like the gesture would wipe it off her face. I stared at her in disbelief, but felt a smile tugging at the corners of my own mouth. The urge to laugh didn't make sense, after the awful things we'd just seen and felt. But I didn't care. I wanted to laugh too, and so I did. Big, echoing laughs that would've made my belly hurt if I were alive.

Andrea did the same, closing her eyes and giggling right alongside me.

When our laughter subsided, I realized the dogs that had been howling in the neighborhood had gone quiet. So had the wind.

We sat in silence for a few minutes. Then Andrea held her hand out again.

It was my turn to show her what Dennis had done to me.

I gathered my courage, bracing. In both life and death, I'd walled off the memories of Dennis in my mind as completely as possible. What was the point in remembering? They were part of me, of course—a festering Tell-Tale Heart. I never told another living soul what Dennis had done to me when I was sixteen. Never even talked about it again after that night my parents sent me to my room instead of sitting me down to get the whole horrible story. Nobody would believe me, I told myself. Nobody would ever understand.

But now? Now, everything had changed. There were a lot of reasons that being dead sucked. This, though? This was the best kind of magic I could imagine, even if it was going to hurt like hell.

I met Andrea's gaze and took her hand, bringing her back with me to that dark night in the church building with the scratchy wallpaper.

33

SABINA

The first thing I did when I got back to the Airbnb was call Joel. I kept him on speakerphone while I relayed everything that had happened at the underpass, typing notes while I talked to make sure I didn't forget anything I'd seen and heard.

It wasn't my baby. But Isabel was somebody's baby. And knowing about her history with Dennis made me all the more determined to give her story some closure if I could.

After I hung up with Joel, I called Nadia, despite how late it was. She needed to know about Isabel—and more importantly, so did Isabel's parents. I had no idea how long it would take the Ogden Police to verify Marlie's story. There couldn't be that many unidentified Jane Does that had died of drug overdoses over the past few years in this tight-knit community. Still, if I were in those parents' shoes, and somebody knew what had happened to my daughter? To hell with procedure.

I might not have gotten any answers that would help me find Andrea. But at least the Palphreymans would know what happened to their daughter.

The thought sent a painful stabbing sensation through my chest. Nadia's choked voice on the other end of the line pretty well captured how I felt. Sadness, relief, and frustration. "Poor Isabel," she murmured. "I can't imagine what she went through, living on the streets like that." She blew out an angry sigh. "Her parents are going to be devastated. I can only imagine how I'd feel if I pushed my daughter away and then—" She stopped abruptly.

I froze too, hands poised in the air where I sat on the bed, typing a note on my laptop.

"That came out wrong," Nadia said in a rush. "Your situation with Andrea is nothing like the Palphreymans'. Nothing at all. Please forgive me?"

The ache in my chest sharpened. "It's fine," I said. But truth be told, I was already on the verge of tears.

As if my distress had summoned him, Joel's name popped back onto my screen as an incoming call. "Hey, my husband is calling," I said as steadily as I could. "I'll talk to you tomorrow, okay?"

I quickly accepted Joel's call, puzzled why he was calling for a second time. It was nearly one o'clock a.m., and we'd already said goodnight when we talked half an hour earlier.

I'd barely said hello when he started talking. "Sabina? Sabina, I found her. Isabel."

"What?" I furrowed my brow in confusion. His words didn't make sense. We'd already had an entire conversation about finding Isabel.

"Sorry, I mean I found her photo. I combed back through the Ogden Police Department's website and social media after we hung up the phone. And I'm pretty sure I just found her picture from three years ago, when they were trying to identify the Jane Doe the police recovered at the underpass. I'm sending the link to you now. It's … it's not easy to look at."

I quickly switched the call to speakerphone and clicked the link he'd just sent.

When the photo popped up on my screen, attached to a Facebook post dated three years earlier, I gasped.

I understood now why Marlie had been so slow to identify the photo of Isabel that I'd shown her. The smiling, blonde girl with the rosy cheeks and long blonde hair bore almost no resemblance to the gaunt, blue-haired woman on my screen. Her high cheekbones protruded sharply above dark hollows, and her short, spiky hair was bright blue in some parts and bleached light in others. Her lips pulled down at the corners in a lax, frozen frown.

"Oh," I whispered, gooseflesh popping over my arms like I'd just submerged myself in an ice bath. It wasn't just the knowledge that I was looking at a deceased Jane Doe. The gray pallor of her skin and her closed eyes were hard to look at, but it was more than that. There was something about her expression—like she'd just squeezed her eyes shut in order to keep from seeing something awful—that made my stomach twist painfully.

The post had two short sentences, describing Isabel as being 18-25 years old, and found near the cemetery in Ogden. It had gotten a handful of likes, a few comments, and five shares. That was all.

It felt like the wind had been knocked out of me. I imagined her parents again, their faces blurry in my mind—since I'd never met them. Their daughter had been here all this time, buried beneath posts about new traffic patterns and police bulletins from the past three years.

Dead, all these years.

"She's buried in the cemetery as a Jane Doe, only a few blocks away from the underpass," Joel said gently. "Grave number five-zero-three. There's a burial record on the Weber County Coroner's website." He drew in a breath. "I'm texting it to you—and then I'll add it to the dossier."

My eyes blurred with tears. "Thanks. I'm sure her parents will …" I let the sentence go, not sure how to finish it. My chest ached with sadness for Isabel *and* her parents—but there was a brittle anger there, too. None of this was fair. Logically, I knew that the Palphreymans getting a measure of closure had nothing to do with my own desperate search. But it still stung that they were the ones with answers. Answers they hadn't even been trying to find.

After I said goodnight to Joel for the second time, I forwarded Nadia the links he had sent me. She'd know how to get in touch with Isabel's parents.

Then I lay in bed with the lights off, listening to the wind thrash tree branches across the window. I kept the laptop screen open on the pillow beside me, staring back at Isabel Palphreyman's Jane Doe photo so long that when my eyes finally closed, I saw a green-tinged after-image burned behind my eyelids.

She wasn't my daughter. I'd never even met her. The grief I felt didn't make sense on the surface, but the gutted hollow in my chest didn't care. Regardless of whether her fate was tied to my daughter's, Isabel was another lost girl whose life had taken a turn for the worse because of Dennis Beaumont.

I decided I would visit her grave before I left Ogden. Maybe by then, it would have a proper marker with her name, instead of Jane Doe.

"Rest in peace, sweet girl," I whispered.

34

SABINA

While I slept, I dreamt of Isabel Palphreyman, nightmares that flashed to life in fits and starts interrupted by the whipping wind that set the dogs in the neighborhood howling all night long. Each time I fell back asleep, exhausted, the cycle would start again.

Maybe it had been a mistake to fall asleep looking at that photo.

In the first dream, her eyes popped open and stared back at me from the computer screen. Her mouth went slack and her chest heaved in a silent gasp, like she'd been holding her breath for a very long time.

Then she mouthed something I couldn't understand, over and over, her lips moving in a wordless dance while her eyes pleaded with me to understand.

"What, what are you trying to tell me?" I kept asking her, leaning so close to the computer screen that her features disappeared into a bright rainbow of blurry pixels.

Tears sprang from her eyes, and I wanted to look away. They were bright blue, matching the strands of hair along her forehead. But the whites were red and bloodshot, like she'd been weeping.

I focused on her lips again, trying desperately to decipher what she was saying. Why couldn't I read her lips? What was she trying to tell me? My brain felt slow and stupid, and with each passing second, my panic ticked higher and higher. I knew just one thing—If I didn't listen to her, nobody else would.

A loud crash from outside the house, maybe a garbage can blowing over in the wind, sent my eyes flying open and the dream skittering into the darkness.

I lay very still, trying to coax the dream back even though my heart was hammering so fast, I had a hard time believing I'd be able to fall back asleep at all—let alone find the thread of the dream. But after a few minutes of tossing and turning, my breathing turned steady and I let the darkness pull me under.

This time, I dreamt that I was back at the underpass talking to Marlie, studying her from the side of the road like I had only hours earlier. Only it wasn't Marlie, anymore.

It was Andrea, wearing a filthy red sweatshirt, her hair long and matted around her shoulders.

I opened my mouth to call her name, dizzy with relief that I'd finally found her. But all that came out was a hoarse-sounding squawk. I looked down at myself in confusion and saw silky black feathers. I was a crow.

Andrea's head snapped toward me, and she grinned—then excitedly tossed a peanut in my direction. Her smile was so beautiful and wide, and I realized I'd never seen a grown-up smile on her face before. I wanted to memorize it, but she was already busying herself with the magazine she was reading, thumbing through the pages and dog-earing a few as she went.

I watched, mesmerized. The scene was almost peaceful, sun streaming around the shade of the underpass where Andrea sat alone—until she set the magazine down and pushed back the tarp covering her shelter.

I craned my crow-neck to see inside, hoping to catch a glimpse of that dirty backpack with the word IZZY scrawled across the white patch in faded marker.

Instead, the dream began to tilt into a nightmare. Inside the shelter, I caught a glimpse of Isabel herself, curled into a ball on her side, bloodshot eyes staring back at me in a desperate plea for help. Her head was cocked at a strange angle where she lay on the dark, lumpy sleeping bag. Like her neck had been broken.

Andrea didn't seem to notice. She pulled a T-shirt from the pile on top of the sleeping bag and let the tarp's flap fall.

I spread my wings and flew toward her and the shelter, but the only thing that came out of my mouth was another hoarse caw.

"Jasper, what's gotten into you?" Andrea exclaimed, holding out another peanut. "You want this one instead?"

I ached to memorize the sound of her voice. It was deeper, softer than I'd imagined. But I was already wheeling backward, wings flapping furiously to keep me a safe distance away from the shelter, away from Isabel.

Because Isabel wasn't lying on the sleeping bag, like I'd thought initially. The reason her head was at such a strange angle was because it was propped against someone's leg.

Dennis Beaumont.

He grinned at me from where he knelt, and peeled back the flap of shelter so that I could see his bulky frame clearly.

Andrea glanced in his direction, unfazed, then reached out her hand toward his mouth, offering a shelled peanut.

"No, baby!" I tried to scream. "No, no, no!" *Caw.* I watched, frozen, as he took the peanut in his lips, but his sharp gray eyes stayed fixed on me.

With one hand, Dennis reached down to stroke Isabel's choppy blue hair. She cringed but didn't move—and it was then that I realized he had her body pinned between his knees. Her lips moved in a wordless flurry of silent words, again and again.

I wanted to help her, but I was a crow. What could I do?

And then, as Andrea drew her hand away from his mouth, he darted forward and took her finger in his teeth.

She glanced at me and shrugged helplessly as he bit down hard, his lips turning red as they sliced down to bone with a sickening crunch.

I launched myself toward him, talons outstretched. Isabel's mouth worked soundlessly.

Dennis let go of Andrea's bloody finger and, before I could make contact with his face, he put both hands on Isabel's head and twisted.

A sickening crack sounded in the muffled chaos.

Isabel's mouth stopped moving. Her face went slack. Andrea screamed.

And I woke again to the sound of my own terrified gasps and the soft glow of the laptop, which should have gone into sleep mode long ago, inches from my face.

I sat up and pulled it closer, studying her slack mouth, trying to remember the motion it had made while she tried to speak.

It finally clicked together as I leaned toward the screen and enlarged the photo, trying to imagine the shape of her mouth with the words.

She was saying, "Look at me. *Look at me.*"

Full-body chills made me wrap the tangled comforter tighter around my sweaty body as I did just that. I looked at her. Really looked.

What I saw made the air whoosh from my lungs like I'd been kicked in the chest.

There were strange bruises near her mouth on the left side of her face. They formed a semi-circular pattern that ended at her bottom lip.

The goosebumps on my arms pulled tighter as the chill in the room intensified.

Maybe I was just tired. Maybe it was the dream I'd had. Maybe Isabel's skin was—like I'd originally imagined when I scanned right past those marks—spotted with lividity, dirt, or any number of scuffs she might have gotten while living on the streets.

But those tiny, faded bruises, consistent in spacing and moving from larger to smaller, looked like a human bite mark.

35

ANDREA

Isabel and I sat on the bed beside Sabina and listened with fascination while she told Joel about the vivid dreams she'd had—and the bite marks she'd noticed on Isabel's face.

The morning had long since faded into afternoon. Between the howling dogs and the fitful sleep, Sabina hadn't gotten much real sleep during the night. When her alarm had gone off at 8:00 a.m., she'd blearily turned it off, and we'd finally let her sleep.

"The dreams were so real ..." Sabina said, the laptop screen still open, the same way it had been when Isabel and I came inside at nearly 3:00 a.m. to see her photo glowing dully. "You see the bite marks on her lip, right? I'm not just imagining them? I just texted Nadia, and she agreed."

Joel went quiet on the other end of the line. Finally, he said, "Yeah, I see what you're talking about." He held a long pause. "She was living on the street though, Sabi. Those marks might've come from anywhere."

Next to me on the bed, Isabel reached up absently to touch her lower lip. Last night, she'd shown me exactly how she'd gotten those bite marks. The memory, still fresh in my mind, made me shake with disgust and anger.

"I know," Sabina cut in impatiently. "But after that dream ... I can't help thinking that it meant something, Joel. I didn't even notice those bruises on her face when you first sent me the photo. Did you?"

"No," he admitted. "And I'm not saying you're wrong. By all means, tell the police, and Nadia. All I'm saying is, you're there to find out what happened to Andrea, right? I know this Isabel girl crossed paths with Dennis Beaumont at some point, and I'm not trying to minimize what he did to her. But is this rabbit hole worth going down? Or maybe it's better to hand off the baton to her parents?"

Sabina's mouth tightened into a slim line. It was the first time I'd seen her look upset by anything Joel had said.

I could tell that Isabel was getting frustrated, too. The feeling came off her in little electric waves. She stood up from the bed and paced the carpet. "If I were her, I'd probably listen to him," she muttered, shaking her head. "I don't think the dream was enough. And why should she care about me, anyway? I'm not her kid."

I sighed. The dream hadn't worked quite like I'd hoped. The one we'd *tried* to send her while she slept, wrapping our arms around her body, had shown Sabina exactly what had happened to Isabel. Every awful, gritty detail. But, hearing what she'd just re-counted to Joel, some pretty big wires had crossed.

I wasn't sure why the dreaming thing hadn't worked like it had last time—when Sabina had whispered "sweet girl," then told Joel how she'd dreamed of the exact memory I was trying to show her. There wasn't an instruction manual that came with life, and I guess there wasn't an instruction manual that came with death, either. Best I could tell, the difference had some-thing to do with the fact that Sabina and I had both experienced our shared memory at one point, while Sabina didn't have any shared memories with Isabel.

There was really no way to know for certain. All we could do now was hope that garbled dream had gotten the job done. Had thrown a wrench into the current theory that Isabel had died of an unfortunate drug overdose while living on the streets, like the coroner's report claimed.

Sabina closed her eyes and rubbed her temples in slow circles, the same way I used to when I was alone in my room at night, scared that Dennis would visit me. "I know you're trying to look out for me. And maybe I *am* just diving face-first down an emotional rabbit hole. I can't explain why this feels important. But it does, okay? You know I love your Peter Parker brain–and I love the dossier you made. You've been so helpful. But … my Spidey senses are going off here."

Isabel stopped pacing the room and studied her, waiting. Another prickle of hope moved through me.

Joel laughed softly, like he'd heard her say this exact phrase before. "Message received. I know better than to try to out-logic your Spidey senses. I'm sorry. I love you, and I miss you. I need to go. Mom has a doctor's appointment. But I'm going to do some more digging on the Beaumonts this afternoon, okay?"

"I love you too," Sabina said, her eyes still fixed on that open laptop where Isabel's photo had been enlarged as much as the pixels would allow. As she moved her pointer finger to end the call with Joel, a number with an 801-area code popped onto the screen.

Sabina answered without hesitating, putting the call on speakerphone. "Hello?"

"Hello … Sabina? My name is Mary Palphreyman."

Nobody in the room, living or dead, moved or spoke for a long moment. Isabel's mouth formed a small O as her expression ping-ponged wildly between disbelief, anguish, love, anger, and sadness.

"Hello?" Mary repeated. "Is this Sabina Turpin?"

Sabina finally broke the silence. "Yes, I'm sorry. Arc you … are you Isabel's—"

"Mom," Isabel said softly, in tandem.

"I hope it's all right that Sister Ramos—Nadia—gave me your number. And I'm sorry to call like this," Mary said, her voice light and apologetic as if she were talking about some last-minute favor instead of the daughter she hadn't seen for years.

I looked at Isabel, who ignored me completely, eyes fixed on the phone lying on the bed.

"It's totally fine," Sabina said in a rush. Then, more slowly, "Did the police …" She let the sentence fade, wincing as she balled her hands into fists to grab some of the comforter. It was Mary's turn for silence as the question filled the room. Did she know her daughter was dead yet?

"Yes," Mary rasped, like her throat had suddenly gone dry. She cleared it. "I'm driving away from the police station now. To … to the cemetery. My husband is out of town for work." Her voice strained higher, like a wobbly bow across a violin string. "He's flying home now, so we can—" Her voice broke on the last word, and a tiny wail pierced the silence.

"Oh, Mary. I'm so …" Sabina began, but the wail on the other end of the line swelled into a sound like I'd never heard. Part scream, part keening howl that filled the room with so much raw pain, I had to force myself not to shrink away from it.

The computer screen went dark, erasing the pixelated close-up of Isabel's face, but Sabina didn't even notice. She bowed her head and pulled the phone against her chest, as if she were giving it a hug. Tears dripped from her tightly closed eyes while the wail coming from the phone's speakers turned into gasping sobs.

Isabel stared stone-faced at Sabina and the phone, like she refused to react, but there was no mistaking that the torrent of grief lashing the room was hers, too.

"All this time, I told myself she'd come back to us," Mary cried. "We raised her right, so I was sure she would come back someday. That was all I wanted. I knew she would, I prayed she would. Like the prodigal son in the Bible. That's what my husband Corey said would happen." She sobbed harder. "I'm sorry," she repeated between gasps. "I'm sorry. I don't even know why I'm calling you. I'm sorry."

Isabel got up and walked out of the bedroom, into the kitchen. The storm cloud that moved with her told me she wasn't interested in being followed.

Sabina opened her mouth as if to speak, then shook her head. "I'm so sorry, Mary. You couldn't have known—"

"No. But I could have gone looking for her," Mary interrupted in a voice so loud, Sabina winced. "I could have asked her to stay when she told us she was moving out. I could have helped her find a proper place to live, at the very least. Was she living at that underpass all these years? Did I pass her in my car, I know I drove that way once or twice." She sniffed loudly. "I never even tried to find her, though. I didn't want her to think I approved of the path she was headed down. She was so angry, so full of hate … and she didn't want anything to do with us or the church!"

Some appliance from the kitchen made a series of erratic beeps, and Sabina flicked her eyes toward the tiny ruckus then back at the phone. Her chest rose as she drew in a long, steadying breath and she wiped her cheeks with the sleeve of her pajamas. Her frown told me she didn't like some of the things Mary Palphreyman had just said. But she didn't kick the woman while she was down, either. And I loved her even more for both of those things.

"Mary," she said softly. "I don't know what Nadia's told you. It must be enough that you're calling me, though—"

"She texted me this morning. Told me you were the one who found Isabel's backpack at that … at that homeless camp," Mary said, her voice wobbling again. "So I asked her for your number. I just wanted to speak to you. I don't even know why." She drew in a loud, painful-sounding breath. "The police said that they found her with drugs. That she'd overdosed." She said the last word as a whisper.

Sabina sat up straighter and folded her arms tight across her chest over the covers, like she was steeling herself. "Did you see Isabel's photo yet? The 'Jane Doe' photo from the Ogden PD Facebook page?"

Mary let out a shuddering breath. "Yes, I've seen it. She looked awful. I wouldn't have even known she was my daughter if I walked past her on the street."

There was another loud beep-beep-beep from the kitchen, but Sabina just kept staring at the phone. "Mary," she said slowly, "did you see the bruising pattern near her lower lip? Maybe I'm wrong, but it looks like bite marks to me. I don't want to tell you what to do, but if she were my daughter …" She squeezed her eyes shut and hurried on. "I would ask for an autopsy."

36

ISABEL

I'd stormed out of the room, but I couldn't stop myself from hovering near the bedroom door so I could hear every single word my mother said.

"She was so angry, so full of hate."

"She looked awful. I wouldn't have even known she was my daughter if I walked past her on the street."

"Like the prodigal son."

Her words landed like arrows. The pain of hearing them was worse than I'd imagined it would be, while I was living beneath that underpass, toying with the idea of finding a payphone and calling my family. Because it wasn't just disappointment I heard in her voice. It was love, too. And pain. And sadness. All mixed up in a poisonous stew where there was no more separating the parts that would build you up from the parts that would destroy you.

I was so angry. I was so hurt. And I missed her so much. I missed my dad and my sisters, too.

And maybe they missed me. I was willing to believe that now. But I also knew, in the deepest parts of me, that the news of my death meant that I would be frozen in their memories as a broken, lost girl.

And then Sabina broached the idea of an autopsy.

I rushed back inside the sun-streaked bedroom, stunned. I knew that Andrea and I had convinced Sabina to see the faint bruising on my lip and cheek—but I hadn't let myself hope she would push things that far.

"Yes, yes! Please do the damn autopsy," I begged, catching Andrea's wide eyes, not sure whether I was addressing Sabina, the universe, my mother, or all three. There was DNA on my body. They'd find my fractured ribs—and maybe they'd even realize that I didn't have any drugs in my system.

"That seems extreme," my mother said hesitantly, in response to Sabina. I could almost imagine her crinkling up her forehead in horror at the idea of unearthing my body and demanding it be re-examined. "The police already did an exam ... they know how she died. We're ... we're making arrangements to have her moved to our family plot at Myers Memorial. The idea of planning a funeral ..." Her voice broke again, and I could tell she was crying softly once more.

Sabina pressed her hands against her cheeks, eyes focused on the phone lying on the white duvet in front of her crossed legs. "I don't think it's extreme. I'm sure the coroner does post-mortem autopsies all the time—"

My mother interrupted by clearing her throat. "In her text, Sister Ramos asked how I felt about putting that photo of Isabel— with the horrible blue hair—on your Facebook page. At least she *asked* this time. But I don't see what that's going to accomplish. Our daughters didn't know each other, outside of attending the same church for a little while. They weren't even close to the same age." She made a muffled sound, something between a grunt and sniff, and I could almost imagine the distasteful look on her face.

"Just get the autopsy," I hissed.

Sabina bit her lower lip and leaned forward, brows furrowed in concentration. "The page has been getting a lot of activity. I know it's still a longshot to think that Andrea's case is connected to what happened to Isabel. But Dennis Beaumont—"

"No!" I cried, but there was no pulling back the words Sabina had just said.

Saying his name had been a mistake.

"Connected?" my mother said shrilly, and I watched the horrified realization hit Sabina too late. Andrea looked between us in confusion, but I didn't bother explaining. My mother was about to lose her shit—and she'd explain why, herself.

My mother didn't want to talk about Dennis Beaumont. She never had. And she definitely did not want to believe that my death had anything to do with Andrea's disappearance.

Instead of anger, I felt an unexpected stab of clarity—and empathy. Of course my mother didn't want to talk about Dennis Beaumont. Of course she didn't want to believe that my death was connected to Andrea in any way. Because if Dennis Beaumont was somehow connected to my death, it meant that I'd been telling the truth all along about what he did to me in that interview. It meant that she and my father should have listened to me, helped me—instead of sending me to my room and asking me to repent for my sins. It meant that life might have taken a very different path. One where her daughter might be sitting at her dinner table instead of lying in the ground.

And those thoughts were too much for her to bear.

"I don't—I didn't mean—" Sabina fumbled.

"I'm very sorry about your daughter," my mother said icily. The tears had dried up, and so had the wailing. Her voice rose in volume as she continued. "I know how desperate you must be to find her. But if this is a witch hunt for Dennis Beaumont, then I want no part of it. I have a funeral to plan." Her voice faltered on the last word.

I sat down on the bed in defeat, briefly imagining the funeral my family would hold for me at the church meetinghouse. The chorus of "God Be With You Till We Meet Again" swelling through the same pews where I'd once sat as a teenager, surrounded on all sides but so alone.

"I'm sorry," Sabina said helplessly. She was standing now too, clutching the phone in her hand. "I misspoke—"

"I need to go," my mother said abruptly. "We haven't even told her sisters yet."

Then the screen blinked off as the call disconnected.

"Shit," Sabina whispered, sitting down heavily on the side of the bed. "Shit." Then she stood and stomped into the kitchen.

Andrea moved toward me, but I turned away, my mother's words still ringing in my ears as I allowed myself to imagine my sisters' faces.

Abish would be twenty-six by now. Had she already gotten married, had her first baby? Was the wedding what she'd planned, at the Salt Lake temple with a long-sleeved lace wedding gown and a bouquet of pink roses? Had she married Brady Oaks, the boy in our ward, like she'd always said she would?

Eve would be twenty-seven. She'd been partway through her degree in Elementary Education at BYU when I left home. Was she a teacher, now? Ms. Palphreyman, to a class full of kindergarteners like she always wanted? Or was she at home with tiny children of her own, running barefoot across a yard in the same neighborhood as my parents?

Sariah would be twenty-nine, so grown-up I could barely imagine her. She'd just gotten married when I left home—a wedding in the temple I hadn't been allowed to attend. At her reception, held in the same church building where Dennis Beaumont tried to corner me in his office, she'd stepped out of the receiving line to wrap me up in a hug. Then she'd invited me to dinner at her new apartment. Promised she'd make me my favorite dinner, chicken and broccoli casserole.

I suddenly wished more than anything in the world that I'd said yes.

And for a moment, while I stood there in the unfamiliar Airbnb, I felt more lost than I had while I was tucked beneath that underpass. But then I knew what I wanted to do.

"I need to go to them," I told Andrea. "My family."

Andrea was staring at me like I'd lost my mind. "Wait, what? You're leaving *now*?" She glanced in the direction of the kitchen, where the coffee maker had just hummed to life, despite the fact that it was nearly dinnertime. Her disbelief turned to crestfallen disappointment. "I know we just met, but …" She raised an eyebrow ever so slightly, and I knew she was thinking about the memories I'd shown her last night about my parents and Dennis.

"If I can convince my parents to get the autopsy, it'll change everything," I said softly. "Maybe she'll listen to me … like Sabina seems to listen to you."

She nodded slowly, understanding dawning on her face. "Yeah. Okay, yes. That makes sense."

I didn't try to explain the rest. It wasn't just that I wanted my parents to order the autopsy—and I did, badly. The autopsy might be the puzzle piece that finally put Dennis Beaumont in the hot seat when it came to both our deaths. The police could finally get a warrant. Dennis would go to jail.

So yeah, I wanted that autopsy pretty bad. But it was more than that, too. I didn't try to explain it to Andrea, but I suddenly wanted to see my family again. My sisters, my dad, my mom. A seed of hope had worked its way inside my head that maybe they missed me—more than I'd thought.

The memories I'd shown Andrea, the ones that had hurt me, were hard to stomach. But they weren't the whole story of my life with my family, either.

And at the end of the day, my mother and father finally were, like I'd imagined so often over the past three years since Dennis Beaumont stole my last breath, coming to find me. They would take my body to the beautifully landscaped cemetery where both sets of my grandparents were buried beneath a giant row of oak trees. They would call my sisters home from wherever they'd gone in their grown-up lives. They would lay me to rest.

And I needed to be there when they did that.

When I saw them, I would hug them tight in the only way I still could, hoping they would feel my presence nearby, the way Sabina seemed to.

"I'll come back as soon as I can," I promised Andrea, taking a step toward the hall. "I promise."

She shook her head, and I could feel the frustration and loneliness rising up in her. "How will you know I need you? How will we find each other again?" she demanded, sounding like the teenager she was. "What if Dennis comes for Sabina? He's got that tracker on her car, remember?"

I'd been thinking about this, and I had an answer even if I wasn't totally sure it would work. "You remember that memory from church? The one where I was sitting in the pew with my family? When you touched my arm and spoke to me, it brought me right back inside that memory with you. At the time, I was sitting next to Marlie in the underpass while she read a magazine. And then *bam*, I was there in that memory with you. I could see *you* standing in front of me—not just the toddler-Andrea that was in my original memory." I thought for a second then added, "I'm sure we have other memories that overlap, but we know that one works."

She considered this. "So if something happens, I just go back to that memory and grab your arm?"

I nodded. "Yeah. And this time, I'll stay. We can talk to each other, and find each other again."

"Okay," she said reluctantly. "Do you know how to find your way home—to your family?"

I shrugged. I'd always known—or at least, I'd always been pretty sure I could figure it out if I spent enough time wandering the city streets. But right now, I was going back to the cemetery. My mother had just said she was on her way there.

"I've gotta go," I said, moving away so she wouldn't feel the ripples of sadness running through me. We'd only met a day ago, but the reality was, she already knew me better than my own family in a profound way, and I hated to leave her.

I suddenly had the thought that maybe someday, when my parents and sisters died, they would know me that way, too. And I'd know them. *They see as they are seen.*

That thought gave me the most hope I'd felt in a very long time.

37

SABINA

I regretted the late-afternoon cup of coffee as soon as I took the first sip, knowing it would almost guarantee another sleepless night. I finished it anyway though, staring out the living room window of the Airbnb at the shady oak in the front yard.

I'd tried pulling up Joel's dossier again to make a plan of where to go next, who to speak with, but nothing felt right. Maybe it was the dreams or the fact that I'd slept the day away. Maybe it was the coffee churning in my otherwise empty stomach. Maybe it was that awful conversation with Mary Palphreyman. Or maybe it was the fact that Nadia had just texted to say that she'd gone ahead and posted the new photo of Isabel to the page—and made me an admin on the Facebook page, too. My thoughts were spiraling like an out-of-control carousel.

All of those thoughts led me back to questions I couldn't answer, and a sense of dread at the idea that I might never find out what had happened to my baby.

Was there really any chance that I could do more than the police were already doing? Or, like Joel had gently hinted, was I starting to follow desperate rabbit trails?

Maybe the dream I'd had about Isabel was just a dream. Maybe Isabel wasn't connected to Andrea's disappearance at all.

Maybe I was grasping for answers, because I didn't know where else to turn.

I closed my eyes and tried to steady the shaky adrenaline pumping through my veins with no outlet. The only thing I really knew at the moment was that I needed to go out and find something to put in my stomach besides black coffee. Then I could do the logical thing and keep working my way down the list of potential leads and people I'd written down in my notes and in Joel's dossier. But this morning everything felt like a yawning maze, branching deeper and deeper with endless forks and dead ends. Was I lost inside it already? Was I wasting precious time?

I'd lost nearly an entire day. But did that really matter? I didn't know where to go next. How much longer could I actually stay here?

The reality was creeping up that I couldn't stay in Ogden forever. At what point would I pack up and go home to my husband, answer the work emails that were no doubt piling up? With each hour, each day that passed, I was inching closer to the point where I'd have to give up and go home. For now, there was no clear path forward.

I shook my head and blinked into the sunlight, already blinding from the west. I wasn't going home today. But even that thought gave me little comfort. I felt paralyzed by the possibilities of what to do with my time, what would bring me closer to finding my daughter.

I opened my laptop at the kitchen table and tapped the ON button, since the computer had managed to turn itself off. Then I scrolled to the JUSTICE FOR ANDREA page and hit "accept" on the admin request Nadia had sent.

The page refreshed, popping the recent post onto my screen—the Jane Doe photo of Isabel that the Ogden Police had posted back in 2012, which they'd updated this morning, to show her real name.

"UPDATE," Nadia's post read. "We are both grateful and devastated to learn that Isabel Palphreyman has been identified as this Jane Doe. Our hearts are with the Palphreymans at this time. If you have any information about Isabel's death, we urge you to contact Detective Monte Barker with the Ogden Police."

There were already a few shares, hug emojis, and sad face emojis. But the first comment seemed to echo the dark thoughts spinning through my mind. "I'm confused. Why are you posting about this random girl? Who is actually running this page?" asked someone whose name I didn't recognize.

Beneath it was a reply from Jenny Johnson. "Pretty sure the true-crime nut jobs are bored. Sad. Let the police do their job."

Blood boiling, I reached out to shut the laptop screen. But as I pulled it down, a bell chimed, and a direct message to the administrators of the Facebook page popped onto the corner of my screen.

"I might know something about Isabel. But I don't wanna talk to the cops. Or online. If you want to talk in person, I might."

The rolling boil in my veins slowed, and I clicked on the profile. There was no photo. No friends. And, like Jenny Johnson, the name—Amy Sue—sounded so generic I immediately decided it was fake.

I stared at the message and drummed my fingertips across the keyboard, trying to decide whether to respond, ignore it, or text Nadia.

Unable to help myself, I typed a response. "Hi. Thanks for reaching out. Can you tell me a little more?"

"4900 S., 80 E. Apartment 8. 10:00 tonight. Do NOT come any earlier. Do NOT say anything to the police."

The sour coffee churned harder in my gut. Was this another Dennis Beaumont spam account? Did this person actually think I was going to show up alone to a random address?

I glanced at the clock on the computer. That was only a few hours from now.

A chime notification sounded, and another line of text appeared.

"I might know something about Andrea, too. That's all I'm gonna say here."

I froze, re-reading the message thread, goosebumps prickling across my arms despite the morning sun bathing the kitchen in light.

This person was saying they knew something about both Andrea *and* Isabel.

Barely breathing, I started typing out a response.

Before I could even hit ENTER, the messages disappeared. And the name next to the blank profile image turned from "Amy Sue" to "Facebook Profile User." When I clicked the icon, the words "Content Unavailable" appeared.

"No! No, no, what the hell?" I hissed, clicking back and forth and kicking myself for not taking a screenshot as soon as that very first message appeared. Hands shaking, I opened up my notes page and tried to remember the address, but my mind had gone completely blank. "Dammit!" I cried in frustration. I'd only seen the address for just a second. There was no way I could remember it.

I searched the corners of my memories. Was it 4600 South? 60 East?

I tried inputting different street numbers into the Maps app on my laptop. Nothing.

I stared at the screen, tears filling my eyes.

And then, in a way that made no sense at all, the address popped back to the front of my mind with uncanny clarity. Like someone had briefly broadcast a projector there.

Goosebumps dotted my arms as I typed it into the blank cursor field.

4900 S., 80 E. Apartment 8. 10:00.

I sat back in the kitchen chair, feeling the hair rise on the back of my neck. "Thank you, baby," I said softly, and moved my hand to my heart.

When I closed my eyes, I saw her in my mind's eye. My wide-eyed baby girl with a shock of auburn hair and a rare gummy-mouthed smile.

For a moment, the sour churn in my stomach settled into calm, and the quilt-wrapped feeling held me tight.

I popped the address into the Maps app. Then I zoomed in on the dot, switched to street-view, and saw a squat, two-story build-ing that was so run-down I wondered if it was actually occupied. The windows were barred unevenly, and one was covered in some kind of plastic sheeting. Even in the grainy photo, I could see that the siding on the jaundice-yellow apartments was warped and miss-ing in some sections.

"Yikes," I whispered. Was I really willing to go there at night? Should I do what "Amy Sue" had warned me not to do and call the police? The apartment complex looked like the set of a hor-ror movie in daylight. I could only imagine what it would be like in person, at night.

Zoom out. The hunch elbowed its way through the chaotic thoughts in my head.

Without hesitating, I listened.

At first, nothing stood out. It was just a map of North Ogden, the street numbers climbing and falling with each section of the grid.

Then my eyes landed on the mortuary. And a familiar set of locations I'd plugged into my Maps app last night: the soup kitchen and the encampment by the underpass.

I released the breath I'd been holding in a quiet whoosh. This had to mean something. My heartbeat picked up, The colors in the tiny kitchen seemed to intensify, and the lingering smell of coffee turned sharper.

This meant something. I couldn't explain how I knew it—or what I'd find—but I knew it.

I'd always joked with Joel about my "Spidey senses." While he tended to think with his logic, his research skills, his left brain, I tended to check my gut first. It rarely steered me wrong, but I'd generally made light of the fact that I felt my way through life with my heart.

"You're one of the most intuitive people I've ever met," my friend Kat had told me in amazement one day after I called her out of the blue to chat—and learned that her beloved dog Sasha had just died.

I spent a few more minutes scanning the map and the surrounding area for anything else that stood out.

Then my eyes moved back to that dot, marking the address.

The safe thing to do would be to call the police. But that's exactly what my gut was urging me *not* to do.

38

ISABEL

I made it to the cemetery half an hour before my mother. She'd said she was on her way when she spoke to Sabina, but as the sun sank lower in the sky, the shadows lengthened, and I stood waiting in the parking area just outside the front gates, I started to wonder if I'd misunderstood.

Maybe she wasn't coming for me tonight, after all. I knew the cemetery gates closed at dusk, and we were almost to that point.

I was about to leave, ready to start wandering the streets in the gathering dusk until I made my way back to the house I'd grown up in, when a shiny white Audi I didn't recognize pulled into the nearly empty lot.

A shiver of recognition zipped through me. It was her.

I stayed where I was, watching as she maneuvered into one of the far-back parking spots then got out of her vehicle.

For a few moments, she just stood there, with the driver's side door open and her face turned away from me, staring out at the sprawling, sloped cemetery. A few families and single people stood beside graves among the trees, and I wondered which ones she could see. And which ones, like me, were dead.

Her hair, still highlighted pale blonde, was shorter than it had been, hung just past her chin. She wore a sage green cardigan and an ankle-length paisley skirt. She clutched a cream-colored purse beneath her arm so tightly, the boxy shape folded in slightly.

"Mom, I'm right here," I said, hurrying toward her, unable to stop myself even though I knew she couldn't hear.

It hurt anyway, when she kept her back turned to me, eyes scanning the rows and rows of headstones tucked into the grass.

If she knew what she was looking for, she'd be able to see the tiniest portion of the roof of the eight-plex where I'd spent most of my time after leaving home. And if she turned to face me and the hum of cars moving along I-84, she'd see the walls of the underpass where I'd spent my last days.

Hesitantly, I moved closer until I stood beside her and the car.

To my surprise, she almost looked younger than when I'd last seen her. Smooth skin, high cheekbones, and barely a wrinkle in sight. Her eyes, red-rimmed and wiped free of makeup, were the only part of her that looked undone.

"Mom," I said again, laying a hand on her arm and feeling a strangely specific but overwhelming sadness that if I leaned in to hug her, I wouldn't be able to smell her. Did she still wear the expensive perfume my dad had gotten her for Christmas, the one that smelled like honeysuckle and pear? Was there still a hint of chlorine beneath it, from her morning swims at the rec center?

She pursed her lips and shifted the purse in her arms, away from my outstretched hand, still staring out at the cemetery.

When I followed her gaze, I saw a group of women wearing ankle-length dresses emerging from the trees by the nearest row of gravestones beside the gate. Some of them wore bonnets, their hair tucked inside the hats that framed their faces. One young woman in a pretty, robin's egg blue dress with pleats along the tiny waist carried a little girl in her arms, pointing at the Wasatch Mountains while she walked.

As if she sensed me staring, she tilted her head and glanced over her shoulder in my direction.

A small guide sign indicated that the pioneer section of the cemetery was located to the right.

For some reason, I didn't even wonder if they were dead—Ogden had its share of pioneer re-enactors and "Trek" marches—until the little girl wriggled down from her mother's arms and slipped easily through the chain-link fence.

My mother didn't see them, just like she didn't see me.

With a shuddering sigh, she straightened her back and turned toward the mortuary entrance.

I followed her—just as I felt a familiar falling sensation, and found myself back inside the memory of my old church building, with my mother and sisters on either side of me. The memory felt heavy and charged, exactly like it had last time this happened.

Andrea stood in front of me with her hand wrapped around mine and a pleading expression on her face. The words tumbled out of her in a rush. "Hey, I know it's only been a few hours, but somebody sent a message to the page and said they know something about you, and their address is pretty close to the cemetery. Somebody named Amy Sue? It might be a fake name like—"

"Doesn't sound familiar. My mom just barely got here—to the cemetery," I said, trying not to sound impatient even though I knew by now that she could read my emotions like a book. "I can't come back yet, okay?"

Andrea's shoulders sagged and she looked down at the ground. I felt her disappointment as much as I noticed it. "Okay. But hurry? I think this is important."

I flashed her a quick smile and then gently pulled my hand away from hers, the memory dissolving as quickly as it had appeared. My mom was already negotiating the too-long grass in her sandals, frowning as she scanned the rows of graves. The frantic hum of fear in Andrea's voice worried me, but I needed to convince my mom to get an autopsy while her heart was still tender.

How, though?

A wave of anxiety rose up inside me, and a flurry of tiny black birds shot skyward, from where they'd been perched along the gnarled oaks separating the pioneer gravesites from the rest of the cemetery.

My mother startled, drawing her hand to her chest.

I fell into step beside her as she scanned the rows of graves. "This way, Mom," I told her quietly, taking her arm and pointing even though I knew it was futile.

To my surprise, she tensed and swatted at the place on her arm where my hand lay, as if shooing away a mosquito before it had a chance to bite. However, she changed course slightly as she did it, then walked toward the desolate, far south corner of the cemetery, more or less arm-in-arm with me.

A mourning dove who-whooed in the distance, and my mother scanned the rows of marked graves, looking for the number that had been seared into my mind for years.

1002.

I tugged gently at her arm, and after a few seconds she stood in front of the laminated marker that stated "Jane Doe, found January 10th, 2012," and my post-mortem photo.

Her purse fell onto the grass.

"Oh, Isabel," she whispered, leaving the purse slumped where it lay. Then she wobbled, knees buckling beneath her, and sank to the ground in front of my grave. "Oh, Isabel." She bowed her head and closed her eyes as if in prayer, moving her lips in words I couldn't decipher while tears slipped from the corners of her eyes.

I sat beside her in silence, among the gathering shadows that sent the other mourners trudging back toward the gates.

My mother stayed where she was, tears dripping down her cheeks and into the collar of her cardigan. She didn't wipe them away.

When her eyes finally opened and she shifted a little, I thought she might be getting ready to leave. Instead, she leaned forward and whispered again, "You should have come home. I wanted you to come home, Isabel."

I stared harder at the dark blades of grass between us. "I wanted to come home. You have no idea how much I wanted that," I told her quietly.

"Should I have stopped you? Locked you in your room like a toddler? Grounded you?" she asked, her voice suddenly angry, shaking with emotion. "What else could I have done? You were nineteen, an adult. You made the choice to leave."

I kept my eyes lowered to study a ladybug that clung to a bouncing blade upside down, its wings opening and closing in frustration. "You forced me to. You didn't believe me about Dennis," I said so softly I could barely hear my own words.

"He was the first counselor in the bishopric!" she insisted, reaching forward to snatch at a handful of grass, ripping it up by the roots and narrowly missing the ladybug. "He … he couldn't have done what you said he did. His calling came from God. And God wouldn't make a mistake like that. You were just angry about Archer, weren't you? *Weren't you,* Isabel?"

Any hope I had of tenderness in her heart evaporated. She was angry. And now so was I.

"No!" I cried, all the old hurt and betrayal pulling me into its depths like a whirlpool of brackish water. It had been a mistake to come here. How could she still be so blind, so dogged, after all this time? After she'd realized I was *dead*? "I wasn't lying! I ran all the way home thinking you'd help me. And you didn't! You acted like … like you didn't even love me anymore, because you were so disappointed in me."

My mother looked up at my photo on the laminated sheet, her mouth pulled tight in a desperate grimace. "I went to see the bishop the night you came home from your interview with Brother Beaumont. He told me to 'Trust in the Lord with all my might.' Like Abraham, when his only son was on the altar." She squeezed her eyes shut and let out a keening moan.

I stared at her, stunned. I didn't know she'd gone to talk to the bishop that night. And I'd always hated that story about Abraham. What kind of God asked a man to prove his faith by sacrificing his only son?

"I tried to have faith. I tried so hard. But it wasn't like Abraham. God didn't bring you back to me." She was sobbing again now.

"Fuck Abraham," I snapped and got to my feet. "Ask for the damn autopsy, please! Look what he did to me!" I grabbed her arm and tried to show her the memories of what Dennis Beaumont had inflicted, the way I'd shown Andrea.

She whipped her head violently, crying harder as she tensed and pulled her arm away from my outstretched fingers.

And then she reached for the purse, unzipped it, and pulled out something from inside.

39

ISABEL

My mother held a photograph—a glossy Polaroid that glimmered in the sun—from the family vacation we'd taken to Bear Lake when I was fifteen. The last summer before Sariah went to BYU.

The summer before everything fell apart.

The photo focused on me, standing knee-deep in the turquoise blue waters of the lake, sunburned and windblown and grinning ear to ear. My hands were on my hips, linked at the elbows with two other sets of sunburned arms out of frame. My sisters.

"I love you, Isabel. And I'm sorry," my mother sobbed, her trembling hands sliding the photo into the plastic sheeting to cover up the Jane Doe image that had been taken of me in the morgue. "I don't know what to believe anymore," she whispered, like she was confessing a secret.

The anger burning through me cooled ever so slightly. And for the first time, I considered that maybe two things were true. She had failed me. And she had loved me fiercely. Like Abraham must have, while he held the knife.

I let myself sink inside the memory of the photo, and watched my sisters and I coat our blonde hair and faces with "mud masks" from the soft, silty sand beneath our feet in the warm waters of the lake. Abish was laughing so hard, she squealed, "You're gonna make me pee my pants!"

"You can't! You're not wearing pants!" Eve cackled and whipped her muddy hair back and forth like some kind of head-banging mermaid.

I wrapped myself tight around the memory of pure bliss and belly laughter, watching my fifteen-year-old self float on the salty surface of the lake to fan out my hair, still giggling. It was a perfect day.

My sun-kissed, beautiful teenage self started up a game of Marco Polo, dashing through the waist-high water as Sariah closed her eyes. As she did, I turned to look at the flapping blue shade shelter, where my mother was sitting in a camp chair beside my napping father, an open book on her lap and her hand on top of his, watching us.

I moved away from the splashing, close enough that I could see my mother's serene smile, and her eyes behind her sunglasses. They were crinkled up in pure joy. Pure adoration.

After a few minutes, she stood, smoothed the front of her modest black swimming suit coverup, and set to work arranging a picnic of ham sandwiches, Capri Suns, and peanut butter cookies she'd made to bring on our trip. "Girls, I've got lunch for you!" she called, her smile widening as her four teenage girls came rushing back toward the shelter with excited squeals, then sat down on towels to wolf down the food without a thank-you. My father stretched in his chair, yawned, and put a hand on her back as he stood up. "Thanks, hon. That was great."

"Are there more cookies?" Fifteen-year-old me asked hopefully, wiping her hands on her swimming suit.

My mother, who had just pulled the last cookie out of the tin for herself, smiled and gave it to me instead. "You betcha. You girls have been playing so hard."

The Isabel in my memory flashed her a smile and took the cookie from her outstretched hand. "Will you and Dad come play with us? Chicken fight? *Please*?"

My mother hesitated, glancing at the book on her lap, open to pages two and three. I knew what she really wanted was to spend a few more minutes reading. And I knew the game was her least favorite, since her carefully styled hair would inevitably get wet and sandy.

But I also knew that she'd say yes.

"You're sure lucky I love you so darn much," she teased, taking off her swimsuit coverup and kicking off her flip-flops. "Come on then, let's go. You too, Corey." She nudged my father in the side.

Then, whooping like a child, she lifted her arms up and ran into the sparkling blue water, with us girls and my father following her with our own happy cries.

Later that day, we got raspberry shakes after my parents managed to drag us back to the vacation rental to clean up. Then my sisters and I stayed up far later than we were ever allowed at home, watching old *Little Rascals* movies on VHS.

I reluctantly drew back from the memory and searched my mind for others like it.

They glowed like stars emerging among thick clouds at night, endless and sparkling like something new, even though they'd been there all along.

The day I came home crying after school in third grade, because a boy on the bus kept pulling my hair. She got on the bus with me the next morning, the only mom I'd ever seen there, and told him very politely that if he ever did it again, she would ride the bus home with him to talk to his mom.

When I was eleven and embarrassed to buy my first bra, she took me to the store after hours—one of the women in our ward was the store manager—and let me try on every single one until I didn't feel ashamed.

The summer I turned fifteen and failed my driver's test twice. When I told her I wasn't trying again, she took me to an empty parking lot at six o'clock on a Saturday morning and set up orange traffic cones and a cinder block with googly eyes that she named "Judge Judy" so I could practice.

When I told her I hated her and meant it—really meant it—a few months after the incident with Dennis Beaumont. She made my lunch for school the next morning and added a note in the bag that said, "Still love you. Always."

When I turned eighteen and told her that I didn't believe in the Church anymore, and that I didn't want to attend on Sundays, she stood silent at the counter for what felt like an hour, preparing dinner. Then she put my favorite casserole in the oven and said quietly, "You'll still eat, won't you?"

The night I left home for good, and came back to grab a few more items of clothing. I found her on her knees in my bedroom, praying. "Just stop," I'd told her angrily. "Why are you doing that?" She stayed on her knees but lifted her chin in a mirror image of the same defiant look I was giving her. "I won't stop," she insisted, and her voice broke on the last word. "I don't know how to reach you anymore, but I have to believe that God does."

In the cemetery, an owl hooted softly, like a warning that dusk had fully arrived. I latched onto the sound of it to pull myself back from the sea of memories and into the present.

"Please forgive me, Isabel," my mother was murmuring.

I didn't know what she meant by that. I wished I could ask her. But even more than that, I wished I could tell her that I could finally see the stars through the clouds again.

And they were as beautiful as the clouds were dark.

"I know you tried, Mom," I said, holding onto those memories tight and tentatively laying my hand on her arm again.

This time, she didn't flinch away.

And this time, I didn't try to persuade her to think about Dennis Beaumont. I focused all my thoughts on those bright pinpricks of memory that lit up the sky through the darkness.

There was no way to tell if it worked. But after a few seconds, she took a shuddering breath and wiped her tears, eyelids moving back and forth in tiny movements like she was dreaming while she stared at my photo on the grave marker.

"Do it for me, Mom. Because you love me despite everything. Please," I whispered.

Her eyes flew open.

40

SABINA

I was a ball of nervous energy when I got in the car and headed out in the direction of the address "Amy Sue" had given me.

I didn't need to leave quite this early, but I couldn't stand staying at the Airbnb another second.

I kept picking up my phone to call Joel and Nadia, to tell them about the deleted messages from "Amy Sue" and the meetup tonight. Something stopped me every time, though.

I'd told myself I would do it as soon as I showered.

Now, I told myself I'd call them as soon as I got some food in my stomach. I was nearly sick with anticipation and jitters from the coffee I'd downed, and all of it was starting to make me question my own sanity. Was I really considering going to that address at 10:00 tonight? Clearly.

But I couldn't stop thinking, what if this was the lead that broke the case wide open? What if this was my chance? What if I did the safe thing, the reasonable thing—and never found out what happened to my daughter? Amy Sue's message had been clear. If I showed up with the police, she wouldn't talk.

I wavered back and forth, and I shoved my phone away at the last second before hitting CALL every time.

But I was going to have to make a choice soon. Because I was nearly out of time.

Against my better judgment, I took the long way as I drove out of the neighborhood, going past Dennis and Bunny's house.

I just wanted some sign they were home. To reassure myself that Dennis wasn't waiting for me at the address I'd popped into my Maps app. Best I could figure, this was probably technically against the rules of the bullshit restraining order they'd filed against me. But if I stayed in my car, I'd be a hundred feet away from their front door, surely? Besides, I rationalized, my Airbnb was in their damn neighborhood. And it wasn't like they'd be able to recognize me behind the tinted windows of my car.

My chest tightened as I drove along the empty road, and my skin prickled in warning as I glanced out the passenger window to see the shuttered windows, patchy lawn, and drooping branches of overgrown elm trees in the wooded backyard. There was no sign of Dennis or Bunny anywhere.

I slowed the car just a little, but as I did so, I noticed a flash of movement in my rearview mirror.

There was a white car turning onto the street maybe two hundred yards behind me.

I brought my own vehicle up to speed and continued driving.

My eyes flicked back to the rearview mirror as I approached a bend in the road. To my horror, the white car screeched into the Beaumonts' driveway at an angle, and Dennis Beaumont leapt from the driver's seat.

"Shit," I hissed.

I only caught a glimpse of his open-mouthed, red face stalking down the driveway and raising a fist in my direction before I rounded the corner. The interaction was enough to send my stomach churning dangerously. He was at home—for now. That was good. But he'd definitely seen me. That was bad. Was he about to call the police? Would I be in violation of the bogus injunction if

Dennis had managed to get a cell phone video of me on his street—potentially less than an exact hundred feet from his house?

"Stupid, stupid, stupid," I muttered to myself through clenched teeth as I pulled out onto the main road.

I pushed the interaction out of my mind. Right now, I needed to get a hold of myself—eat something—and then buckle down and make the phone calls.

I pulled into the nearest drive-thru and wolfed down a burger while I stared at the inky skyline, my fingers hovering over the dial button.

My mind felt like an overheating computer, stuck and slow while it tried to work through everything I'd thrown at it over the last few days.

Just reset, refuel for a few minutes, I told myself while I forced another bite of the bland chicken sandwich I'd ordered.

I chewed, swallowed, gritted my teeth, then hit dial before I could talk myself out of it.

Nadia picked up on the first ring. "Sabina! I'm so glad you called. Have you seen all the shares the new post has—"

"Yeah, I saw them. It's great …" I hurried to say, feeling bad for interrupting but even worse about the numbers on the car's clock. The meeting time was coming up fast. "I'm guessing you didn't see the direct messages we got on Facebook before they disappeared?"

There was a short pause. "No, I don't think so?"

I took a steadying breath and filled her in, starting with how I'd assumed Amy Sue was another bot—like "Jenny Johnson"—and then realized that the address was near the underpass right as the messages disappeared.

I wasn't sure what kind of reaction I expected. But when Nadia let out a long breath and said, "I don't know what to think, except that we probably should take this to the police," I knew instantly, forcefully, that it was the wrong thing to do. That certainty didn't make sense, because I'd toyed with the same thoughts ever since I'd seen that message.

Of course we should tell the police. Surely they'd be able to handle this situation better than two untrained women who were playing detective.

And yet.

"She said she won't talk if the police show up," I argued feebly, even though I knew I'd already mentioned this detail. "I was hoping that … you'd go with me. I just get the feeling that this 'Amy Sue' person might—"

Nadia cut me off. "Sabina, *no.*" And for the first time, I heard fear in her voice. "I still can't believe you went to that underpass by yourself. Ogden is pretty safe, but that area isn't a good part of town."

I ignored her concerns. "What about your husband? Would he come—"

"No," Nadia said firmly, her voice rising a little. "We had a fight tonight," she added, tone softening. "He thinks all of this has gotten way out of hand. He's the second counselor in the bishopric in our ward, and some of the people at church on Sunday … well, they're upset about the tone of the Facebook page. They think it reflects badly on the Church, since both girls were Mormon."

I opened my mouth to reply, but no words came out. I couldn't believe this was even a factor.

"I stood up to him," Nadia said defensively, even though I hadn't said a word. "I think he's dead wrong—that's why we had the fight. But he's not going to be any help," she muttered.

"Please," I said, not even trying to soften the fact that I was begging now. "She said she knows something about both Andrea and Isabel. What if she's telling the truth? What if …?"

My throat closed around the words I couldn't say out loud. *What if this is our chance? What if I never find my daughter?*

"And what if 'Amy Sue' is some creep? What if it's Dennis?" Nadia countered. "I'm sorry, but we need to call the police so they can—"

"No!" I cried, shouting into the phone so loudly that I wouldn't have blamed her for hanging up on me. "Let's just think about it a little longer, okay? We have time," I lied.

"When is this meeting supposed to happen?" Nadia asked.

I hesitated for a fraction of a second. I'd left that part out intentionally. "Midnight, tonight If you still want to call the police by eleven, then we'll do it. That's plenty of time for them to get to the address."

I winced, hating that I was lying to her about the meeting time. Nadia had been so kind, so helpful. And if I were in her shoes, I'd probably want to call the police too—and stay the hell away from that apartment complex. But in my shoes? I couldn't help but believe Nadia would make the same choice I was about to.

I would be careful. I would have my phone with me, and the police would be just a call away.

And I wouldn't be alone, either.

My daughter might be dead, but she wasn't gone. And I was scared shitless, but it was the least I could do for her.

Nadia sighed into the phone. "All right," she relented. "But I'm not changing my mind. Whoever this person is needs to talk to the police, not us. What does Joel think?"

"I haven't told him yet," I said truthfully. "But I need to. I'll talk to you later tonight, okay?"

I hung up with Nadia and stared at my phone. Joel would be even more insistent that I loop in the cops. He'd call them himself if I told him what I was planning to do. Still, I needed his support—and a lifeline to safety—more than ever. So I took a deep breath and made the call.

He answered on the first ring, and the sound of the familiar voice I loved so much almost made me abandon the half-truth I planned to tell him.

Almost.

Squeezing my eyes shut, I blurted out, "I'm meeting up with someone tonight who says they have information about Isabel. Nadia can't come, and the apartment complex looks kind of rundown. Will you come with me—on speakerphone—until I know I'm safe?

He hesitated, and I could feel him wrestling with how to respond. Even with all the information I'd left out, this meetup sounded borderline dangerous.

"Of course I will," he said after a long moment. "You know I will. Usual code?"

Relief washed over me. We'd done this before, at family functions and social gatherings. Three quick throat-clearings meant *I'm okay, all good.* Three quick coughs meant *SOS, get me out of here.*

41

ISABEL

My dad—and my sisters, and their children—pulled into the driveway a little after 9:00, shortly after my mother and I got home from the cemetery.

When I heard the twist of the doorknob and the sound of solemn voices coming up the front walkway, I felt so nervous, I could barely contain the frenetic energy thrumming through me. It made the dishwasher beep erratically and the plants hanging from macrame holders sway gently above our heads, but my mother hardly noticed. She'd been like this ever since the cemetery. It was as if she'd retreated inside herself.

Both of us sat frozen in the dark living room, sitting on an uncomfortable-looking brown leather sofa that I'd never seen before—as the door burst open without a knock.

There they were, swarming inside and turning on lights to illuminate the room, like my memories brought to life.

I stood close to my mother as my sisters hugged her, imagining that they were putting their arms around me, too. How much had they thought about me while I'd been gone? Had they talked about me? Cried about me? Or had I lived in the silences where all the unspeakable things seemed to go in our home?

My father looked exactly like I remembered, except for the white hairs creeping into his hairline. His eyes were red, like he'd had a long day of travel. Or had been crying, maybe. I couldn't remember ever seeing him cry. He stood beside my mother and sisters as they hugged, his hand on Eve and Sariah's shoulders, his mouth in a tight line that trembled the tiniest bit at the corners.

Abish, who was clearly very pregnant, her blonde hair longer than I'd ever seen it, held the hand of a familiar lanky, bearded man with kind brown eyes. Brady Oaks, all grown up, I realized after a moment. When was her baby due? How had Brady proposed? Where did she live now? I wanted so desperately to ask her these questions.

Sariah looked so much like my mother, I couldn't stop staring. Right down to the cardigan she wore buttoned up to the neck. Her husband, a firefighter named Rob, wasn't here, but I'd caught a glimpse of her three little girls—maybe two, five, and six years old —before they had hurried upstairs to play. They looked like carbon copies of my sisters and me.

Eve had cut her hair short into a chic pixie that made her cheekbones look like cut glass. She held a bald, wiggly, wide-eyed baby girl in her arms who was squawking at being left out by the three children who had hurried upstairs to play. "Just a few minutes," Eve called after them tiredly. "It's already past bedtime." But the girls were already out of earshot.

"You're beautiful," I told the baby, reaching for her impossibly tiny hands and wishing I could kiss her chubby cheeks.

She stopped fussing and struggling on Eve's lap, and her rosebud lips made a little "O" as her tired eyes opened wide and stared right at me in wonder.

"I'm your aunt," I told her, and then, on impulse, I made a silly face like I'd see photographers do when they tried to get a little kid to smile.

Her face broke into a wide smile, and she reached for my outstretched hand.

When her delicate fingers failed to grasp mine, her fine blonde brows crinkled in frustration, and she wriggled on Eve's lap.

She sees me! I wanted to call to everyone excitedly. *She actually sees me!*

But in an instant, the moment was over and the baby had busied herself with reaching up and trying to grab a handful of Eve's short hair.

They were so alive and together, it hurt to look at them as they huddled in the living room, talking about funeral plans in hushed voices.

"It's late, so we can talk more tomorrow," my mother was saying, her voice a barely audible monotone. "But Sister Hendrix will take care of the flowers. Really, everything is taken care of ..." She trailed off, then forged on. "Sister Anderson—the Relief Society President—is handling all of the food. She did a wonderful job with the Merrick boy's funeral ... she just needs to know how many people will be coming into town, but I told her we wanted to keep the funeral small and quiet."

She looked up sharply at Abish, as if expecting pushback.

Abish pursed her lips and laced her fingers tighter through Brady's hand, but didn't say anything. As she shifted on the couch, I was shocked to notice two piercings at the top of her left ear. Two discreet gold rings that blended in with her hair. While multiple piercings weren't technically disallowed for members of the LDS church, they were definitely frowned upon, and I wouldn't have expected it from Abish. I wanted so badly to ask her about them—and to know what my mother thought she might have to say about keeping my funeral small and quiet.

"For hymns, I was thinking 'I Know That My Redeemer Lives,'" Eve said. Her voice wavered. "We sang that one together in primary one time, and I know she liked it."

I bristled. I didn't want any hymns. But maybe that didn't matter. Funerals were for the living.

"Yes, that would be nice," my mother said absently, folding her hands in her lap.

Abish squeezed her husband's hand tighter and cleared her throat. Her eyes were blazing. "I still don't understand how she was living right here in Ogden and we had no idea. And I'm sorry, but Izzy wouldn't have done drugs. She knew better."

"Yes, yes," I exclaimed, shooting Abish a grateful look I knew she couldn't see.

My mother didn't respond for a moment, and I rushed to her side. This was her chance to bring up the idea of the autopsy. I reached out to place a hand on her arm like I had at the cemetery. "Please. Please, Mom." I was so sure we'd connected earlier, that she might at least be considering it, softening. And now Abish was bringing up doubts. Surely she'd say something.

Instead, my father spoke up. "We never thought she'd do a lot of things, Abish. All I know is that Heavenly Father has the answers. We need to have faith that—"

"You'd *have* answers in this life if you did an autopsy!" I yelled, and the baby on Eve's lap began to cry hard, like she'd been pinched.

"Sorry," I whispered, but she just looked at me with wary, tear-filled eyes.

"If people ask questions at the funeral … about Isabel's death … you can remind them that the funeral is about remembering her as our daughter—and sister—who we will see again one day." My mother clasped her shaking hands tight together as she said the last part, like it was the glue holding her together.

I listened in a daze while my father took up the baton again and relayed the details about where I would be buried, two graves down from my grandparents in the family plot.

My eyes went to a photo of the Salt Lake temple hanging above the red brick mantel. The rest of the living room had been redecorated in soft grays and whites instead of the pastel blues that I remembered. But this photo, at least, was familiar. It had been taken at Sariah's wedding. I stood on the edge of the wedding party, unsmiling, looking like I was about to come out of my skin in the dress my mother had insisted I wear.

It wasn't a great photo of anyone except Sariah and her husband, glowing in their wedding attire. But still, it hung on the mantel.

I realized it must have been the last family photo taken before I'd run away.

My dad cleared his throat. "I'd like to offer a prayer to set the tone as we go through this hard time together."

Everyone bowed their heads except me and the baby, who stared at me in fascination from her mother's lap, fussing softly.

And Abish. She kept her eyes open and her chin up as she looked around the room, tears running down her cheeks as she shook her head.

I couldn't read her mind, but I could read her emotion.

She was sad, like the rest of my family. But she was brimming with frustration, too.

My father cleared his throat. "Heavenly Father," he began, his voice thick. "Our hearts are heavy, but we come before Thee in faith. We are grateful for the plan of salvation, for the knowledge that families are forever. We are most grateful for Thy Son, Jesus Christ, who died that we might see our daughter Isabel again. We ask for the Spirit to guide us, and we ask for Thy comfort and blessings at this time. We say these things in the name of our Savior Jesus Christ—"

I stood abruptly as the sound of their "amens" filled the living room. Not because I was upset, but because my dad's prayer just gave me an idea of how to reach them.

It was a long shot, but long shots were all I had left.

42

ANDREA

It wasn't until Sabina lied to Nadia about the time of the meeting with "Amy Sue" that I knew for sure she was actually going to the meeting.

That's when I started to get scared.

I told myself she'd have Joel with her—on speakerphone, at least. But I couldn't shake my sense of unease.

The moment I saw that address on the map Sabina pulled up—right by the cemetery, not far from the underpass—I knew it was important. The address wasn't very far from the place where Isabel had died. Maybe this person had seen something all those years ago that would be able to link Dennis Beaumont to Isabel's death, and set the dominoes falling.

That was what I was hoping, at least. A best-case scenario.

But even in a best-case scenario, it still wasn't a good idea for Sabina to go out there by herself. I'd been so sure that Nadia would come along. If "Amy Sue" was Dennis, she was in danger. So far, he'd been skulking in the background, watching her every move. But when would he decide she was getting too close to connecting the dots? What would he do then?

Cornered animals were prone to bite.

All I really knew was that he was still following her—keeping tabs on where she went—but from a distance. It had been no accident that he just "happened" to be behind her in the neighborhood while she drove past his house.

What exactly was he waiting for?

I suspected I knew the answer to that question. He was making sure he knew just how hot or cold she was getting to finding answers. That idea was terrifying all by itself. But the real terror lay in the question, what would happen when she got too close?

I was desperate to talk to Isabel again, but I made myself wait until I really needed her. She was doing something important, too. I needed to give her space.

Sabina crumpled the wrapper of her sandwich and glanced at the clock for the umpteenth time: 9:31 p.m.

The pressure valve inside me was hovering near red. It was all I could do not to let my jumbling emotions spill out and turn the check-engine light on uselessly. I didn't want to waste that ghost juice. Not when I might need it later. Because tonight was important. I just knew it.

Then an idea floated to the front of my mind.

If Dennis *was* Amy Sue, maybe I could find out—and warn Sabina.

If Dennis *wasn't* Amy Sue—then I could distract him before he realized what Sabina was up to.

Which meant I needed to pay a visit to Dennis.

I frowned, pulling up the memory of the map Sabina had loaded on her laptop earlier, routing the course to Amy Sue's address. Yes, I could find my way there alone if I had to.

Then, with my mind made up, I checked the time on the car's dashboard one more time—9:34—and squeezed my body through the tiny crack in the passenger window, watching in fascination as my arms and legs dripped through it, bit by bit like water.

I ran the half mile from the fast-food drive-thru back to Dennis and Bunny's house, moving as fast as I could go, not stopping until I slid through the crack in the screen door and stood in front of the banged-up microwave in their dingy kitchen. I came to a stop just in time to watch the clock change from 9:34 to 9:35. I already knew I was inhumanly fast, but I didn't know I was *that* fast.

"Just leave it alone, Dennis," came the rusty-hinge whine of Bunny's voice, coming from the living room.

"Why the hell should I? She won't damn well leave us alone," he shot back, followed by the sound of a fist hitting a wall.

From the sound of it, they were talking about Sabina's drive-by ten minutes earlier. I bristled at the sound of them fighting. There were a hundred memories baked into my subconscious that sounded exactly the same. From the way Bunny had always talked, I got the feeling they'd genuinely liked each other at one point. Based on our smiles in the few family photos that had been taken of me as a baby, they looked happy enough. But I'd never actually seen them hug or hold hands or say "I love you" to each other, and they'd definitely never kissed.

Sometimes I'd wondered if that was because of Dennis's nighttime visits to my bedroom.

Meeting Isabel and learning about her experience with him confirmed what I already knew: He was a fucking pedophile.

I walked into the living room to face them, my disgust boiling hot at the surface.

Bunny sat on the couch, cringing away from Dennis, wringing her hands on the knees of her ratty pink robe. Dennis stood above her, rubbing a reddened fist tenderly.

The wall behind the couch, maybe a foot from Bunny's head, had a telltale, fist-shaped indentation where the drywall and paint cracked in little spiderwebs.

There were plenty more like it throughout the house.

"Don't you tell me what to do. You're the one who let that bitch in our house in the first place, probably gave her the idea that we had something to do with Andrea running away. If you'd used your goddamn brain …"

They eyed each other in wary silence, and I got the feeling that this argument had been going on since Dennis saw Sabina drive past their house.

"Just let it be," Bunny muttered after a long silence. "I'm sorry I let her inside. I shouldn't have done that." To my surprise, tears sprang to her eyes and her lower lip began to tremble. "I'm sorry, Denny. I don't wanna fight."

Dennis grunted and waved her off, pulling his phone out of the pocket of his jeans to check the screen. I tensed, ready to distract him—and reining back the wave of emotion as hard as I could at the last second. He'd already seen her car drive by. If he saw she was just going to get a bite to eat, that was good.

A five-minute-old notification in a blue bubble had appeared on his lockscreen, with the words, "BITCH is on the move." A second notification beneath it declared, "BITCH IS AT 2781 E. 37 S., DEL POLLO SABROSO."

He rolled his eyes and shoved the phone back in his pocket.

Bunny hefted herself to her feet and edged around him with careful steps, like he might lunge at her. Then she shuffled toward the stairs. When she got to the landing, she stopped and turned to face Dennis. "That lady's barking up the wrong tree giving us all this hassle, but you know what?" Her lower lip trembled. "She's doing a hell of a lot to try to find Andrea."

Dennis didn't answer.

Bunny stared at him for a moment longer as she stood there. Then, in a voice so quiet I barely heard it, she added, "What if she didn't run away after all, Denny?"

For reasons I couldn't explain, hearing that made me want to cry.

* * *

I watched Dennis like a hawk for the next twenty minutes, finding a way to distract him every time he reached for his phone to check the screen.

It was working, too. The time was currently 9:55 p.m., which meant that Sabina would be arriving at the apartments any second. And Dennis had no idea.

That was good.

And even better? Dennis didn't seem to have any intentions of leaving the house tonight. With each passing minute, I felt more confident that he *wasn't* Amy Sue.

I was terrified for Sabina all the same. Who was this person she was meeting? What were they about to tell her?

All I knew was that the man who had murdered me and Isabel was standing right in front of me. And for right now, the best thing I could do to protect Sabina was by keeping him so occupied he wouldn't check that phone screen and see where she'd gone.

When Dennis had finished his argument with Bunny, he stalked outside to the shed.

The second he reached for his phone, I managed to burn out the single bulb that hung overhead.

When he hauled out a ladder to change it—without turning off the light switch—I somehow managed to send a pulse of electricity through the element that shocked him so badly, he swore out loud, then went pinwheeling backward. The ceiling in the shed was low enough that he was only two rungs high on the ladder, but he still landed hard on his tailbone with a satisfying crunch and a howl that brought Bunny rushing all the way over to the shed.

She stood in the doorway squinting into the darkness, looking him up and down, eyes flicking to the ladder in annoyance. I studied the faint crow's feet and marionette lines of her face and wondered for the first time how much younger she was than Dennis. As a kid growing up, they'd always both just looked standard-parent old to me. But now that I looked at Dennis's weathered, liver-spotted head and saggy neck compared to Bunny's skin, I realized she might be significantly younger than he was.

I still hated her. She hadn't ever lifted a finger to keep Dennis away from me while I was alive, and I was convinced that she knew what he was up to. But after what she'd said to him in the living room about hoping that Sabina found me, I was finally convinced she had no idea Dennis had murdered me. Maybe he'd even hurt her, too.

When Bunny realized Dennis wasn't seriously injured, she heaved a sigh and walked away without helping him up.

Dennis swore some more and struggled to his feet. When he'd finished successfully changing the "damn lightbulb," he reached for his phone again.

I managed to send a teetering saw blade hanging above the workbench clattering down in his direction, scattering tools and nails.

"Goddammit," he cursed, eyes wide as he studied the saw blade that had landed mere inches from his arm. "What the fuck is going on?"

A tiny shadow scurried a few inches from his hand as he picked up a fallen wrench from the clutter on the workbench and hung it on one of the hooks that lined the wall.

When I leaned closer, I saw a large brown spider with long, delicate legs hunched in a defensive position inside one of the dusty work gloves on the counter.

I leaned as close as I could to the greasy, hair-clotted entrance to Dennis's ear. It was about a million times more revolting than the spider, but I pressed my lips so close that I was practically cozied up beside his eardrum. Then I whispered, "I should put on gloves, so I don't get splinters while I clean up this mess."

For a few seconds, he didn't seem to react. Just grabbed a rusty screwdriver, examined it, then hung it beside a few others on the wall.

Then he grabbed the nearest glove, wriggled his meaty hand inside—and roared.

He yanked the glove back off, and his eyes nearly bugged out of his head when he saw the enormous brown spider scuttle down his arm to the workbench.

I watched with satisfaction as his hand swelled up around a painful-looking bump and he spent the next half an hour hefting the bench back and forth in an attempt to locate the spider.

When he gave up and kicked the workbench, sending the screwdriver clattering behind it out of reach, he put a hand into his pocket to grab his phone.

This time, it was harder to harness the emotion in time.

I managed to make the spider reappear at his feet just in time to make him set the phone down—and grab a wrench.

"Shit," I whispered, staring at the notification on the lockscreen of his phone.

BITCH is at 4900 S., 80 E. announced the little blue bubble.

43

ANDREA

I froze and stared at Dennis, who was bent over kicking the retreating shape of the spider, which had leapt onto the floor.

Could I make the little blue bubble disappear from the lockscreen if I concentrated hard enough?

I already knew that the answer was no. I'd been working so feverishly to distract him, I was running dangerously low on ghost juice. Sort of empty and tired. But I tried anyway.

I focused my attention on the now-dark phone screen first, conjuring up memories of that hole Dennis punched in the wall. His disgusting ear. Bunny saying she wished I'd come with a return policy.

With a little luck, he'd go inside to ice his spider bite, pour himself a mug of the Ovaltine he loved so much, and go to sleep.

My luck had run out, though.

As Dennis snatched the phone from the workbench on his way out of the shed, he hit the side button to light up the screen.

The message was right there, glowing blue.

BITCH IS ON THE MOVE.

I slammed myself into his ear. "She's not worth the trouble. Leave it alone. Ice that hand, drink some Ovaltine!" I demanded with as much energy as I could muster.

He did no such thing. Instead, his eyes narrowed beneath his sparse, graying brows and he opened up the app to view the path of the location tracker.

"Slippery bitch," he hissed, his voice a mix of shock and—unless I was imagining it—worry.

His face darkened and he hurried inside, grabbed the keys to the car without so much as a goodbye to Bunny, then rushed to the driveway.

As the tires zipped backward down the driveway, I threw myself into his car through the tiny crack between the back door and the window.

There was no doubt in my mind that he was headed straight for Sabina.

"No, no, no!" I screamed, but the sound was hollow even to my own ears.

"You've gone just about far enough," he muttered at the phone notification angrily, yanking the gear shift into drive then zooming through the empty streets in the direction of that blinking dot on the app's map.

"No! Go back home," I screamed at him in desperation. "Leave her alone!"

I scrambled to harness the rage, the disgust, the horror that had been fueling me for the past twenty minutes.

Hardly anything happened, though. No sirens. No check-engine light on his car. No shutdown of his phone, no incoming call from my old cell phone number. Just a flicker of the check-engine light.

I was all burned out. No more pressure, no sparks of electricity burning inside me. Only an empty nothingness.

Every part of me screamed that something bad was about to happen. But there wasn't much I could do about it at the moment.

I needed Isabel.

44

ISABEL

My family had always been the "early to bed, early to rise, makes a man healthy, wealthy and wise" type. And thankfully, today was no exception.

By nine-thirty, everybody was tucked into bed and the house had settled into an uneasy silence. Abish, Eve, and Sariah slept in their old rooms, their daybeds replaced by queens. The toddlers slept in Pack-and-Plays, in what had once been my room.

As I moved down the dark hallway, I felt a sharp tug and a falling sensation that warned me I was about to be drawn back into the church-pew memory with Andrea.

Only this time, I resisted it forcefully, focusing hard on the soft-looking gray carpet beneath my feet that had replaced the beige I remembered from before, the pretty glass chandelier that now hung in the hallway, the photos of my sisters' smiling children that lined the walls.

And to my surprise, it worked. I didn't get sucked back into the memory.

I felt bad about it. I knew Andrea needed me, and I wanted to be with her. But this was important, too, and I didn't know how long it would take.

"Just hold on a little longer," I muttered to nobody in particular, then hurried down the hall toward Abish's room.

I would start with her and move as quickly as I could.

She lay in the queen bed beside her husband, curled up in a ball on the edge of the mattress. His hand lay a few inches away from her back, like he'd been reaching for her—and she'd rolled away from him—right before they fell asleep. In the dimly lit room, I could barely make out her features pinched in a frown, but her chest rose and fell steadily.

Repeating exactly what Andrea and I had done the night before with Sabina, I snuggled up next to my sister and put my lips to her ear.

"Hi, Abs," I whispered. "I need you to listen to me, okay? It's Isabel." Then I wrapped my arms around her and focused as hard as I could on the memory I wanted us to relive, hoping it would work. Neither of us had participated in the memory directly, but the story was so ingrained in our family's lore that I felt like I had.

My parents had told the story so many times while we were growing up—during Family Home Evening or testimony meetings—that it felt like part of my DNA, like one of my own memories even though I wasn't even there when it happened.

When my parents were newly married and Sariah was a baby, they lived in Elk Ridge, a newer community out in the foothills of southeastern Utah. It was the middle of January, a Sunday before church, and there was a skiff of snow in the forecast. A freezing cold, miserable winter day, but nothing to worry about.

As my mother told the story, Sariah was a crying mess that morning. Two blowouts through two dresses and her special fuzzy blankie, and no morning nap. By the time they got her loaded up in the car to make the twenty-minute drive to the chapel, there was no way to avoid being late to church. And my mother hated being late to anything, especially church.

But as they pulled out of the driveway and started down the lane that led into town, my mother had a prompting from the Spirit.

Words that struck her as clear as if my father had said them. *Go back for a blanket.*

It was a strange thought. Sariah's baby blanket—the one she loved—was in the wash. And the only other baby blanket at home was a thick, too-big thing that would be a little unwieldy to carry around during the three-hour church meeting. And besides, Sariah was already starting to fuss in her car seat. They should keep driving.

But the Spirit whispered again. *Go back for a blanket.*

When she told my father, he looked at her strangely and said, "You know, I was just having the exact same thought. Let's just get the blanket."

So they did. Then they got back in the car and headed to church, arriving nearly half an hour late.

During the meeting, the predicted flurries of snow started— and worsened—into a storm that turned Elk Ridge into a snow globe. The bishop actually ended the church meeting an hour early, so that everyone could make it home, since the blizzard showed no sign of stopping anytime soon.

My parents and baby Sariah had made it halfway home when the car's brakes locked as my father tried to slow down for a stop sign, sending the car into a skid that sent them spinning into a rocky ditch.

Nobody was hurt, but the brakes were completely shot, so my father killed the engine.

Then he went into the blizzard for help while my mother huddled in the car with Sariah in the freezing car.

Things might have gotten bad fast if it hadn't been for that big, thick blanket that covered them both up snugly while they waited nearly two hours for my father to return with help—and find the spot on the long highway where the car had gone off the road, since the snow had completely covered the ruts where we slid.

While she waited, my mother said a grateful prayer. When she told the story to our family later, she always added, "Never ignore a prompting from the Holy Spirit. It doesn't matter if it's inconvenient, or strange. You listen."

When I was finished, I watched the rapid flutter of Abish's eyes, moving back and forth behind her lids while she slept. Then I nudged forward one last memory. A brief flash, from a weekend when I was ten years old and had fallen off my bike while riding through the neighborhood. My wrist had popped backwards in a sick crack when it hit the cement, and even the motion of walking had hurt it while I made my way home.

When I finally opened the front door and came inside, I could hear everyone in the kitchen, bustling around and getting lunch ready.

"I need help, I'm hurt!" I cried from the entryway, voice wobbling and tears finally rushing down my cheeks now that I'd made it home. "I fell off my bike."

Eve came into the hallway first, and her eyes went to my scratched-up knees. My parents were behind her. "Aw, let's get you some Band-Aids," she said.

"I think I need a doctor," I cried, holding up my throbbing wrist so they could see the angle it was hanging at.

"Oh, Isabel!" my mother had cried, rushing to me as my father went for the car keys. "Hurry, we need to go to the hospital now."

Abish whimpered softly in her sleep as I let the memory fade, then rolled onto her left side and reached for her husband's hand. She sighed when she found it, but her brows stayed creased in worry.

I lingered a little longer with my hand on her cheek. "Are you listening, Abs? I need your help. They need to do an autopsy on me, okay? It's important." I wrestled with the sadness rising up in me, not wanting the smoke alarm to start beeping or something. "I love you so much. I missed you every single day that I was gone. I think you missed me, too."

A sudden spinning, falling feeling gripped me, and I could feel Andrea trying to call me into the church-pew memory with her again.

I resisted being pulled into the memory again, focusing hard on the star-shaped gold of Abish's ear piercings, the soft blonde of her hair spread across the pillow to ground me in the present.

"I'm sorry, Andrea," I murmured guiltily. "I'll hurry."

Then I rushed into the next room where my parents were sleeping and repeated what I'd just done with Abish.

My father, as stoic in sleep as he was awake, barely reacted. The only indication I was getting through to him happened when I showed him the memory of my broken arm—and his mouth turned down in a deep frown.

I expected the same from my mother, given how she'd shut down after the cemetery. But the moment I moved to her side of the bed and lay my hand on her shoulder, she began to tremble, tears slipping down her cheeks like winding rivers. When I reached the memory of my broken arm, she whispered the words out loud with me. "Oh, Isabel! Hurry, we need to go to the hospital now."

My heart cracked open, and I lay my cheek against hers. "That's right, Mom. I need you."

Her tears came faster. "Is … is he the one who hurt you?" she asked in a halting, childlike whimper.

I froze, hardly daring to believe what she'd said. Was she talking about Dennis Beaumont? "Yes. Dennis is the one who hurt me."

Her whimper stretched into a thin sob and her eyes squeezed shut tight, like she was bracing for some kind of impact. "He hurt you. And I didn't help you. Oh, Izzy, I'm so sorry. I'm just so sorry. I love you so much."

"I love you too, Mom," I whispered back, needing to believe that when she woke up, she'd remember this moment. Then I hurried on to Sariah's room.

There were no guarantees this would work—whispering the same memory to each of my family members while they slept. But I felt sure that if they woke up and realized they'd all had the same dream, it might be enough to convince them that the message of the dream was important.

The Spirit spoke through dreams, after all. I just hoped they'd understand what I was trying to convey:

Do what needs to be done, no matter how inconvenient.

And, *Isabel needs our help.*

It was the best I could think to do.

45

SABINA

With each step I took along the crumbling walkway that led to the dark apartment complex, I wondered if I should turn back.

The pepper spray I clutched in my right hand, and the phone I gripped in my left—with Joel listening silently on speakerphone—offered some comfort. So did the sparse street lights. But with every step I took, I braced for something or someone to leap out at me from the overgrown juniper bushes flanking the walkway that my shoulders were practically up to my ears.

The streets were quiet, the wind that had whipped through the night before just a whisper now, but somehow that made my hackles rise even more. In the distance, toward the cemetery and the underpass, I could hear the faint rush of traffic from I-84.

"Shit," I whispered as a cat trotted past without looking at me, hunching then diving into an opening in the bushes.

Something squeaked, then went silent. I clenched my teeth, whispered, "It's fine, just a cat," for Joel's benefit, and kept moving.

The complex hadn't looked particularly ominous from what I could see on Google maps. But now, in the dark, the structure loomed like a crouching animal. As I got closer, I caught the whiff of something that smelled like mildew and stale cooking oil, along with the faint scent of rot. One of the exterior lights was flickering just enough to make the row of mailboxes beneath it look like they were shuddering in a repeating stop-motion.

I clutched the pepper spray tighter as my eyes scanned the shadows for any sign that I'd walked right into some sort of trap set by "Amy Sue" or "Jenny Johnson."

I was hoping that the quilt-wrapped feeling would pull me close for a moment, make me believe that I wasn't really here alone, about to walk down a flight of concrete steps into a dimly lit breezeway.

But there was nothing.

Biting down hard on the inside of my cheek, I scanned the empty courtyard then hesitantly went down the steps.

I could barely make out a number eight in black wrought iron, hanging on the brick beside the nearest apartment door.

You can turn around and go home, offered a terrified voice in my mind, urging me to rush back to the car and drive back to the Airbnb.

But I knew better than to listen. The Airbnb wasn't home. Not really. Home was Oregon. Home was Joel. Home was the daughter I'd amputated from my life like a piece of my heart. And right now, this was the way back home—real home—knowing that I was trying as hard as I could to do right by her.

Before that terrified voice could get any louder, I hustled forward and knocked softly on the door, heart hammering.

For a few seconds, nothing happened.

Then a quiet clink as the knob turned, and the door opened a crack and I caught the smell of stale cigarettes. There wasn't a light on inside the apartment, and I took a step back even while I squinted to see the person hidden inside. "Hello? Are you—"

"Are you here by yourself?" A woman's voice cut me off. And she sounded absolutely terrified.

It wasn't Dennis. I let out a whoosh of breath and moved my finger away from the pepper spray. My hands were trembling so violently I was afraid I might depress the trigger by accident.

"Yeah, it's just me," I told her, glancing around to verify that the breezeway was still empty. I wasn't sure if I'd be more terrified by an invitation to come inside the apartment, or standing out here in the dark.

"You came. I didn't think you would after I deleted the message. My name's Rita," the woman whispered, opening the door to reveal herself.

Her close-set, black-lined eyes scrutinized me as she ran one hand self-consciously through her hair. It was dark at the roots, reddish at the ends, and her bangs hung across her forehead in a choppy fringe. She wore a tight-fitting green bomber jacket over a white tank top, and jeans with a rip across the thigh that showed a patch of skin on her skinny legs. After a few seconds, she seemed to have decided I'd passed some test and said, "Sorry I gave you a fake name," and opened the door a little wider to invite me inside.

"Sabina," I said, holding out a hand. The fear I'd felt a moment earlier melted into tentative hope.

My Spidey senses were telling me this woman wasn't dangerous. If anything, I needed to reassure *her* that *I* wasn't a threat. So for the moment, I held my tongue instead of releasing the stream of questions I was dying to ask.

I cleared my throat three times as Rita shut the apartment door, giving Joel the signal that I was okay. Then—knowing that Rita would freak out if she heard any kind of noise from Joel and realized I had someone on speakerphone—I carefully hit the side button to end the call. My heart clenched when I imagined Joel with that phone placed carefully in front of him, waiting for it to ring again when I was finished.

Rita pointed to a sagging sofa against the wall in the tiny, dark living area, inviting me to sit. "Sorry I have the lights off," she said. "I don't want anybody to think I have company this late."

I nodded and sat, resisting the urge to inspect the cushion before settling down. The smell of cigarette smoke in the apartment was powerful, mingling with the odor of old sweat.

Rita shot a suspicious glance at the phone in my hand as she took a seat beside me. "That thing's not recording, is it?"

"No, it's not. I promise," I told her, showing her the blank home screen, both relieved and disappointed that I hadn't thought of doing that very thing.

I opened my mouth to start asking questions, then shut it again. *Not yet. Let her talk.*

Neither of us spoke for an agonizing few seconds. Then, finally, Rita sighed and pulled her knees to her chest, drawing herself up into a ball on the couch. "Why do you care so much about Isabel?" she asked finally, and I could tell the answer mattered to her. "You aren't even from here. I looked through your Facebook profile."

I nodded slowly. "You're right. I didn't know Isabel's name until a few days back. I came to Utah because Andrea Beaumont is my daughter. I gave her up for adoption seventeen years ago." My voice caught. "I thought I was giving her a better life. But then I got a letter from the police that she was a missing person. And then … then I met Dennis and Bunny Beaumont. I'm pretty sure they did something to her," I said, trying to steady my voice. "I've been following every lead I can over the last few days, and one of those leads is Isabel Palphreyman. Dennis assaulted her when she was sixteen."

I watched out of the corner of my eye as I told her the bare bones of what I'd learned, looking for reactions.

She laced her fingers together tighter around her knees when I mentioned Andrea again. She shook her head, rocking back and forth slightly, when I said Dennis's name. When I mentioned Isabel's assault, she went completely still.

"Rita, why do you care so much about Isabel?" I asked her gently, turning the question around.

She didn't meet my eyes, just stared at the door, keeping her hands locked around her knees.

Then, in a choked voice she finally whispered, "Because it's my fault she's dead."

46

ANDREA

I slipped through the keyhole of the deadbolt in unit eight just in time to hear the woman sitting on the couch beside Sabina say the words, "Because it's my fault she's dead."

For a moment, all of my frantic energy evaporated. Because I knew this woman. Or at least, I recognized her. Rita was her name. She'd appeared in one of the memories Isabel had shown me, from the night that Dennis found her and attacked her.

This was the apartment where Isabel had lived for three years after she ran away from home. I'd recognized the breezeway immediately when I rushed to follow Sabina, and I just knew that if I went upstairs, I'd see a crooked number plate in front of unit four —Isabel's old apartment.

"Oh my gosh," I whispered, dumbfounded.

When "Amy Sue" sent that message earlier with this address, I hadn't recognized it. Isabel would have, but the address didn't ring any bells for me.

But now that I was here, looking at this woman, at the dirty carpet, at the bare walls in the apartment that looked nearly identical to the one that had been Isabel's, I was sure of where I was.

A fresh rush of panic surged through me, sweeping away the brief moment of calm.

Isabel needed to get here now. I didn't know how long it would take until I could flex my limited ghostly abilities again. All I knew was that I felt wrung-out, helpless, and desperate for help. But Isabel continued to shut me out.

This was important, though. Rita had seen Isabel the night she left. And whatever she was about to tell Sabina mattered enough that she'd gone to the trouble of sending that Facebook message, even though she was clearly terrified. Her face had gone white as a sheet, and one hand kept reaching for a pack of Marlboros lying beside an ashtray on the side table, then drawing back.

Sabina sat beside her on the couch with a calm expression on her face—but the energy of a coiled spring—waiting for Rita to speak.

Rita finally grabbed a cigarette with trembling fingers and shook her head. "I'm sorry, I just need a second. I think I might throw up," she whispered, then ran down the hallway.

Sabina stayed frozen where she sat, eyes wide as the sound of retching and then a flush came from the bathroom.

For a moment longer, I stayed frozen too, not sure what to do.

From the memories Isabel had shown me, I knew that Rita saw Isabel the night she slipped away from this apartment complex. She'd also seen the fresh bruises on Isabel's face. What else did she know? What else had she seen?

I was desperate to find out, but that wasn't the only pressing issue right now.

Sabina, and probably Rita, needed to be very, very careful. Because out there on the street, parked just around the corner from her car, was Dennis.

He was as scary as I'd ever seen him tonight, in the car on the way over here. And that was really saying something. Because I'd seen him choke the life out of me.

He knew Sabina was here, somewhere in this apartment complex. And if she was here, he knew she might actually be getting close to finding out the truth of what happened to Isabel.

And the truth of what happened to Isabel would unravel the truth of what happened to me.

Those sirens would be real if Sabina walked out of here with information that could directly link Isabel's death to Dennis.

And he wasn't going to let that happen.

On the drive here, he'd kept reaching for an extension cord lying on the passenger seat of the car, running his fingers along the length of it, and I knew all too well what Dennis could do with something like that.

"Shit," I whispered again.

I hesitated, torn between listening intently to what Rita was about to say, rushing back out onto the street where I'd left Dennis raging in the driver's seat of his white Accord, and trying to reach Isabel one last time.

I'd tried everything I could think of to dissuade Dennis from following Sabina on the car ride here—but he hardly even blinked at the faint flicker of the check-engine light. Just gritted his teeth, wrapped his hands around the steering wheel tight like he wished it was Sabina's neck, and kept fingering that extension cord on the seat beside him.

The toilet flushed again, and Sabina stood from the couch, calling out, "Are you okay? Do you need anything?"

"I'm okay. Just a second," came Rita's voice, then tentative footsteps along the carpet.

I finally made my move, rushing to grab hold of the memory of the church pews with Isabel.

This time, I didn't reach for her arm. I slapped her straight across her cheeks. "Isabel! You have to come *NOW*," I screamed at the teenage girl with the beautiful blonde hair and the modest

Sunday dress. "Dennis is coming for Sabina, right now! 'Amy Sue' is Rita. We're at your old apartment complex. I don't care what you're doing right now, I need your help!"

I thought I saw her mouth open into a surprised O before I drew back from the memory so I could listen to what Rita had to say.

I just hoped it was enough to get her here.

47

SABINA

If I hadn't actually heard Rita throwing up in the bathroom as soon as she ran down the hall, I might have chased her.

And when she came back with tears cutting smudged black trails down her cheeks from the thick mascara and eyeliner, I wanted to grab her by her skinny shoulders and demand she start talking. It was her fault that Isabel was dead? What the hell did that mean? *Tell me, please God, tell me now.*

Instead, I reached out a hand for hers and grasped it tightly. Her thin fingers were ice cold. My gut was telling me she'd had enough people push her around in her life. And if I started doing the same, she might disappear behind those hooded eyes again and ask me to leave.

So I held the stampeding horses in my mind back and squeezed her hand for a few seconds while she wiped her eyes and took a sip from the half-full glass beside her pack of Marlboros.

She swallowed hard. Looked at me. Then finally, finally, the words tumbled out of her. "I didn't know Isabel all that well. Not as well as I know some of the other girls here," she said in a low voice. "She was nice, though. Seemed like a sweet kid."

"When did she live here?" I asked.

Rita cocked her head and took another sip of water. She seemed to be calming down. "She was here for a few years, maybe three?" She held up her fingers and counted. "I remember the week she moved in, because it was Cassie's birthday, and she got some wine for everybody after we were done for the night. Isabel stayed in her apartment. The other girls thought she was rude, but I think she was just scared. She was only a baby." She sighed sadly. "This isn't any place for a girl like that."

"What kind of place is this?" I asked, pretty sure I already knew.

Rita looked down at her hands, rolling the unlit cigarette back and forth. "You know," she muttered. "Us girls see ... we see clients here."

She flicked her eyes to meet mine for the briefest moment, and I nodded. "I get it," I said softly, needing her to know that I understood—and that I wasn't judging her.

Rita shrugged. "There's plenty of worse places, and the guys who run this place aren't so bad. They don't have to give us our own apartments. One girl—Misty—stayed someplace in Nevada where they were packing *five* girls into a one-bedroom, using the couch for tricks, making them take clients at all hours of the night." She picked at a loose thread unraveling from the couch. "It's better than living on the street, especially in the winter. Pays for food and some extra stuff. Could be a lot worse."

She said the last part so quietly I barely heard it. My heart was starting to pound as I considered where this story might go, and how it might involve my daughter. Had Andrea been to this place? I'd never even met Isabel, but my heart ached when I thought about her living here, taking "clients."

When Rita didn't go on, I squeezed her hand again.

She drew in a deep breath, let it out, and continued. "I had this pretty regular client. Middle-aged white dude who wheezed when he got ... uh ... worked up. So that was his name. Wheezy. Not that I ever called him that, or anything else, to his face." She gave me a side eye. "He liked the younger girls a lot, so the managers always sent him to my apartment. He didn't come by very often … maybe a couple times a year?"

I didn't react, even though my stomach was flipping. I just nodded and studied her downturned face more closely. I'd been thinking she was at least forty years old based on the makeup, the fine smoker's lines ringing her mouth, and the way she was dressed, but when I looked at her hands—slender and baby smooth —and the set of her brows and jaw, I realized that she might not be much older than mid to late twenties.

She tugged harder on the thread coming from the couch. "So yeah, Wheezy wasn't like a regular or anything. There's dudes who stop by twice a week. But this guy? I thought about him all the time, even if he wasn't here. Because he was the worst. Really rough, really rough. And he had this smell …" She trailed off, and I knew better than to ask questions by the pained expression on her face. "He always did this weird little knock on the door, two short knocks, then a couple of knocks with long pauses in between. So I'd know it was him, I guess. I wanted to throw up whenever I heard it. Could already hear the sound of him breathing."

I couldn't stop myself from asking. "Was the guy … was that Dennis?"

She looked up sharply, and her eyes bored into mine like she was trying to read my thoughts. Like she was trying to decide whether she'd made a huge mistake and wanted to push me out the door instead of answering the question directly.

"He never told me his actual name," she said. "But he was one of a kind. Had these big old meaty hands, rough nails like he'd bitten them off instead of using clippers. A nasty beard and a greasy combover. And he had dark spots all over his head that looked like cancer or something." She made a disgusted face.

Dennis. That's Dennis. He was here.

My hands were shaking now. I pulled them into my lap and stayed quiet, not wanting Rita to stop talking even though I was terrified to hear what she was about to say next.

"Then one night, I heard that same knock—only it wasn't on *my* door. It was up there. Above me." She pointed to the ceiling. "I figured maybe I got too old for him, and he'd asked the managers to give him somebody younger." She let out a shuddering sigh. "I was relieved, you know? That Wheezy didn't want me anymore. Somebody else's problem."

My stomach heaved violently, and I wrapped my arms tight around my stomach.

Rita kept going, her voice small and thin. "It was Isabel's apartment. It … sounded bad in there, but that's how he liked things …" She drew in a ragged breath. "I waited until I heard the door slam overhead and he left. It was late by that point, so I didn't have any more customers for the night. For a while, I stood around smoking in the breezeway, trying to decide whether I should go upstairs and say something to Isabel." She looked up at me sharply, like I might be ready to scold her. "She'd been here a while by that time. It wasn't like she was the new girl or anything, but that guy was something else …"

She stopped talking then, finally giving up on the couch thread and holding up the unlit cigarette she'd been clutching in her palm. "I'm sorry, but do you mind? I need a smoke, and I don't wanna go out into the breezeway to talk."

"Do whatever you need, just please … please tell me what happened next," I begged.

She lit the cigarette and inhaled deeply, blowing the smoke toward the air-intake vent on her side of the couch. "I'd just decided I was gonna go back inside and mind my own business when I heard footsteps on the stairs—and saw Isabel coming down wearing a backpack. She looked … he'd messed her up real bad."

"Bad, how?" I whispered.

"Not much you could see on the outside. I think he bit her lip and her cheek. But I could see from the expression on her face … it was like she didn't want to live in her body anymore. She was trying so hard not to cry," Rita said quietly, taking another drag. "She told me she was leaving. Didn't want to come inside and talk to me, just wanted to run. Her eyes were huge, like a scared animal. She was terrified of that fucker." Her voice wobbled on the last word, and she squeezed her eyes shut and went silent.

I waited, but she didn't continue. I could hardly find the words past the rage licking at my ribs like red-hot flames but I managed, "Rita, that's not your fault. He was the one who hurt her—"

She balled her fists so tightly the knuckles went white. "I'm not finished."

48

ISABEL

I was in the middle of whispering dreams to Eve—she was the last person in my family I needed to reach—when I felt Andrea yank me into the church-pew memory with so much force I found myself face to face with her before I could resist the pull.

When I heard what she had to say, I stopped what I was doing and rushed out of Eve's bedroom, down the dark halls of my family's quiet home, and through the dark streets of my neighborhood at a dead run, scrambling to find my way.

If I'd been alive, it would've taken me hours to run that distance.

Tonight, it took only a few minutes.

When I finally saw the underpass, then the dark abyss of the cemetery in front of me a short distance away, I knew I was close. Just another mile. As I ran, I caught a glimpse of the pioneer women I'd seen earlier in the day. They stared at me curiously while I whipped past them, rushing through the silent cemetery and weaving around grave markers, coming out the other side onto the streets until I reached the apartments where I'd lived when Dennis Beaumont found me.

When I finally saw the familiar, squat eight-plex, I went straight to Rita's old apartment and slipped inside to find her sitting on the couch beside Sabina, and Andrea.

Her shaking fingers clutched a half-spent cigarette. And she'd just said the words, "What happened to Isabel is my fault."

I stared at her, dumbstruck, and moved closer to the couch, desperate to hear what she'd say next. She looked older than when I'd seen her last, heavier makeup and fine lines ringing her lips. We'd never been friends, really. The only reason I'd thought about her over the years was to regret taking that bag of goodfellas she'd thrust into my hands the night I left. If I hadn't had those drugs on me when the police found my body, would they have investigated my death more thoroughly? Would they have realized that someone had murdered me, and done forensic testing on my body, instead of stuffing me in a morgue's freezer then burying me in a Jane Doe grave when nobody came to claim me?

Was that what she meant by "What happened to Isabel is my fault"?

Andrea patted the small space next to her on the couch cushion where she was curled up beside Sabina. She looked exhausted—and terrified. I had a hundred questions for her. But Rita started speaking again.

"She didn't tell me where she was going or anything. And I didn't ask. But I had a pretty good guess. She didn't have a car, and there's an underpass maybe a mile that way." She waved a hand vaguely. "It's walking distance to a food bank. A lot of the girls who live in this complex have stayed there at one point."

When I heard that, I expected the wind to start howling outside, shaking the trees. Or at least for lights to start flickering, or the microwave to start beeping. But nothing happened. Instead, I just felt numb and depleted from spending the last hour filling my family's heads with dreams, trying as hard as I could to communicate with them.

My mind spun as I tried to process what I was hearing. Rita knew exactly where I'd gone when I left the apartment complex.

And from the stricken look on Andrea's face, she was thinking the same thing I was. That this must have been how Dennis had found me at the underpass.

I watched the realization spread across Sabina's face, too, as Rita kept talking. "He came back here a couple weeks after Isabel left." She swallowed and shook her head slowly, eyes on her lap. "Isabel was gone. So he was back here knocking on my apartment door."

Sabina didn't move. Her eyes shone with tears.

Rita blew out a cloud of smoke, not bothering to aim for the air-intake vent, but Sabina didn't flinch. "He was worse than ever … but I just told myself to get through it, same as I had before, and then he'd leave. But then he started asking about Isabel. The managers didn't know where she'd gone, and I doubt they cared. They'd replaced her with a new girl the day she left. Someone older, in her thirties. So obviously he didn't want her."

Sabina bit her lip hard, like it was taking everything in her to let Rita keep talking instead of bursting in with questions.

Rita shot her a pleading look. "I told him I didn't know where she went at first. Acted like I didn't even know who he was talking about. But he wouldn't leave without an answer … started saying that he'd hurt me if I didn't tell him. So … so I said maybe I knew where she went. I hated myself for it, but I was afraid. He was holding my arm so hard while he asked the questions, getting up in my face."

Rita clasped her hands together as if in prayer. "When I told him about the underpass, his eyes went … I don't know how to describe it. Sharklike, or something. Dead, black. It really scared me. And then he … he grabbed my throat so hard I thought he was gonna strangle me. Told me to forget I ever saw him. And, 'Forget you saw her, too, because if you don't, I'll make sure you disappear.' That's what he said. And that nobody would care that much about what happened to a 'filthy whore' like me." She snubbed the cigarette out on an ashtray then put her face in her hands and began to sob. "I'm sorry. I'm so sorry. I told myself she would be okay, and I didn't let myself think about either of them after that, because he never came around the apartments again. And then yesterday I was on my phone looking through Facebook and I saw your post …"

Andrea reached for my hand, and I took it, finding some comfort in the fact that she was reeling every bit as much as I was.

The numb feeling was threaded through with sadness and horror, but I didn't really blame Rita for what she'd done. Hell, he probably would have strangled her if she hadn't told him what he wanted to know.

I probably would've done the same thing if I'd been in her shoes. Anything to get him to leave. Anything to get those shark eyes and ragged fingernails out of my apartment.

I'd heard enough, though. There would be time to sort through this particular tangle of awfulness later. Because right now, the thing blaring through my mind like a tornado siren was what Andrea had shouted earlier, when she yanked me back into that memory. *"Dennis is coming for Sabina right now!"*

I felt the urgency of those words now. After listening to everything Rita had told Sabina, there was no question now that she was in real danger the moment she left this apartment. I could see from the way she sat, rigid and ready to jump off the couch and rush back to her car, that she knew Rita was the missing puzzle piece that tied my death to Andrea. The police would see it, too.

And so would Dennis. He knew about this particular puzzle piece better than any of us. And if he knew Sabina was talking to someone in this apartment complex—maybe was even watching to see movement in the breezeway by Rita's door—he knew full well that she might be learning information that would send him directly to jail.

And I was pretty damn sure he'd do whatever it took to keep that from happening.

"She needs to call the police right fucking *now*," I said.

"Yeah, I know," Andrea said with just a hint of reproach. "I tried everything I could to stop him while he was driving over here, but he's here, and he knows where her car is parked. He—he's going to do something bad, Isabel. There's nothing we can do." Her eyes were huge, and she kept shaking her head like she was in a daze. From holding her hand, I knew she was just as exhausted—and depleted as I was.

"Talk to her," I demanded. "Try again!"

"Call the police now, don't leave the apartment," Andrea begged, wrapping her arms around Sabina's shoulders and leaning closer to her ear. "Please, Mom. He's outside. He's going to hurt you."

But Sabina was still focused only on Rita. She moved her hand to her chest, where it rested perfectly square on top of Andrea's. After a beat of silence, she said, "I mean what I said earlier. It's not your fault what happened to Isabel, okay? It's his fault. He did that to her, not you."

Rita squeezed her eyes shut and shook her head, new tears cutting paths through the mess of mascara staining her cheeks. "You don't have to say that."

"Please," Andrea begged. "The police, you have to call the—"

Sabina pulled her phone from her back pocket and unlocked the screen. In the split second it flashed to life, I saw a flurry of missed texts from Nadia, demanding to know why Sabina hadn't called her back, where she was, the address that "Amy Sue" had given.

"The police will see it that way, too. I'm going to—"

"No!" Rita cried.

315

Before Sabina could blink, she'd knocked the phone out of her hand, like it was a rattlesnake about to strike.

Sabina froze. Her voice went quiet, stern. "Rita, you asked me to come here for a reason. I know you're scared, but—"

Rita shook her head wildly, eyes on the phone, muscles tensed like she was ready to dive for that little black rectangle on the floor at Sabina's feet the second she moved to grab it. "*No.* I'm not ready to do that. You know how scared I was to send you that message? You know how many times I said, 'fuck it' and told myself to forget it?" Her voice rose in pitch. "The last girl who ratted on the managers after a client nearly beat her to death wound up in jail for turning tricks."

Sabina shifted uncomfortably. "But when you tell them what you know, they'll arrest—"

Rita's eyes were blazing now. "Ever since I contacted you, I've been getting ready to make a move, get out of here so he won't be able to find me. But I need a couple more days. Then I'll talk. But there's no way we're calling right this goddamn minute."

My heart sank.

Rita lifted her chin. "I'm sorry for what I did, and I hate that motherfucker, but I'm scared. Not just of him. The guys who run this place ..." She set her mouth in a hard line. "Yeah, they treat us decent compared to some other places, but that doesn't mean they give a shit. And it doesn't mean they won't slap me around if I get out of line. I've got nowhere else to go, and I'm not gonna talk until I can get on a bus the second I've said my piece, given the cops a statement or whatever. Police are gonna be all over here trying to talk to the managers and the other girls—and they're gonna know pretty quick that it was me who squealed."

Sabina looked stricken. She held out her hands in front of her, like she was trying to coax a jumper off the ledge of a bridge. "I'm sorry, please, I'm sorry. You're absolutely right. I don't want to put you in any danger."

"No!" I cried. "No, you have to let Sabina call them right now. Please, Rita!"

If something happened to Sabina when she walked out that door, I had no doubt in my mind Rita would disappear the second she realized that Dennis was making good on his threats.

There wasn't time to wait. Sabina had to call the police *now.*

"Mom, make her listen," Andrea added desperately, eyes wild.

But Sabina just nodded slowly, pointing down at the phone Rita had knocked to the floor. "I'm going to pick that up now, okay? But I'm not going to call anybody. I promise. Not until I know you'll be safe."

"Shit," I hissed.

"We have to find a way to keep her here—or distract Dennis," Andrea cried as Sabina stood and gave Rita a tentative hug, talking in low voices as they moved toward the apartment door.

But I was out of ideas on how to do that. I didn't feel powerful or fierce like I had when I made that windstorm blow over Marlie's shelter so Sabina would see my backpack, or when I was whispering dreams to my family.

I was wrung out.

And all I felt right now was dread.

49

SABINA

Blood pounded in my ears in a strange cocktail of horror, sadness and excitement, as I clutched the pepper spray canister in one hand, keys in the other, and rushed away from the blinking orange lights of the apartment complex. The lingering smell of mildew and urine surrounded me as I rushed back into the night, heading for my car.

I was desperate to call Joel and Nadia—and even more desperate to call the police. But the last thing I wanted to do was blurt out everything Nadia had just told me in confidence—and risk one of her managers overhearing through a cracked window. So instead, I raced toward the car. I'd call Joel, then Nadia, as soon as I was safely locked inside. They would both be upset, but then again, my instincts—or maybe it was Andrea—had been right on. "Amy Sue" had information. She was terrified, and rightly so. She never would have talked if I had brought the police in right away. Given all that, I figured that Joel and Nadia would forgive me for being reckless.

I would apologize as soon as I could. But first I had to catch my breath. After what I'd learned over the last hour, I doubted I'd be able to string together a coherent sentence.

Dennis Beaumont killed Isabel Palphreyman.

Those words pounded in my head with every step I took.

I knew Dennis had done it. This new information from Rita would be enough to make her parents reconsider the autopsy. This would be enough for the police to get a warrant to search his house, to look for evidence of foul play. My stomach churned when I thought about what Rita had described when she last saw Isabel in this apartment complex. I could only imagine what he'd done when he found her at the underpass.

I could only imagine what he'd done to Andrea.

Tears stung my cheeks as I came around the hulking line of juniper bushes. One short block to the car, and the keys were already laced between my fingers.

"Mother—fucking—bastard," I whispered between ragged breaths. It felt good to run, good to do something with the adrenaline that had been screaming at me to act, to fight for my daughter, and for Isabel.

There was a rustle behind me, then the slightest scrape, from the thick line of bushes I'd just rushed past.

I turned my head, but not in time to see anything or anyone.

Before I could even fully understand what was happening, I felt something cold wrap around my throat. A cord, a thick wire, I couldn't tell. It bit into the skin like a garrote, so forcefully I nearly fell backward as I tried to lurch forward.

I gasped—or tried to—but I couldn't. No air came in or out.

The strap pulled tighter as rough fingertips dug into my neck with relentless pressure, pulling me backward against a thick blocky frame.

"Fucking *bitch*!" a voice hissed.

I didn't need to see him to know who it was.

No, no, no, no.

I clawed at my neck, scrambling to reach the car alarm button on the key fob or mash the trigger on the pepper spray, but everything was moving too fast.

The key and pepper spray fell to the ground, useless, as I stumbled backward against him then went down on my knees, bucking wildly.

The world tilted, stars swirling above me. My vision flashed white.

I barely felt the pain. Just the pressure that screamed, *You're going to die,* and the primal terror that screamed back even louder, *You have to fight!*

My lungs spasmed uselessly, my mouth gaping like a fish out of water. I couldn't make a sound.

He panted like a dog behind me, grunting each time he pulled the cord a little tighter, stumbling backward a few steps as my weight pressed against him.

A sinking, falling sensation filled my stomach, like I was in an elevator plunging downward. I was going to pass out. It was only a matter of seconds.

Go dead weight, demanded a stern voice somewhere inside me.

And then, I saw her, standing before me.

Andrea. My daughter.

Not the chubby baby I'd handed to the social worker. But the seventeen-year-old from the high school photo. Her eyes were wide with panic, and she looked as desperate as I felt. And even though my lungs were spasming from the lack of oxygen, I couldn't help thinking about how beautiful she was. My precious, precious girl.

Fight for me! Go dead weight, she demanded, her eyes wild. She bent her knees abruptly, miming the motion.

This time, I obeyed, and for just a moment, he lost his grip on the cord as I crumpled to my knees.

Elbow him hard! Now! Use your left arm!

The cord around my neck slackened the tiniest bit, and I gasped in a lungful of air. Then I lifted my left arm forward as far as I could and swung the sharp point of my elbow directly up into his groin.

The sound he made—half yelp, half gurgle of shock and pain—sent a fresh jolt of adrenaline spiking through me. The white dots vanished from my vision. So did Andrea.

The cord fully loosened, and my fingers clamped down around the cord, yanking it free and tossing it as far as I could while he fell backward onto the cement.

I heard a rustle as the cord landed somewhere out of sight, then a dull *crack* on the pavement followed by a muffled howl of pain.

I pushed to my feet and ran. I didn't look behind me to see how badly he was hurt. I lunged forward away from him. My legs felt disconnected from the rest of my body, and so did my fingers, but somehow both obeyed, propelling me back in the direction of the dimly lit apartments.

Could I make it back to Rita's apartment? Would anyone else open up to banging on their door at this hour? Surely someone would come into the courtyard to see what was wrong. It didn't matter who it was. Anyone. A witness, a helper, I'd take what I could get right now.

But when I tried to scream, all that came out was a croaking hiss.

"Call the police!" I tried to say as my clumsy fingers grabbed hold of the cell in my pocket and hit the home button. But the words were too quiet, too garbled. Nothing happened when I glanced down at the screen.

I kept running forward, trying to pull up the keypad to dial 9-1-1.

I'd made it as far as the walkway that circled the apartment courtyard. In just a few seconds, I'd be out of the darkness beyond the juniper bushes.

And then, for the second time tonight, I heard footsteps on the pavement and felt someone grab me from behind.

50

ANDREA

"Don't look back," I screamed, "Hit him again, just keep running!"

She didn't, though. Instead, Sabina froze mid-stride like she'd just hit an invisible wall, body trembling in the half-light, phone clutched in her right hand. The fingers of her left hand hovered over the screen, its glow turning them a pale blue.

The first two digits of the attempted call, 9-1, blinked uselessly on the screen.

Then I realized why she'd stopped trying to fight him.

Dennis had a new weapon.

He held the sharp ridge of a broken bottle, against the soft skin of Sabina's throat. He was pressing it so tight that I couldn't help imagining the pale skin splitting into a gaping red smile.

"Drop the fucking phone, now," he hissed in her ear. Flecks of spit peppered her cheek. His eyes glinted huge and black in the moonlight, gleaming with rage—and pleasure, too. The way he was breathing, labored and fast, told me she'd hurt him when she elbowed him.

And he was going to make her pay for it.

Sabina tried to speak into the phone, but the only sound that emerged was a gasping rattle, a broken croak. Even the breeze that had picked up earlier as she walked away from Rita's apartment had quieted down into little more than a whisper.

The loudest sound in the grimy courtyard was Dennis's breathing, wheezing and ragged, as he held that jagged glass to Sabina's throat.

For half a second, nobody moved.

Then from behind me, Isabel let out a scream.

A raw animal sound as she launched herself at Dennis, clawing at his back, clawing at his eyes like a feral cat.

"Help, please, we need help!" I screamed, even though I knew that nobody could hear me.

And nobody would help.

"I said, drop your phone," Dennis growled, yanking Sabina's hair roughly with one hand while pressing harder with the bottle edge. A red bead welled up beneath the glass, and I whimpered for my mother as Isabel clawed harder, still screaming like a banshee.

Sabina still didn't comply, though. Her thumb was moving, shaking, slipping across the screen. She was trying to finish the call —hit the last button that would send it through to the police. She couldn't see the screen, though. Her head was twisted too far skyward because of the way he was holding her hair and the angle of the glass shard pressing into the front of her throat.

"A little to the right!" I begged, pressing my lips to her ear.

9-1-2.

Sabina couldn't see the screen. But Dennis could.

The barest smile worked the corner of his lips as he saw what she had tried—and failed—to do with the phone. Then he cranked her neck roughly as she fumbled for the call button one more time.

The call still didn't go through.

And Dennis knew it.

His gaze flicked from the screen to her throat. Then, with a snarl, he let go of her hair for the briefest moment—and slapped the phone from her hands. It sailed through the air, spinning over the pavement like a skipping rock when it landed before vanishing into the shadowy tangle of junipers.

Sabina seized the opportunity and lashed at him with her feet, kicking hard.

"Yes," I cried as Isabel clawed uselessly at his eyes and Sabina's first kick connected with his side. He grunted as she reared back and went for his groin again.

The blow never landed, though.

Dennis didn't try to flinch away from the kick. He caught her ankle midair and yanked hard.

Sabina crumpled onto the pavement with a sickening thud, bone on concrete.

I leaped toward her, covering my body with hers as I saw him lunge.

I felt the jagged glass move through me like so many dust particles.

And I watched up close as he drove the bottle into her neck.

He didn't say anything else to her. No pause while he confessed everything he'd done to me, to Isabel, before he delivered the blows. Not even a moment's wait while he recovered his breath. Just raw, abrupt violence and blood.

As the blood gushed down her throat and into the hem of her shirt, he lifted the jagged glass and rammed it into her chest. Then again. And again. Her arm, her side, her ribs.

The blood dripped onto the sidewalk in messy ribbons, pooling on the pavement and soaking into the cracks.

"Mom!" I cried, curling myself around her even though I knew it was useless. Like maybe she could feel me in her final moments.

Her hands jerked with each impact and her mouth opened wide, gasping in mute shock. The only part of her that wasn't dripping red was her face and it tilted in the direction of the apartment complex, eyes locked on the silent building.

The porch lights were still flickering, but I didn't see any sign of movement behind the rows of dark, slatted blinds covering the windows that faced the courtyard.

If someone looked outside right now, sorting the shapes in the darkness for just a few seconds, they would see Sabina's body lying on the pavement, covered in blood.

But not one set of blinds parted.

Not one door opened.

Dennis raised the bloody bottle yet again, his eyes on Sabina's chest where part of her shirt was still clean and unbroken.

I braced, waiting for him to deliver the blow that would make my mother stop writhing and go still.

Every part of me wanted to protect her. Every part of me wanted to wrestle him for that broken bottle.

I couldn't do a single thing.

And then, out of the corner of my eye, I saw Isabel stop frantically—uselessly—pummeling Dennis's head and turn toward the juniper bushes.

She gasped quietly. And, then she called out, "Please, do something, please help us!"

51

ISABEL

At first, when I saw the shadowy figures at the edge of the courtyard, I thought that some of the girls from the eight-plex had finally come outside to see what was going on.

Then I recognized the gingham fabric, the full skirts, the bonnets the women were wearing.

The woman nearest to me was holding the hand of a solemn toddler wearing a black cap, and a wide-eyed baby perched on one hip.

The women I'd seen walking through the cemetery. They were ghosts, just like me and Andrea. My heart sank. They wouldn't be able to help us. Not really.

And then I saw their faces.

Each of the women in the small group was staring at Dennis with pure, undisguised hatred in their eyes as he lifted the jagged bottle above his head and prepared to plunge it into Sabina's chest yet again.

The woman wearing a blue gingham dress—the one holding the baby—hissed something to her young son and let go of his hand. Then she hefted her baby onto her hip and moved forward alongside the other women like a military flank, fanning out in a circle around me and Isabel—and Sabina and Dennis.

"Leave her be," one of them cried, lifting her hands out in front of her body toward Dennis in a brace, like she might push him away.

He didn't move.

"Leave!" another woman cried out, her voice high and angry.

The air crackled with fresh energy, replacing the numb static that had been humming through me for the past hour. And suddenly, the awful silence in the courtyard split with a loud series of bangs as a row of garbage cans along the nearest wall of the courtyard went toppling to the ground.

A large raccoon scurried away into the shadows as Dennis lowered to a crouch, bottle still raised at his shoulder, but hesitating like he was debating whether to bring it down one more time on Sabina's lifeless form.

His eyes narrowed and he took a step back, looking wary, scanning the courtyard for any sign that the noise had drawn someone's attention. He stared down at Sabina's body, his upper lip curling in disgust as he took a tentative step away from her, breathing hard, eyes roving across the shuttered windows and dark doorways, cursing under his breath.

Dennis still didn't run away. Seemingly satisfied that the courtyard remained empty, he took a step back toward Sabina, observing. She was breathing, but barely. Could he see the subtle rise and fall of her chest like I could?

Andrea curled her body tighter around her mother, like maybe this time she could stop the bottle from coming down. We both knew better.

Andrea's scrunched face was turned toward the nearest pioneer, a gray-haired woman wearing a simple black dress that hung to her ankles.

The pioneer woman's face softened for a moment. Then turned back to stone when Dennis took another step closer to Sabina. Time seemed to slow as the elder looked between me and Andrea. "You know this man?" she demanded. "He's the one who stole your lives?"

"Yes, he … killed us," I said, unsure how else to answer her.

The old woman's eyes blazed. "You know his secrets. His power. Bring them to light. Take his power. *Now!*" she urged.

"What do you mean, 'take his power'?" I asked, frantic.

There wasn't time. Dennis was lifting the dripping bottle once more, cranking his arm above Sabina. I looked at Andrea, and our eyes locked.

Then Andrea blurted the words on the tip of my tongue. The same words that had been burning inside of me for three years. "Shh. Don't fuss. The more you fuss, the worse it'll be."

"Together!" the old woman boomed.

I did what she asked. And this time, the other women circling tighter around us repeated the words with me and Andrea. "Shh. Don't fuss. The more you fuss, the worse it'll be."

Dennis's eyes went wide and his mouth went slack, like he'd just been slapped. Still holding the bottle, he whirled around and scanned the dark windows, then down at Sabina as if she might have spoken those words.

The emotion flowing from the women in the courtyard—hatred, rage, defiance—swelled.

He looked terrified, shocked. Had he somehow actually *heard* the words we were repeating?

"Oh, he hears us," the old woman snarled. "Now tell him that you see him."

"He's right over there! In the courtyard! I saw what he did to that woman!" I screamed into the night, saying the first words that came into my head. The words I knew Dennis would be most afraid to hear.

Andrea and the other women repeated the words in unison as quickly as I said them.

Dennis let out a sharp wheeze and cut his eyes toward the far end of the courtyard, where a dim light had finally turned on behind the blinds in one apartment.

"Shit," he muttered. Eyes still on that window, he slunk down like a scared dog as he backed toward the breezeway, then toward the line of juniper bushes.

He needed to leave *now*. Sabina was running out of time, and I could already feel the pioneer women's energy dissipating, cooling.

As if on cue, the women circled tighter around Sabina and Andrea. I moved with them. I didn't know how they'd learned to do what we'd just done—throwing our voices like that. I'd been silent and invisible since the day I'd died. The memory of my church camp leader telling a story about a pioneer graveyard—supposedly haunted—flashed through my mind, and all I could guess was that these women had been around a very long time. Long enough to learn some things.

Dennis's mouth tightened into a frown as he flicked his eyes back to Sabina one more time.

She had curled tighter into a ball, trying to protect herself, and her body was shuddering slightly now, jerking erratically.

She was dying.

"Call the police!" Andrea called out, frantically. We were completely circled around her and Sabina now, shutting Dennis out of the circle we had formed.

We all lifted our voices and boomed together, "Call the police, *now!*"

The blinds in the lit window moved a fraction of an inch.

And then Dennis finally ran.

52

SABINA

One second, there was only red-hot pain that tore through my body, bathing me in my own slick blood.

Then everything blurred—including the pain.

I wanted to beg. I wanted to scream. But all I could do was lean into the blur, because it was the only way out of the agony.

I clung to it like a life raft. Because Joel was in the blur. His smile, his off-key whistle while he made coffee and cinnamon pancakes on Saturday mornings. The smell of his aftershave and the warmth of his cheek against mine when he pulled me into him.

Andrea was in the blur, too. Her chubby baby hands, her lashes wet with tears and impossibly long against her cheeks when she had finally cried herself out. Her fingers wrapped around my hair while she slept in the basement recliner for a few peaceful moments.

And then, suddenly, the pain stopped and the blur disappeared, taking my husband and baby with it.

No more terror. No more Dennis Beaumont with his rage-filled eyes and grunting noises.

Just the dark apartment courtyard, where a woman lay unmoving and blood-soaked on the dark ground beside two strangers: one who was hovering just behind the body, and one who was stroking her hair.

It was *my* body lying on the ground, I realized with a shock. *I* was the blood-soaked woman.

Was I having an out-of-body experience? Was I dead? Who were those two people? Had they been the ones who chased Dennis away?

"Rita?" I whispered, peering through the darkness, doubtful she could hear me but unable to help myself.

The woman who was standing beside my body looked up sharply, and I took in her chiseled, petite face—and pale blue hair.

Isabel Palphreyman.

We stared at each other for a split second, and then her eyes moved to the shadowy figures darting away at a fast clip along the side of the apartment complex. Dennis? The police? But there were no sirens, no flashing lights.

And then the woman kneeling beside my body, her back to me, whirled around to face me. The cowlick in her auburn hair caught the orange glow of the nearest blinking porch light and her hazel eyes went wide.

Somewhere, distantly at the far edge of the courtyard, a new light blinked on behind someone's blinds, and I heard voices.

I ignored them and stared at the woman barely two feet away from me, forgetting all about the unbearable pain I'd felt moments earlier, and my broken body lying motionless on the sidewalk. Forgetting all about the shock that I might be dead. Forgetting all about the shards of glass I'd been carrying around in my chest long before Dennis Beaumont broke the skin of my throat and ribcage.

"Andrea," I whispered.

"Mom," she said in a trembling voice, and held out her arms to me like she had when she was a baby on that afternoon when we'd walked with the stroller.

And this time, I didn't hesitate. I dropped to my knees and scooped her up tight, shocked by the way my arms could wrap around her body yet not feel a thing except the love radiating through me. "I love you, I love you so much."

"I love you, too," she cried. Then grabbed my hand.

And in an instant, like a movie reel whirring in blinding fast-forward, I saw what she'd been through. What Dennis had done to her and where he'd buried her body. The person she had become since I'd last held her in my arms as a baby. How this moment meant as much to her as it did to me, despite the despair.

Then somehow, impossibly, I squeezed her hand back, letting her see a flurry of moments and emotions. How I'd missed her every second since I'd let her go. How much I'd wanted to believe that she was happy and loved with her adoptive family. How sorry I was for letting her down. How much I wished she could have called me "Mom" and Joel "Dad" and walked along the beach in Neskowin, searching for sea glass after the storms that rolled through the coast.

"I've been looking for you," I told her, the emotion rising up in me and wrapping both of us in that quilted feeling that was so familiar now.

I could hear the wail of sirens close by, drawing nearer.

Andrea managed a smile, but her eyes moved to my body on the ground. "I've been with you this whole time, trying to help. I tried to stop him, I tried to tell you he was outside the apartments—"

"It doesn't matter," I told her firmly. A car door slammed beyond the apartment complex, followed by feet pounding the ground, muffled voices, more sirens.

We both looked up sharply as two EMTs rushed into the courtyard.

One held a case containing defibrillation paddles under the crook of his arm.

They were going to try to revive me.

I couldn't bear the thought of leaving my daughter yet, though. Not when I'd only just found her again.

I drew back from Andrea's embrace to look at her, to memorize her, panic souring some of the pure joy at having her in front of me.

The EMTs quickly knelt and felt for a pulse, some sign I was breathing.

I wasn't.

They charged the paddles, and I looked at my daughter helplessly. She was staring into my eyes, hers flashing. "If they can bring you back, go. I would have … I would have gone back if I could. You have Joel."

The EMTs pressed the paddles against my chest, and the body at our feet—my body—jolted.

I gasped as the pain returned and Andrea's face disappeared into dark for a split second. I felt myself being wrenched away from her. Back to my dying body. But still I resisted.

"I love you," I told her again, and again. "We'll see each other again."

I meant the words to come out as a question. Instead, they emerged as a promise.

The paddles charged again, then moved back toward my chest.

"Go," she demanded. "I'll still be there. You'll feel it. I love you, too."

The pain came rushing back, and the world whirled sideways into darkness.

And then she was gone.

53

ISABEL

Dennis ran faster than I would have expected a man his size to move.

He was covered in sweat and Sabina's blood, eyes wild and wide by the time he reached his white Accord, which he'd parked on the far side of the cemetery.

The pioneer women and I kept pace, flanking his sides like a wolf pack, our eyes every bit as wild as his and our jaws tight with anger.

Dennis's fingers shook as he opened the car door and wiped a smear of blood against his pant legs.

Our anger swelled as we surrounded his car. There were sirens in the distance, getting louder as they moved in the direction of the apartment complex.

Not loud enough, though. Dennis was going to get away.

Everything had spun sideways so fast.

He'd killed me. He'd killed Andrea. And probably Sabina, too. Nobody had seen it happen. There was no way Rita was going to speak to the police now.

Maybe the cops would investigate Sabina's death more thoroughly than mine or Andrea's. There might be DNA he'd left behind. Skin under Sabina's fingernails.

Maybe. But even if both of those things happened, Dennis wasn't an idiot. He had to know that he'd left a mess he couldn't contain.

In all likelihood, he was going to get in that car and vanish into the night right now.

He shut the driver's side door, let out a long wheezing exhale, and reached for the ignition button.

The engine revved.

The woman in the gray dress looked at me, like an Army captain awaiting orders from a general. "No more running!" I screamed, "No more running!"

They were the last words he'd said to me that night he found me at the underpass.

The other women repeated the words, surrounding the car, banging on the hood in soundless slaps.

I could see Dennis's face behind the windshield. He was losing his shit—but he was still driving away.

Tires squealed, and the Accord screamed down the road, headed in the direction of the underpass.

"Hurry!" cried the woman in the blue gingham, pointing to the underpass. "What we practiced." She shot me a glance and then grabbed my hand. "Come on."

There wasn't time to ask questions.

I could feel the rage burning through her—along with something else. Determination—and a flash of what we were about to do. "Just keep hold of my hand," the woman said.

And so I did. All of us were on the move again, a pack of wolves, impossibly fast, cutting across the cemetery in the direction Dennis's car was disappearing.

We made it to the street right before Dennis did, going at least fifty miles per hour.

Then we fanned out across both lanes of the narrow road, directly in front of his car.

We all linked hands. I stared into the oncoming headlights, maybe ten feet away, barreling toward us.

Then, right before the car hit, the woman in the black dress—the eldest of the group—turned to me. "Make him see you," she demanded. "He couldn't snuff you out. You're s*till here.* You can do it."

For a split second, I panicked, not knowing how to do what she was asking. I was invisible. I couldn't make him see *anything.*

But there was no time to second-guess. I had to try.

A wail rose in my throat that was so loud, so intense, I could hardly believe it was mine. *"Look at me,"* I demanded in a roar, calling up every bit of horror and indignation and grief that he'd made me invisible to the world. "I'm still here."

As the car made contact with my body—and the line of women holding tight to my hands—I looked through the windshield, where I saw Dennis's face through the headlights.

It was only a split second. But in that split second, his mouth opened into a horrified O, and I knew he saw me. The girl he'd killed.

There was no other explanation for why he abruptly jerked the steering wheel hard to the right and down an embankment. His head slammed against the driver's side window as the car flew down the steep slope. His body jerked sideways.

He screamed.

And then the white Accord crashed head-on into a utility pole.

54

SABINA

I was clinically dead for two minutes, the doctors estimated.

It was a miracle, they said. He stabbed me with that jagged bottle nine times, one blow missing the major artery in my neck by two centimeters. I'd lost so much blood.

I'd cried so hard in the ambulance, mouth open in a silent howl, my throat a maze of deep bruises from the cord Dennis had pulled across it, that one of the EMTs gave me a shot of Lorazepam, to help with the shock.

He'd said they were rushing me toward the surgery center at the Ogden Regional Medical center, and he kept trying to ask me questions I couldn't answer about my name, where my phone was, who they should contact.

I'd just cried and closed my eyes, trying to memorize every single detail of those two minutes with my daughter. I never wanted to forget them.

When I woke up in the hospital, with Joel squeezing my hand tight, I started to cry again. Big wracking sobs that made Joel cry too—and made the doctor and nurse in the room look at each other like maybe I needed another shot of Lorazepam.

It wasn't that, though. I just kept thinking of my baby's face. Her big green eyes.

Kept wondering whether the quilt-wrapped feeling was her beside me right now, or just the drugs.

It was her, I told myself. *It's her.*

"I'll still be there. You'll feel it. I love you," she'd told me.

Rita was the one who had called the police and brought the EMTs to the courtyard, finally gathering up the courage to step outside to see what the scuffle was about.

She swears I was the one who shouted, "Call the police *now.*"

I knew I hadn't spoken those words. None of the women the police interviewed at the apartment complex had said them either. There were no witnesses, no passers-by to see Dennis raise the jagged glass edge again and again while I lay bleeding on the pavement.

I hadn't told Joel everything that had happened yet. He'd gotten bits and pieces from the doctors, from the police, and from the sentences I'd typed out on the laptop he'd gently placed on the rolling table at my bedside.

Eight hours after the attack, I still couldn't actually talk. I was woozy and sick. And my throat was on fire, even with the pain medication. Swollen and bruised so badly that the doctors had been forced to intubate me to keep my airway from completely swelling shut. It'd been a feat to communicate with Detective Barker, who took my statement via that laptop as soon as I was conscious.

While Joel went to get a cup of coffee, I stared back at the first run-on sentence I'd typed, wincing at the stark, sterile words that held a world of pain.

Did you catch Dennis Beaumont, he did this to me, he killed Andrea, and Isabel, they need to do an autopsy, Andrea's body is buried under the cement slab of the house on the other side of the woods. The one Dennis built. He was working on it when he killed her.

Detective Barker had looked at me in stunned silence. Then he typed out, *Dennis is dead. Car crash.*

The sound of the humming, beeping machines in my room went silent, eclipsed by the pounding in my head. Dennis was dead.

Dennis. Was. Dead.

Part of me rejoiced that he was gone, that he'd never be able to hurt anyone else ever again. The other was outraged that he wouldn't have to stand trial for what he'd done to Andrea, to Isabel, to me.

I blinked over and over, trying to focus, because Detective Barker was already typing again.

Bunny is in custody. We've got a warrant and are searching their house now. Where did you get that information about the cement slab?

I'd closed my eyes, considering how I wanted to answer that question. If I wasn't ready to tell Joel the whole story of what I'd experienced with my daughter, I certainly wasn't willing to tell Detective Barker. Maybe I was afraid they'd look at me like I was crazy—that I'd seen her as the neurons in my brain fired while the life drained out of my body and shut down my heart. That maybe I would start to question what I'd seen, what I'd felt.

He told me, I finally typed out, slowly, reluctantly. *You'll find the other butterfly earring there, with her. I want them both back when you can give them to me.*

The quilt-wrapped feeling snugged tighter, and some of the pain in my throat dulled into numbness.

Detective Barker gave me a skeptical look. Then he typed out, just as slowly, *The Palphreymans let me know this morning that they are going to allow the autopsy to be done. We'll have more information soon.* Then he erased the words and met my gaze. Clearly something he wasn't supposed to share.

His kindness made my eyes fill with tears all over again. Because I could tell he believed me. And not only that. He had a trail paved with evidence to follow.

They would find Andrea's body. They would learn what had happened to Isabel. Rita would speak to the police.

The scales of justice were tipping.

In a few days, I would go home with Joel.

And, even though it wasn't in the way I'd hoped, I would go home with my daughter, too. I would take her with me every time I walked along the beach with Joel in Neskowin after a storm rolled through, looking for sea glass and sand dollars.

And for now, it would be enough.

I would live my life, breathe in as many lungfuls of air as I could.

And then I would find her again.

EPILOGUE

ANDREA

Bunny didn't fight the court request that would allow Sabina and Joel to bring my body to Neskowin for burial.

I still wondered about Bunny sometimes, when I sat on the porch beside Sabina as we stared out into a gathering storm moving fast across the Pacific Ocean toward shore. Had she ever cared about me like a daughter? How much did she know about what Dennis did to me, to Isabel? Did she think about me from that prison cell, or did she still whisper the words "Little bitch" while she cried for her dead, disgusting husband?

Once, I went back to a memory from the day her and Dennis brought me to Utah.

She held me in her arms all that night while I cried, making little shushing sounds while she walked the floors in the upstairs nursery. *"You're ours now,"* she kept murmuring next to my ear, rocking me faster in her arms when I wouldn't stop wailing.

But I heard her say those same words again, in a memory from when I was eighteen months old—and threw a tantrum before church. And this time, she said them through clenched teeth. *"You're ours now. Get used to it."*

Sabina and Joel had purchased a plot in a lush, shady cemetery near their house. Joel chose it, because it was within walking distance of their house and they could visit easily. The police hadn't released my body quite yet. It was an arduous process just to excavate it from the cement. But soon, they said.

It didn't matter, though. I already knew that aside from the day of my funeral, when the broken pieces of my body would be laid to rest, neither Joel nor Sabina would spend much time at the cemetery. Not after what Sabina told Joel she'd seen the night Dennis nearly killed her.

I watched his eyes while she told him the story. How we'd spent two precious minutes together before the EMTs restarted her heart and rushed her into the ambulance. How she'd felt my presence beside her long before that, even though she hadn't been able to see me. How I'd told her where to find my body.

I expected Joel to stare at her in disbelief. Raise an eyebrow, at least. Instead, his eyes filled with tears and shook his head back and forth until he finally choked out, "I've felt her too, ever since I got to the hospital in Ogden. I thought it sounded crazy, I didn't even know her, but ..." He trailed off and let the tears fall.

It was moments like this when I wished even more that he'd been my dad. I just knew he would've loved me the way he loved Sabina. Would have taken care of me the way he did his mom, driving to her house each day to help with physical therapy and bring her lunch. He would have let me paint my room any color I wanted. He would have told me he loved my eyes, because they looked just like Sabina's.

But knowing he believed her about seeing me for those two minutes—and knowing that he could sense me nearby—would have to be enough for now.

Isabel and I had perfected the "Time travel game," as we'd started calling it, drifting deeper through our memories each time we met. I knew her better than anyone now. And she knew me, too.

We see as we're seen, she said once, when she showed me a memory of a cloudless summer day at a city pool in Layton, Utah where she took swimming lessons, and I showed her a memory of my old dog Pollie learning how to roll over. I didn't ask her what that phrase meant. I didn't really care because it was so beautiful.

Isabel's family held her funeral the week after her autopsy was completed, a small private ceremony—including Nadia and Paloma. And, in the spaces behind the pews, stood some of the pioneer women next to Isabel.

They'd been sharing memories, too. And they'd quickly realized that one of them—the elderly woman in the black dress—was Isabel's fourth great aunt who had come across the plains from Illinois to Utah.

Most of those old pioneers in that section of graveyard had long since moved beyond the living world and into the depths of their memories and their loved ones. A small group had stayed, though. There were still some long-buried secrets, some stories that hadn't been told among the living.

Those women intended to stay in that graveyard until that happened. And in the meantime, they'd perfected the art of the haunt.

Sometimes, Isabel talked to me about nearly getting lost in her own memories, like she was walking through a house of endless doors and hallways. Not in a scary way, but in a way that was full of possibilities and discovery and knowing. She was meeting more family members she'd never known about, learning their lives, seeing their memories. They greeted her like long-lost friends. There was a family acquaintance who had died while Isabel was little. Two sets of grandparents. Even a beloved cat that had been run over by a car when she was six.

She said that sometimes, when she waded deep enough into a memory with another dead person and they got to talking inside the memory, she could feel her connection to the living world closing.

And that maybe that was all right with her.

There were endless worlds to explore.

But I wasn't ready to cross over yet.

When Isabel showed me the memories of her funeral—since Sabina wasn't in any condition to travel back to Utah—I was amazed by what I saw. The last time I'd heard Mary Palphreyman's voice, she'd been furious. When I saw her kneeling beside Isabel's new gravesite, she was offering a tearful, heartfelt apology to her daughter.

"I love you. I'm so, so sorry I trusted him instead of believing you. I was wrong. I miss you so much. Please forgive me."

When Isabel showed me that memory, I knew those words meant more to her than the autopsy results, which had uncovered five fractured ribs, trauma to her cheek and upper lip, and no proof that her cause of death was a drug overdose. And Dennis's DNA.

Her cause of death was officially changed from overdose to homicide. Death by asphyxiation and blunt force trauma.

I also knew that it was the last thing she needed before she could move on.

This morning, Sabina was taking her first walk on the beach since coming home to Neskowin. One of the blows had severed a tendon in her hip. Another had sliced through her abdominal wall. It would be a long time before she was ready to set off down the miles of coastline just outside the back porch. But today, Joel held her hand and I looped my arm through the other as we set out for a short stroll to the surf and back.

The wind gently whipped her auburn hair and the sun made her squint across the horizon. I imagined the feel of the sun on my face and the way the wind would tangle my own hair with salt and spray, and the feeling of it swelled up inside me like its own type of sunshine. From the way she squeezed her eyes shut and drew in a shaky breath, a hint of a smile playing across her lips, I hoped she could feel it, too.

I almost ignored the pull when Isabel drew me into the memory of the church pews, hating to leave the moment.

But something told me I'd better not.

And I was right.

"I think today's the day," she said gently. "My grandma and my great aunts—I just love them. I want to know them better." She squeezed my hand across the church pew and looked at her mother, her sisters, her dad. "It's not really goodbye," she added. "They'll find me again." She locked eyes with me. "And you will, too. Okay?"

"I'll still be able to find you here, though, right?" I said, gesturing at our meeting place, and suddenly unsure.

She shook her head slowly. "Once I cross over, we won't be able to talk like this anymore. It'll pull you to the other side. But I'll be there when you're ready."

I nodded, already feeling the sharp sting of grief. I'd never lost Isabel—not the way her parents had. She'd always been dead. Like me.

"I'll miss you," I whispered. "Think about me sometimes, okay?"

She grinned, and I suddenly realized that her blonde hair had changed to short, vibrant blue before my eyes.

Her modest dress turned to a short red skirt and velvety pleated top.

She pulled me into a hug. "Always."

The meeting room dissolved into ocean and sky and the sound of Joel's and Sabina's tentative footsteps on the sand beside me.

The sun glittered across the water, and I came back to the moment with Sabina and Joel, this half-life that I intended to wrap myself around for now. Maybe for their whole lives, until the day we found each other again, face to face.

I wished my mother could see me beside her. I wished my life hadn't ended so soon. I wished I could feel the salty air fill my lungs. I wished there were more memories to be made.

But then I thought of Isabel and her grandmother. Her great aunts. The new worlds they were exploring and reliving together. The conversations they were having. The way they were seeing each other for the first time.

Maybe there were still memories to be made after all.

And maybe mourning was just waiting, while holding onto the ones we love in the only ways we could.

For now.

AUTHOR'S NOTE

While this book is a prequel to *Ask for Andrea,* it's also inspired by the very real story of Cathy Terkanian and her daughter Alexis (whose name was changed to Aundria Bowman when she was adopted by Dennis and Brenda Bowman).

I'd always intended for *Ask for Andrea* to be a standalone novel, but something kept pinging at the back of my mind, insisting that there was more to be written. When I watched the documentary *Into the Fire,* in which Cathy Terkanian described the feeling of her daughter "haunting her," leading her on a journey to solve her murder, I knew I'd found the spark for this story. Cathy's story is distinct, and *Forget You Saw Her* is only loosely inspired by it. However, her tenacity, courage, and love for her daughter are very much the same as Sabina's. Cathy's remarkable and determined efforts to find out what had happened to her daughter also unearthed and solved the cold-case murder of Kathleen Doyle, another victim of Dennis Bowman.

I highly recommend watching the documentary *Into the Fire* if you want to learn more about the real Alexis (Aundria Bowman), Kathleen Doyle, and Cathy Terkanian.

ACKNOWLEDGMENTS

I want to take a moment to express my gratitude to some truly amazing people who helped bring this book into the world.

To my fellow authors, friends, and early readers—Caleb Stephens, Faith Gardner, and Steph Nelson—thank you for your honest, thoughtful, and vital feedback. Your support means more than I can ever say, and your insights helped shape this story into something I'm proud of.

Huge love to my author assistant Jacob Robarts—your executive brilliance and uncanny ability to dream up perfect TikTok ideas has kept this chaotic ship sailing straight. I don't know how I did this without you before, and I'm definitely not going back.

To my editor, Deborah J. Ledford—thank you for your keen eye, your immense skill, and your saintly patience with my reckless overuse of italics. I'm so lucky to work with you.

To Erica Ruth and Jess Lourey—your kindness and encouragement as I stumbled toward the finish line of this book meant the world. Thank you for being a soft place to land when I really needed it.

To Dan Blewitt and the many, many other bookstagrammers, booktokers, and book bloggers who have been cheerleaders for my writing and become friends from afar, I can't thank you enough. Your tireless support of authors and books is a true gift.

Special thanks to Freida McFadden, John Marrs, Tracy Fenton, Karin Slaughter, and Sydney Blanchard. I couldn't believe it when I realized you'd read *Ask for Andrea,* and your generosity in taking a chance on an author still trying to make her mark on the world means so much.

To Jason Pinter and the crew at Simon Maverick, and narrators Andi Arndt, Carlotta Brentan, and Brittany Pressley, thank you for treating the audio version of this book with such care and intention.

To my agents, Ethan and Ezra Ellenberg—you two have always been in my corner, fighting for me with heart and guts. I couldn't ask for better champions.

To Patti Geesey, my incredible proofreader—I'm endlessly grateful for your sharp eye and grace under pressure.

And finally, to Nate—my partner, my best friend, the love of my life. I'll absolutely haunt you. In the best possible way.

Read on for a thrilling excerpt
from Noelle W. Ihli's novel *Such Quiet Girls*.

1

JESSA

Soph had another nightmare ...

That was all the text message said.

The after-school daycare bus shuddered as I killed the ignition, letting out a sigh that pretty well captured how I felt: tired as hell, going nowhere.

I unbuckled my seatbelt, leaned over the aisle, and shoved my phone with more force than necessary into the cubby labeled MS. JESSA.

I knew exactly what those ellipses meant without my sister having to spell it out for me.

My daughter, Sophie, had another nightmare ... about *me*.

I blew out a breath and sat back in the driver's seat, eying the double doors of Northridge Elementary's main building. I was early for my first pickup, but just barely.

I shifted my gaze back to the four-by-four row of cubbies that had been retrofitted just inside the bus door, above the handrail. Each cubby had a little plexiglass door, labeled with a name that belonged to each of the students who would burst through the shiny blue doors of the elementary school as soon as the final bell rang.

A sign fixed to the top of the cubbies read, THIS BUS IS A NO-PHONE ZONE! in cutesy, curly purple font that arced above the Bright Beginnings Childcare Center logo: a bunch of children staring lovingly, and directly, into the sun.

"Very bright," I mumbled to myself, same as I had every day this week. The childcare center was supposed to be getting a new fleet of buses soon. Maybe they'd spring for a new logo, too.

When I'd started this job—only a week ago—I'd learned that the childcare center had a strict no-phones policy for its bus drivers *and* students. That was fine with me, but I'd been surprised by how many of the kids already had phones in elementary school. One of the first-graders. Both of the third-graders. All but one of the fourth-graders.

I side-eyed the cubbies and thought about reaching into the box labeled MS. JESSA to type back a quick reply to Lisa's text. I knew I should ask my sister how Soph was doing. Find out whether I could come by the house after my route. I could offer to bring pizza for dinner. Or just ask for details about my nine-year-old daughter's nightmare.

That was the right thing to do. The good-mom thing to do. I'd really sucked at that lately, though.

I appreciated the fact that Sophie had been able to live with Lisa instead of being funneled into the foster-care system. But it still hurt that I'd had to ask about my daughter's well-being like a game of telephone for the past three years.

So I left the phone in its cubby and shifted in the driver's seat, craning my neck to gaze in the rearview mirror so I could scrutinize my own face in the harsh, late-afternoon light. Then I forced a smile that didn't reach my eyes and wiped the beads of sweat collecting beneath the thick mop of bangs I'd cut just before moving back to Idaho three months ago.

The bangs had been yet another mistake.

I'd been trying for fresher, younger. I got neither. Combined with the "luxe mahogany" box dye I'd splurged on, the bangs made it look like I was wearing a too-bright red wig on top of my former blonde, middle-parted hair. Before the hair hack job, I'd looked every day of my thirty-eight years. Now I came across as at least mid-forties.

Maybe my hair color was the reason Soph was having nightmares, I thought hopefully. Because I looked so different from before.

I pushed the thought away before I could really latch onto it.

I knew better. That wasn't the reason.

CLANG.

"Shit." I startled at the noise—more gong than bell—that announced the end of the school day. I put the key back into the ignition, ignoring the fast thud of my heart and the fizz of anxiety that bubbled in my stomach.

"Just get through it," I whispered under my breath, trying to keep the smile on my face as I pulled the lever to open the bus doors. After a week on the job, I felt more confident that I could handle the lumbering bus and the kids. I'd nearly had a panic attack on the first day, so even a little confidence was progress.

"Hi, Ms. Jessa," a solemn little boy with auburn hair and freckles mumbled as he boarded the bus, his eyes landing on my name tag near the speedometer.

"Hi, Ked," I replied as soon as I saw which cubby he was sliding his phone into. *Ked.* Who named their kid after a shoe?

Two little girls with messy black curls dashed down the sidewalk and boarded the bus after Ked. Sage, a lanky sixth grader, and her first-grade sister—and shadow—Bonnie.

I pasted a smile onto my face then glanced away. With her long hair, freckles, and thick pink glasses, Bonnie could've been a rewound version of my Sophie. Sage, with her bob haircut and pierced ears, looked like the fast-forwarded version.

"Hi Sage, hi Bonnie," I chirped, proud of myself for remembering their names—and sounding perky.

"Just sit with Rose," Sage told her sister, ignoring me completely. Then she plopped down in the front seat and set her backpack in the space beside her.

"But I want to sit *here*," Bonnie whined.

Sage sighed like she was being asked to donate a kidney. "I'm *saving it*."

"Ms. Jessa said we can't save seats. That's against the rules," Bonnie said triumphantly.

Behind her on the bus steps, a little girl with a blonde bowl cut nodded vigorously. "Yeah, you *can't* save seats, Sage."

This was technically true, but I had no idea how I'd actually enforce that rule. My training hadn't covered that, and Sage had a defiant look on her face that told me she was about to argue. So I said, "Sage, put your phone in the cubby. Bonnie, why don't you just sit somewhere else today?"

Bonnie's brown eyes widened, and I knew that look. Unless something changed, she was going to start crying. "But … I want to show her my clay person," she whispered. "We made them today in art."

I gave Sage a pleading look as she rolled her eyes and stood to slide her pink phone into the cubby with her name on it. *Come on, kid. I just want to drive the damn bus. And I don't even really want to do that.*

To my surprise, she relented.

"Fine," Sage muttered, rolling her eyes as Bonnie slid past her into the bench. "What's a clay person, anyway?"

When all of the phones in the cubbies were accounted for—minus the two students absent for the day—I checked the enormous sideview mirror and caught eyes with a random teacher standing at the curb near the bus with her line of students for parent pickup.

I waved at her and smiled a little too enthusiastically.

She tilted her head and waved but didn't smile back.

Shit. I shoved the bus into gear and peeled away from the curb more quickly than I'd intended. The stream of irrational thoughts kept coming like they had every time anyone gave me a funny look.

She knows you lied on your job application.

She knows what you did.

I eased my foot off the gas and pushed the panic down. *Calm down. She's a teacher, not a psychic.*

When I risked another look in the mirror, the teacher was busy helping a little boy find something in his backpack.

I forced in a deep breath and brought my eyes back to the road.

"Ms. Jessa drives like Mom," Bonnie murmured to Sage, interrupting her own speech about clay people.

"That's just how moms drive," Sage shot back matter-of-factly.

I coughed to hide the laugh that escaped my mouth and checked my speed as I turned onto the rural highway.

The Bright Beginnings after-school childcare and rec center was a good thirty-minute drive from Northridge, including a detour for my second pickup at Southridge Elementary. It was a hot afternoon, but with the air-conditioning blasting and the kids safely loaded, the ride was now almost enjoyable. I'd grown up in Idaho, but had been out of state long enough to forget how much I always loved its scrubby beauty. A lot of people complained about the "ugly" brown foothills dotted with sagebrush breaking up the cheatgrass in muted green clumps, but the landscape felt both dearly familiar and beautifully wild to me.

I sat up a little straighter in the lumpy driver's seat and glanced back at the kids, letting myself feel normal for half a second. Pretending I was just another mom with a part-time job. Pretending that my Sophie was one of the kids behind me, instead of taking a different bus home to my sister.

With each zip of the wheels on the road, I practiced the mantra I'd read online in a blog post entitled "9 Therapy Hacks You Can Try at Home."

I accept my past, understand my present, and look forward to my future.

I gave up repeating the phrase before I even reached the exit where the highway crossed the river and moved back toward Boise.

I didn't accept any of it.

Shaking my head, I shifted my attention back to the road as I made the turn off the interstate and onto the empty county highway. My second and final pickup for aftercare was at Southridge Elementary for just one student, and it meant a ten-minute detour into the boonies. I'd gotten lost the first time I drove this route, winding through the switchbacks of rural roads in a panic, too paranoid to grab my phone out of its cubby for directions. One of the kids would definitely narc.

Supposedly, Bright Beginnings was getting a new fleet of buses—complete with dashboard navigation—soon. But for now, drivers were expected to know their routes.

In the distance an orange sign sat in the middle of the road. Was there road construction? It was too far away to tell.

I gritted my teeth in frustration and nudged the bus a little faster.

At this point, my entire life was a detour. The last thing I needed was another one.

2

SAGE

"But Mom said—"

I shot Bonnie the dirtiest look I knew and hunched sideways to look out the bus window, even though doing that always made me carsick.

I already knew what Mom said. Same thing she'd been saying since Bonnie was born. *"Come on, Sage. Let Bonnie tag along."* Or, *"Take care of your sister, Sage."* Or, *"Friends come and go, but sisters are for life."*

Joke was on Mom. I didn't have any friends, because ever since Grandpa's Alzheimer's had gotten worse and he couldn't watch us after school, I'd spent every day on the dumb daycare bus with Bonnie and the babies. That's what Mia said on the playground when she wanted to get me really mad. *"Bonnie and the babies."* Like it was some kind of cringey cover band you'd hear on "Kidz Bop."

I was the oldest kid on the Bright Beginnings bus by two full years. And with my long, skinny legs that came out of nowhere last summer and made me the tallest student in the sixth grade, I looked even older. Grandpa was always saying that sixth grade wasn't meant to be part of elementary school. It hadn't been like that when he was a kid. And I agreed with him. The only reason I wouldn't be going to Bright Beginnings daycare with Bonnie after school next year was because I'd finally turn twelve and go to junior high. And even Bright Beginnings knew that twelve was *way* too old for daycare.

Today was swim day, which was usually my favorite. The blue twisty slide in the indoor pool went so fast it made your swimsuit ride up your butt if you weren't careful. And best of all, the older kids—who could actually swim—got sorted out from the younger kids who had to stay in the shallow pool. But last week, Bonnie had gotten pushed down the slide by a third-grader named Kenan. So this week, Mom wanted me to stay in the baby pool with her. No slide.

I kept looking out the window and ignored the rest of what Bonnie was saying, watching the foothills turn into long rows of cherry trees as we got off the highway. There wasn't really fruit on the branches anymore. The cherry festival in Emmett happened last month, and the harvest was over. But if you pressed your nose to the crack of the bus window, you could smell the last of the ripe fruit that had missed getting picked.

"Ms. Jessa is nicer than Mr. Edward," Bonnie said abruptly, leaning so close to me that the faint, sweet smell of cherries was replaced by the peanut butter and raspberry jam sandwich she'd eaten for lunch. I could still see a little smear of red on her chin.

"How do you know if she's nice or not?" I mumbled, hunching my shoulder and pressing my nose back against the window crack. "She only said you could sit by me because you were blocking the aisle." Bonnie was right, though. Anybody was better than Mr. Edward. He'd made Rose cry at the end of last year, when she dropped the apple from her lunch box and it rolled all the way up the aisle of the bus and lodged under the brake. He'd pulled over to the side of the road and started yelling and swearing like she'd done it on purpose. *"Oh for shit's sake,"* he kept saying while he tried to pick up the pieces of the smashed apple, flinging them into the aisle. *"Fucking hell."*

I'd never heard a grownup use that combination of swears, not even Grandpa, and any other day I might have laughed, but he just sounded so mad and mean. All the kids on the bus had gone quiet, and that pretty much never happened. That was the last time anybody saw Mr. Edward, so that definitely meant he'd been fired.

Bonnie shifted on the bench beside me. To my surprise, she didn't say anything else about Mr. Edward or Ms. Jessa. Instead, she asked, "Why are we stopping?"

I sat up and leaned forward so I could see out the windshield of the bus. We were still headed toward the cherry orchards—and Southridge Elementary so we could pick up Amber Jensen. But we were slowing down. We never slowed down here.

Then I saw the big orange DETOUR sign with an arrow pointing down a dirt lane that looked like it led right through the orchard.

A little ways past the sign, parked on the shoulder of the road, was a big white van. SPEEDY SHUTTLE, it said on the side.

Something about that van seemed strange to me. I almost made a joke to Bonnie about the shuttle not being a very speedy shuttle right now, but I was still mad at her, so I kept my mouth shut.

Ms. Jessa slowed the bus to a crawl, inching closer to the detour sign, as if maybe she wanted to go around it instead of turning right, like the sign said we were supposed to. She was leaning forward, looking down the road past the sign at the parked Speedy Shuttle.

Then she sighed like the sign had been put there just to annoy her, flipped on the turn signal, and turned the bus onto the narrow dirt road into the orchard.

"Um, this isn't the right way," Ked announced, his voice monotone but loud from a few seats behind me. Ked was always piping up about something. "Ms. Jessa, this isn't the right way," he repeated.

Ms. Jessa flicked her eyes up to the big rearview mirror so she could see him without turning around in the driver's seat. "It's all right. There's just a little road construction ... or something."

Out of the corner of my eye, I saw Bonnie lean down, reach into her backpack, and pull her "clay person" out again. It was an ugly, brown squiggle that looked more like a turd than a person to me, but I knew Bonnie would cry if I said that. "Did you see how I gave him hair, Sage?" she chirped, pointing out the tiny squiggles of clay on top.

"Yeah, I saw," I said, keeping my eyes out the window as the bus finished its turn, trying to catch a glimpse of orange barrels or cones in the distance past the Speedy Shuttle. The road looked exactly the same as yesterday, though.

I shrugged and faced forward again.

It wasn't like I was in a hurry to get where we were going. I'd rather drive through the cherry orchard than babysit Bonnie in the rec center kiddie pool, anyway.

The wheels bumped down the narrow dirt road, and some of the kids laughed when we hit a deep pothole, bouncing us in our seats. I smiled, hoping the road would keep us in the orchard for a while. The smell of overripe cherries was all around us now, and it made me think of fall. I closed my eyes as that smell drifted through all the windows while the bus brushed against the leafy tree branches on both sides of the road.

Ms. Jessa hit the brakes as the road dipped then curved sharply enough that Bonnie tumbled against me, pushing my nose into the window. Someone—maybe Rose again—said "Whee!"

"Ouch!" I opened my eyes, pulled back from the window, and rubbed my nose. "Stay on your side, Bonnie!"

"What the hell?" Ms. Jessa said, loud enough for everyone to hear as the bus slowed, then stopped. I felt Bonnie stiffen next to me, no doubt remembering the apple incident with Mr. Edward.

Little gasps prickled across the bus.

At first, I thought it was because of Ms. Jessa's swearing.

Then I sat up tall and looked out the windshield. There was another vehicle completely blocking the narrow dirt road in front of us. Its hazards were on, flashing red.

Bonnie leaned into the aisle so she could see it, too. "What are they doing, Miss Jessa?" she asked.

Ms. Jessa looked over her shoulder at us and scrunched up her forehead so her eyebrows disappeared beneath her bright red bangs. She ignored Bonnie.

"It's fine. They'll move out of the way in just a sec," I told Bonnie. The words felt sticky in my throat, though. Something about the ugly gray van with its brake lights glowing orange felt wrong.

Ms. Jessa just seemed annoyed. She made a frustrated noise in the back of her throat, and her hand hovered above the horn. "Let's go," she muttered and hit the horn.

When nothing happened, she reached for the gear shift to whip the bus into reverse and drive backward, like I'd seen Mom do when we zipped right past a good parking spot at the Merc in Sunset Springs.

Then another sound rose above the low hum of kid voices.

It was coming from behind the bus. The rumble of an engine.

I shifted on the bench, swiveling my head to see out the back window of the emergency exit. A few of the other kids did, too.

The window back there was grimy, but it showed enough.

A big white van was coming up the road.

It came to a stop right behind the Bright Beginnings bus, angled a little bit so that I could just barely see the writing on its side.

Speedy Shuttle.

"Are you serious?" Ms. Jessa tilted her head into a beam of sunlight that made a strip of her hair glow neon red.

Bang, bang, bang.

Bonnie and I jumped as three hard raps came at the bus door. One of the kids shrieked in surprise.

Ms. Jessa made a noise like she'd choked on a sip of water as she stared out the glass of the bus door.

I smashed my face against the window to see for myself.

On the other side of the aisle, Ked sucked in his breath, then he said, "There's a man. He has a gun."